**Praise for Maxie McNabb—
"the most refreshingly original protagonist
to come along in years" (Rick Riordan)**

The Refuge

"Exciting ... Readers will immediately take to the hero-
ine." —*Midwest Book Review*

"Intriguing ...entertaining." —*Publishers Weekly*

The Tooth of Time

"Enjoyable.... Maxie is terrific in her latest caper.... Fans
will want to hitch a ride with Maxie and Stretch as they find
the Land of Enchantment enchanting but dangerous."
— *Midwest Book Review*

"Fans of Henry's Jessie Arnold series will enjoy."
—*Library Journal*

"Should resonate with fans of cozy and atmospheric mysteries." —*Publishers Weekly*

The Serpents Trail

"Hooray! Maxie McNabb [has] dr
right into my heart."

"Devotees of Henry's Alas
lighted to see sixty-three-
Winnebago-driving, free-
gentle whodunit.... Pr
run of adventures."

"Sue Henry, known for her s
she can entertain readers with a

de-
b, the
g in this
d popular
shers Weekly

mysteries, shows
Forty-eight tale."
—*Midwest Book Review*

continued ...

THE REFUGE

A Maxie and Stretch Mystery

SUE HENRY

AN OBSIDIAN MYSTERY

OBSIDIAN
Published by New American Library, a division of
Penguin Group (USA) Inc., 375 Hudson Street,
New York, New York 10014, USA
Penguin Group (Canada), 90 Eglinton Avenue East, Suite 700, Toronto,
Ontario M4P 2Y3, Canada (a division of Pearson Penguin Canada Inc.)
Penguin Books Ltd., 80 Strand, London WC2R 0RL, England
Penguin Ireland, 25 St. Stephen's Green, Dublin 2,
Ireland (a division of Penguin Books Ltd.)
Penguin Group (Australia), 250 Camberwell Road, Camberwell, Victoria 3124,
Australia (a division of Pearson Australia Group Pty. Ltd.)
Penguin Books India Pvt. Ltd., 11 Community Centre, Panchsheel Park,
New Delhi - 110 017, India
Penguin Group (NZ), 67 Apollo Drive, Rosedale, North Shore 0632,
New Zealand (a division of Pearson New Zealand Ltd.)
Penguin Books (South Africa) (Pty.) Ltd., 24 Sturdee Avenue,
Rosebank, Johannesburg 2196, South Africa

Penguin Books Ltd., Registered Offices:
80 Strand, London WC2R 0RL, England

Published by Obsidian, an imprint of New American Library, a division of Penguin Group (USA) Inc. Previously published in a New American Library hard-
cover edition.

First Obsidian Mass Market Printing, March 2008
10   9   8   7   6   5   4   3   2

For Becky Lundqvist,
generous in sharing adventures,
her house in Hawaii,
her Alaskan island refuge,
and many years of friendship, laughter,
and
Farkel.

Acknowledgments

With many thanks to:

Harper's Car and Truck (and Motor Home) Rental of Hilo, Hawaii, for their assistance in providing information and advice concerning RVing on the Big Island.

Chad Oyster and Rob Lanum of ABC RV Sales, Anchorage, Alaska, for information on Lance truck campers like those for rent in Hawaii.

Peter Eseroma and Stephen Schwartzengraber of Island Wide Plumbing Service, Hilo, Hawaii.

All the friendly, helpful people at Hawai'i Volcanoes National Park, Pu'uhonua o Hōnaunau National Historical Park (the Refuge), and Hawaii Tropical Botanical Garden.

Captain Beans' Dinner Cruise, an experience not to be missed.

Helen and Greg Hopkins and their two children, Ruby and Finn, for our sea kayaking adventure on Kealakekua Bay.

My agent, Dominick Abel; my editor, Tom Colgan; and his assistant, Sandy Harding. And to my son, Eric, Art Forge Unlimited, for creating great maps and photographs.

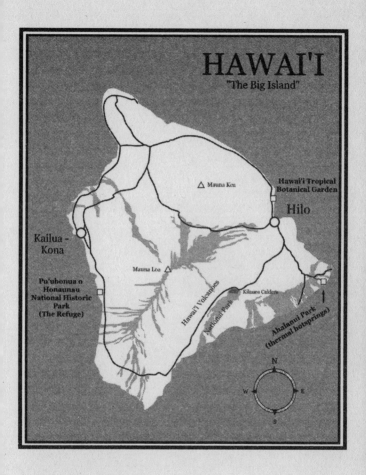

ONE

SOMETIME IN THE DEEP OF THE NIGHT I BECAME VAGUELY
aware of a soft breeze blowing on my face and the gentle susurrus of a window curtain moving above my head.
For a breath or two I didn't move, eyes closed, dreamily
curious and a bit puzzled by those sensations in combination with the sound of rain pouring down outside the
window. Could it have been the low percussion of its
arrival on the roof that had roused me?

I opened my eyes to the shadowy dark, sat up, and
swung my feet over the side of the bed onto—a polished
wood floor, surprisingly cool and certainly not a part of
my well-known bedroom. From what I could see, the
size and configuration of the space in which I found myself was unfamiliar and, in my sleepy state, disorienting.

Sitting there, bemused, I was reminded of other times
I had come awake in the dark of an unfamiliar room,
with the same bewildered reaction: *Where am I?* But
as I assessed the space, one significant clue caught my
attention.

Though most of the room was dark, a kind of half-light

from some artificial outside source illuminated the window curtains that were being ballooned by the breeze and allowed me to see that they were made of a yellow fabric with wide bands of green leaves and red and white flowers—*hibiscus blossoms*! Though known from pictures and southern places I had visited, the print of these curtains was certainly not native to my home in Alaska.

Then the penny finally dropped. *Hawaii!* I was in Hawaii, on the Big Island, where I had arrived unexpectedly, having made no previous plans of my own to visit. I had intended to spend the summer at home in Homer, Alaska, in the house that is most comfortingly mine, recuperating from nine stressful months in the Southwest's Four Corners area of the Lower Forty-eight in my Winnebago motor home, so waking to confusion in the dark made sense. I had never thought to be in Karen's Hilo house, where a torrential, tropical rain could come sweeping in on my first night to rouse and befuddle me. But it was without doubt where I now found myself, tired after a five-hour plane ride.

More awake and feeling better for having identified my surroundings, I sat quietly, appreciating the clean scent of the breeze, the rhythm of the rain hammering on the roof over my head, and the xylophonic water music it made as it fell from the eaves into pools that must have quickly accumulated below. I had read somewhere that Hilo was on the rainy side of the largest island of the Hawaiian chain, so this must be rain that arrived on a regular basis and disappeared almost at once into the soil that, unlike Alaska's, is never frozen, always thirsty for water and damp beneath the surface. No wonder whatever seeds find their way into such soil sprout and grow quickly in rich profusion in our fiftieth state.

Satisfied, I was about to lie down and go back to sleep, when, suddenly, within the splash of running water there was a reminder of something I had half-heard and subconsciously retained—a different kind of sound, just the hint of a clink, soft and metallic that had nothing to do with rain. Listening intently, I waited, holding my breath until it came again, faint and far away, either within the house or close outside. I sat very still, anticipating another repetition; it came almost immediately, bringing me to my feet and across to the door, which I had left half-open to allow circulation in the room.

As I stepped through it and went quietly barefoot along a hallway, I could hear the rain on the roof of the single-story dwelling lessen in intensity. The hall ended at the living room, where I paused again to listen and was once more rewarded with that quiet clink and the scrape of metal contacting metal to my right. Someone outside was trying to insert either a key that didn't fit or some metal tool into the dead bolt of the front door of Karen's house.

The sound was as small as that a mouse might make in gnawing at something within a closed cupboard. Someone was clearly trying to get in—evidently to break in, for with a key that fit there would have been no such trouble in opening the door easily, quickly, and most of all, quietly.

I crept cautiously forward, focused on the door, hands extended in front of me in the obscurity of that dark corner, feeling a bit mouselike myself. Then, unluckily and without warning, my left shin collided painfully with a low stool, and it slid with a screech across the bare wood floor and fell over with a crash. That clatter, along with the curse it elicited from me, was responsible for an instant termination of sound from outside.

There was a long, expectant pause while both I and whoever was on the other side of the door froze to listen in suspenseful silence, but I heard nothing but the slow trickle of water still slowly falling into puddles. The invisible presence beyond the door was the first to capitulate. I heard footsteps go pounding away through the carport that lay just beyond the front step.

Moving as quickly as possible, with care not to encounter another obstacle, I reached the entry, found and fumbled with the knob that released the dead bolt, yanked open the door, and went out onto the step—too late. All I caught was a glimpse of a shadowy figure, no more than a swiftly moving silhouette in dark clothing going away from the carport to disappear around the corner of the house—gone before I could get any real impression of size, age, or gender.

It was no use chasing after the middle-of-the-night visitor, who would, I was sure, have vanished completely before I could reach that corner. So I stood where I was, clinging to the handle of the screen door, looking out at the carport and surrounding yard in the small amount of pale light that filtered in through the branches of a tree from a streetlight perhaps thirty yards away.

The house was situated in the rear third of a large rectangular lot, with a bigger, two-story residence between it and the street. That more formidable building faced passing traffic, turning its back on Karen's single-story rental as if the smaller house were a less acceptable, adopted sister standing a bit too close behind.

The rain had stopped, leaving only a musical drip or two to disturb the puddles beneath the eaves.

"Maxie?" Karen's concerned voice questioned behind me. "Was that someone at the door? What's going on?"

She switched on the overhead light in the living room behind me and I turned to see her standing near the hallway, leaning on the one crutch she could awkwardly manage with casts on both her left ankle and forearm, having hobbled that far from her bedroom.

Half an hour later, with cups of tea I had suggested and made, we were sitting with the dining table between us; she with her back to the kitchen as I explained that it was indeed someone at the door—but evidently not a visitor she would have welcomed—how I had heard the surreptitious sounds of attempted entry, and my blunder in knocking over the stool in the dark that alerted and discouraged whoever it had been.

"Well," she said, "the crash was probably a good thing. It might have been dangerous for you to suddenly throw open the door and confront whoever was trying to get in, don't you think?"

I stared at her, recalling how disinclined to deal with anything disagreeable I knew Karen had always been. She would rather rationalize trouble away or, if possible, let someone else take responsibility for it.

She looked back at me with blue eyes innocently wide, permed blond hair in tangles from her pillow, and yawned. She hadn't changed a bit. A small woman, she looked pretty much as she always had, though there were now lines in her face, darkening circles under her eyes, and, like my own, her jawline had softened under the chin.

Well, I thought to myself, *we're both showing signs of our senior status.*

So I agreed that opening the door might possibly have been dangerous, but I doubted it, considering how fast the intruder had vanished. I wished, though, that I had been able to get more than a fleeting impression that was of no use whatsoever in establishing the identity of the prowler.

Uneasily I wondered what Karen would have done if she had been alone in the house, disabled as she currently was.

"Shouldn't we be calling the police?" I asked her.

Again she shrugged the idea off. "What good would it do? He—she—didn't get in and is long gone now. You can't identify whoever it was and, anyway, I wouldn't be surprised if it's just more harassment from the new owner and landlord. Less than a month after I moved in here the original landlord sold the place to Mr. Taylor and he let me know he wanted me out as soon as possible, though I had signed a six-month lease. It's part of why I decided to move back to Alaska. He's a horrible man who's been harassing me constantly—calling to see if I'm still here, showing up at odd hours, using his key to get in without notice. I know he's been here when I've been out, because things have been moved and once the door was unlocked when I came back. So you see, it could have been him. Maybe he's resorted to trying to scare me away now."

"Coming in without your permission isn't legal. Why haven't you reported him?"

"Oh, I'll be gone soon and he'd just deny it. It didn't seem worth the trouble."

"Why does he want you out so badly?"

"I don't know. He won't say. I've done nothing wrong. Maybe he wants to live here—or has another tenant he wants to move in. The property sits between two office buildings and that makes me wonder if he intends to tear down both houses and sell the land to some developer. Whatever...."

Heaving a sigh of resignation, she rubbed at her forehead with the back of her uninjured hand as if she had a headache, took a sip of tea, set the cup back in its saucer, and leaned back in her chair to say, "If only he would believe that I want out of here as much—maybe more—than he wants me gone. Why can't he just back off to let me get on with it as fast as possible? What have I ever done to make him so unreasonable anyway? Nothing. I've been *hurt*! Why can't he understand and sympathize with that? I was doing okay with the packing until *this* happened."

She lifted her left arm in its cast as example of "this."

"Oh, Maxie. I can't tell you how very thankful I am to have you here. It is so good of you to leave home and—well—just come. Thank you."

"No thanks necessary. You'd probably do the same for me in like circumstances, so you know I'm glad that I could, Karen," I told her. And, at that particular moment, I was—mostly.

I have to admit, though, that it seemed—with a prowler added to the already complicated mix—to be more than I had bargained for when I received a beseeching phone call from Karen and left Homer, Alaska, where I live, and caught the first available Hawaiian Airlines flight out of Anchorage to Hilo. But Karen Parker Bailey was an old acquaintance, though I wouldn't really say friend. She had sounded stressed and frustrated in her request for assistance, and I was without real commitments, except to myself, and free to go. We had known each other for years of sharing somewhat similar lives in the same small town, had even gone to high school together. Our husbands had been friends, which kept us in the same circles. They had both been fishermen and hers, like my first husband, Joe, had drowned at sea, but much later in life, not long after retiring.

As I offered reassurance across the table in those early-morning hours, I took a long look at her that reinforced what I had partly observed and partly suspected on my arrival the afternoon before. Karen seemed suddenly *old* in a way that I assumed had mostly to do with the accident-induced pressure and the strain she had been experiencing, but which I now thought was more than that. There was something about her—her behavior and attitude—that suggested to me that she was in retreat not only from her present circumstances, but, perhaps, from things in general.

Short and artificially blond, a sugar-and-spice girl with a calculated helpless streak, she had always been one to require personal appreciation, with the assumption that care would, and should, be taken of her. Three years older, Lewis Bailey had been exactly what she required. He had adored her and gone out of his way to take care of her. In a childless marriage she had been the childish one while he had become very parentlike, somewhat to the amusement of our small community, where everyone knew everyone else. The roles they had adopted, unrealistic or not, had seemed to work well enough for them, though others often viewed the relationship a bit askance, hiding tolerant grins behind their hands.

When Lewis died Karen had suddenly had no one to support her and seemed at a loss to know what to do with herself. Abruptly cast adrift, she had gone on grieving longer than seemed necessary or appropriate. I remember wanting to give her a shake and tell her to *get on with it,* and perhaps I—or someone—should have done so. But things had seemed to gradually improve and she took over most of her life alone, if not with total confidence, at least with what had passed to keep herself—as one of my neighbors put it—"clean, fed, and out of jail."

Because she and Lewis had bought land just outside Hilo on which to build, planning to retire there, against advice she had insisted on following the path of least resistance and gone ahead with those plans by herself. *It's what Lewis wanted,* she asserted. Shipping her household goods, she left Homer and moved into a Hilo rental before the new house construction even began. It had never seemed to dawn on her that she was leaving the support system of the community in which she had spent her entire life, so it was no surprise to me that she found herself less than happy, or capable, in a place where she knew almost no one who would put up with her helpless expectations.

Now, it seemed, with injury as excuse, she was falling back into as much dependent behavior as she could. So I would evidently have to do one of two things—either accept responsibility for the job of packing her up and moving her back to Alaska, where she had now decided to go, or finally take the bit between my teeth and tell her exactly what I had wanted to tell her before: *Damn it all, Karen! Grow up and get on with it!*

Why, oh, why am I at times such a sucker for someone in trouble? I wondered. *How could I have . . .*

Ah, lovie, I heard Daniel, my second husband, laugh quietly in my mind, *don't chuck a fit. She's always been a silly sheila, but you can at least give it a bash and get it over with. It'll all come good and you'll be back home soon to watch your garden grow.*

My dear Daniel, bless him! It had been no easier to bury a second husband after the first—having been lucky enough to love and be loved by them both. Besides scraps of his colorful Aussie slanguage, he left me with an instinctive knowledge of what he would have suggested in response to many situations, as he was dependably levelheaded, usually encouraging, and almost always in good humor. He had left me well provided for, but had also known that I was totally capable of taking care of myself.

Thank you, Daniel.

So, instead of admonishing Karen, for the moment I kept my opinions to myself in favor of something else that had been on my mind.

"Tell me," I suggested, "exactly how and where you fell."

"There." Karen pointed to an open doorway in the wall behind me, a dark room beyond. "That space used to be a garage, but someone made it into what must have been a family room. It has a cement floor that's two steps lower than this part of the house. I was using it to sort and pack up, and was moving a box of heavy stuff out there from the kitchen. But I couldn't see ahead because of the box I was carrying, felt for the step and missed. My foot came down on the edge of it, which pitched me forward so that I fell sideways on the floor, losing the box as I went down. My left ankle was across the step's edge when the box fell on it. The rest of me landed hard on this arm." She once again raised her cast-encased left arm. "I heard the bone snap in my forearm, but didn't realize my ankle was broken as well until I tried to get up and it hurt—terribly. I had to crawl back up here to the phone to call for help."

"I'm sure it did. And so, because you live alone, they kept you overnight in the hospital."

"Yes. But I came home in a taxi the next day just after noon. I hate hospitals."

"Then you called me?"

"Well, not for a couple of days. I thought maybe I could hire someone from the paper to help me finish packing and getting things ready to ship home. But there simply wasn't anyone reliable, or who was able to do it right."

Or who would make decisions for you, I thought, but didn't say.

"So then I called you. And you *came.* I do so appreci—"

Feeling overly thanked already, I cut her off and suggested that we had better plan on a busy day tomorrow—or today, as the clock now indicated—so we should go back to bed for what rest we could salvage, which we did.

But once again in my bed I found sleep impossible to come by and lay partly considering how to proceed with the job at hand, but mostly remembering the long road and serendipitous circumstances that had brought me back to Alaska for the summer—and, barely a week after arriving at home, in the right place for Karen to reach with her plea for assistance.

None of it had been planned or anticipated. The garden I had left in Homer would probably grow to a wild ruin in my absence. But most of all I missed the company of my inveterate travel companion, a mini-dachshund named Stretch, for, given rabies-free Hawaii's animal import regulations, which require strict and lengthy quarantine, I had been forced to leave him behind. So the quicker I finished with the job at hand, the sooner I could go back to retrieve him from his temporary home with my friend Doris, who looked after things for me when I was away.

Rolling over in frustration and giving my too-fat pillow a thump to flatten it a little, I began to mentally go back over the decisions and events that, mile by mile, had unpredictably brought me to Hawaii for what I foresaw would be no vacation.

Two

"NORA MAXINE STILLMAN FLANAGAN MCNABB? THAT'S quite a name," the agent in the kiosk at the border that separates Idaho and British Columbia had commented with a smile as she reached up to hand my passport back through the window of my Winnebago motor home.

They almost always comment, as I have kept my maiden name and those of my two husbands, good men both, worth recognizing in this small way.

She turned then to the declaration card I had filled out in detail, checking the necessary answers aloud.

"No fresh fruit, vegetables, or plants. Less than the liter limit of alcohol. No firearms?"

I agreed with her assessment, ignoring the small pang of guilt I always feel at border crossings in remembering the shotgun that, hidden away in a secret compartment, perennially accompanies me on my travels. Wandering around North America alone at sixty-four years old, I have no desire for a handgun, convinced that anyone attempting to break into my rig would be more inclined to think twice in confronting an edgy senior citizen with a shotgun in shaky hands.

"Cute dog. Are its shots current?"

At the word *dog* my mini-dachshund, Stretch, turned to look across at her from his padded traveling basket. It hangs from the back of the passenger seat and allows him, being short-legged, to view the world we pass, in which he is almost always interested.

He gave the agent a doggy grin and wagged his tail furiously.

I gave her his veterinary papers.

She gave them a glance and handed them back with a smile for Stretch.

"Carrying more than ten thousand dollars Canadian?"

"Don't I *wish*."

"Don't we all? Going home to Alaska?" she asked.

"For the summer at least. We'll probably be back sometime in September when I run away from the cold weather again."

"I'll watch for you. Have a good trip."

She waved me off and, as I drove away, in the side mirror I saw her leaning out to look after us as if she wished she could come along. Maybe she did.

For me, however, there was more than the usual sense of freedom and satisfaction in that border crossing, a comforting recognition of a familiar road into Canada and the country through which we were and would be traveling for the next week or ten days. *Comforting?* I found myself a bit perplexed at that particular word, though it seemed to fit my mood. From what exactly, I wondered, did I feel a need for comforting? I shrugged it off. There would be time enough to consider it later if the feeling lingered.

On leaving Taos, New Mexico, a few days earlier I had no intention of making the long drive north. Rather than heading for my house in Homer, I simply meant to travel beyond Denver toward the top of the map until I found a place that pleased me, where the temperatures would be cooler than those of the Southwest. Born, raised, and living in the far north all my life has thickened my blood. I can handle cold weather by wearing warm outer clothing, but heat wears me out more quickly, and when I reached southern Idaho the first of June the thermometer was already climbing into the nineties. So I went on through Idaho Falls, turned northwest into the mountains, spent one night in a campground at North Fork on the bank of the Salmon River, crossed over Lost Trail Pass into the beautiful Bitterroot Valley of Montana, and headed for the Missoula KOA Campground, stopping for a few groceries on the way through town.

I then settled us into one of the last available spaces in the KOA Campground and hooked the Winnebago up to water, power, and sewer, plus a line for cable television. The latter I often forgo, preferring music or whatever book I am currently reading, but I wanted a look at the news and weather report, thinking it might help me decide where to go next.

"Well, lovie," I said, leash in hand, to my traveling buddy, who, after a long drink of water from his bowl, was hovering impatiently near the coach door in anticipation, "you've a walkabout in mind, I see."

We strolled, as usual, for most of half an hour and I could see the woman in the office had been right in saying I was lucky there was a space to be had. "Except for one other, we're full up for the night."

Looking at the registration form I had filled out, she had commented on the address.

"You must be going home for the summer. It'll probably be easier to find camping space farther up the road,
especially after Dawson Creek, where the Alaska Highway officially starts. A lot of the folks staying here now
are on vacation and headed either for Glacier National
Park or Banff and Lake Louise. I imagine you'll be going
on up the Icefields Parkway to Jasper."

I had started to shake my head at the "going home"
part, but found myself nodding, suddenly knowing it was
exactly what I, consciously or not, had wanted to do—go
home, to spend the long summer days in my snug little
house a couple of miles east of Homer where the highway ends on the Kenai Peninsula and I could look south
out over the ever-changing colors of the wide waters of
Kachemak Bay to the jagged peaks of the Kenai Mountains. I wanted to spend sunny days putting my flower
garden in order, take Stretch along to wander the long
sandy beaches of the local spit with gulls riding the wind
overhead, see the always visible Big Dipper overhead
in our northern night sky—perhaps through a wisp of
the aurora—and best of all, invite friends for extended
evenings of conversation, laughter, and the sharing of
good food and drink around my large dining table. My
hankering was to simply be back where I belonged and
felt most content—with my hands in the dirt or my feet
in the sand. Sometimes you just want to be in your own
space, with dear and familiar things around you and, at
sixty-four, I have *my own space* quite clearly defined and
actualized in the house in which I have lived half my life.
It is the one place in the world that is a refuge to me in
times of trouble, or joy.

As Stretch and I walked that evening I thought about
it all with some amusement at my self-deceptions, but
the admission that I wanted to be there was enough. I

didn't need to analyze it in detail, or question my sudden change of plans. It felt perfectly clear and correct. I didn't know exactly why, but neither did I feel a burning need to know. It was sufficient to have accepted reality. I would act accordingly and my motives would most likely come clear enough as I did so. Mind made up, I slept well that night and was up with the sun to head farther north in the cool of the morning.

I knew I could anticipate a familiar and pleasant journey up the long highway to my home state. So I made my way up the Idaho panhandle and crossed the Canadian border into British Columbia in good order and a peaceful frame of mind. During the afternoon I went through Cranbrook and passed by the Fort Steele Heritage Town, originally a small settlement born during the Kootenay Gold Rush in the 1860s, with a specific goal in mind—Dutch Creek RV Park, where I had stayed before and where memories overtook me as, late in the afternoon, I settled comfortably in that less crowded campground for the night.

I like driving the Alaska Highway. It is a trip full of spectacular scenery and interesting places to visit, with a friend or two I like to stop and visit along the way. I had met a new friend in that same campground on an earlier trip—Jessie Arnold, an Alaskan sled dog racer from near Wasilla. With her Alaskan husky, Tank, for company, she had been driving a motor home up the road as a favor to a contractor who was about to build her a new log cabin in place of one destroyed by an arsonist. As I moved my padded lawn chairs and a small table outside, where I could relax and watch the sun go down, I recalled having her welcome company in the second chair on a similar evening as we got acquainted over a shot of Jameson Irish and watched our dogs become friends as well.

Though we had journeyed together for much of the way north after that, meeting to park next door to each other in several RV parks and Canadian campgrounds, it was at Dutch Creek that we had met a young runaway also headed for Alaska. Remembering both Jessie and young Patrick made me wonder if he was still in Fairbanks, where he had been determined to go and find a friend who had moved there from Wyoming. I resolved that when I reached Alaska I must remind myself to ask Jessie if she had heard anything from him and what he was currently up to.

It was good to sit and remember, for it had been a long day's drive and I was tired. The campground was peaceful and, next to the river that ran close on one side, refreshingly cooler than Missoula. I sipped my drink and watched whatever and whoever passed along the circular access road. A small girl gave Stretch, leashed and sitting at my feet, a grin and a wave as she peddled proudly past on a pink bicycle that wobbled back and forth on training wheels. A tall man with an ambling gait followed close, but not hoveringly so—obviously her father keeping a close eye on his chick. He smiled, nodded to me, and continued to amble along behind her until they disappeared behind the motor home next door. From somewhere out of sight the whisper of the late breeze brought the sweet, tangy scent of someone's barbecue drifting in to remind me that lunch had been a long time ago and the chips I had brought out to accompany my Jameson were not meant to be dinner. With the crunch of the gravel on the road, a large fifth-wheel pickup rig drove around its curve in search of the space assigned to it. Someone at a distance laughed and a woman's voice called out something unintelligible from where I sat.

It would have been nice to have Jessie sitting in the other chair and catch up on conversation. I decided that farther up the road I would call to see if she would be home and welcome me for an overnight visit at her house on Knik Road. Meanwhile, I would wander along at my own steady pace and enjoy the drive.

Finishing the last sip of my drink, I took Stretch inside, found dinner for us both, and went to bed early to read, but fell asleep over the book—no fault to David McCullough's *1776*, a fascinating account of the early part of the Revolutionary War and those who marched with General Washington in the beginning of our fight for independence. Whatever he writes, it is always a rewarding read.

Once again I woke early in the rear of my house on wheels. Still drowsily content to cling to the perfect, comforting warmth of my bed, I turned over and lay watching the slight motion of some leafy shadows cast on the window shade by the first rays of the sun shining through the branch of a tree outside. *Comforting.* There was that word again. Considering it, I realized that as soon as my decision to go home had been made I had stopped feeling so much in need of it, but was still aware of a vague discomfort that had something to do with the events of the last nine months of my life on the road.

You've had a lot on your plate, old girl, I heard my dear departed say in my head, as he surely would have said aloud had he been there. *It's understandable that stress would make you want to nick off home, where it's safe and predictable.*

Daniel, the second husband I outlived, was an expatriate with a wealth of Aussie-isms he was more than willing to share and which I, of course, picked up and still use occasionally. I talk to him now and then, and like to think I can hear his comments—usually advice that is at least worth considering.

Stretch was his dog to begin with and became mine by default when he died. This developed into an eventual and mutual satisfaction, though we missed Daniel a great deal as we grew used to each other without him—and still do. Once in a while at the sound of feet coming up the steps to the porch of the house at home Stretch will raise his head to stare fixedly at the door listening intently, and I recognize his hopeless optimism that just maybe our lost one is finally returning, as it coincides so precisely with a single breathless split second of my own wish.

I had to agree with the assessment Daniel had provided me concerning the past few months. I had not only lost my best and oldest friend to a murderer the previous fall, but only a few weeks past had become inadvertently mixed into another killing in Taos. Both events had been full of tension and confusion. It was true that the deaths and their eventual resolutions had taken a significant psychological toll—which I had pretty much ignored.

It made sense that my traveling decision had been made with my subconscious crying uncle. Comforting? Yes, I needed some kind of comforting. And going home was the best and most reasonable solution.

"Thanks, love," I told Daniel aloud, which elicited a whine from Stretch, who was sitting up in his basket, needing to go out.

With a spurt of energy I climbed out of my warm cocoon, shrugged on a robe, and let Stretch out on his tether and got the coffee going while I dressed in one of my comfortable travel skirts with the large patch pockets, washed my face, brushed my teeth, and pinned my graying dark hair up in the twist that keeps it off my neck—making myself ready for a day of driving north, knowing that the closer I came to Alaska, the better I would feel.

How was I to anticipate that even home could not always be the perfectly peaceful and most restorative place to be—or that I might not be spending a perfectly ordinary summer there?

THREE

SELDOM HAVE I ENJOYED THE TRIP MORE THROUGH THAT LONG, thin slice of western Alberta, much more of both north-eastern British Columbia and the southwestern corner of the Yukon. The road, now paved and extremely driv-able from one end to the other—better than many in the Lower Forty-eight—was easy going and, except for a couple of semiovercast days and a morning of light rain outside Whitehorse, the weather held clear and sunny.

Wildlife viewing along the route is usually best in the spring, when grass and sunflowers appear first along the verges of the road and herbage-eating animals seek them out, hungry from the winter's deprivation. Birds migrate early, so many are passing into or through Canada in April and May. But this time, in June, like magic, it seemed life was everywhere.

There was a pair of swans gliding serenely on the still waters of a wilderness lake where we paused for lunch. Later a caribou slipped out of the trees as we drove by and I saw moose in several small ponds lift their drip-ping heads from beneath the water to chew the sedges they had browsed from the bottom. A small herd of buffalo lumbered across one section of highway, requiring me to stop and watch them pass. In one meadow a black bear had brought her two cubs into the wide field of sunflowers, where they tumbled over each other in play while she lunched on the fresh greens, paying no attention short of a glance when I pulled to the side of the road to smile at their antics.

I spent nights in an RV park or two—one in Fort Nelson—and of course I stopped to visit my friends Dave Hett and Carolyn Allen at Dawson Peaks Resort a few miles short of Teslin.

Canadian provincial parks and government campgrounds are great and I stopped in several favorites—Whistlers outside of Jasper, Kiskatinaw just north of Dawson Creek, Liard River Hot Springs between Fort Nelson and Watson Lake, Wolf Creek near Whitehorse. I spent my last night in Canada at the Congdon Creek Yukon Government Campground on the shores of Kluane Lake, where I made sure that I arrived early enough to find a space that allowed me to park near the shore where I could sit beside a small fire and watch the almost full moon rise and lay a pale, glittering line of light across those wide and peaceful waters.

It had been a good trip. Driving relaxes me and the closer I came to home the more my spirits rose. Three more days, most of it in my home state, would have me pulling into my own driveway in Homer, where the friend who looks after my house would have made sure it was ready for me.

"Ready to go home?" I asked Stretch, who was lying at my feet and raised an alert head at the word. Even he, it seemed, was aware of and approved our destination.

The next day we crossed the border into Alaska,

spent one night in an RV park in Tok, took the cut-off to the Glenn Highway, and by just after four in the afternoon had gone through Palmer and Wasilla and were pulling into Jessie Arnold's drive on Knik Road. My tires scrunching on the gravel announced our arrival, setting the few sled dogs left in her yard barking, which brought her flying out the door to provide her own welcome with a huge, enthusiastic hug.

"Oh, Maxie, I'm glad to see you. Can you really only stay one night?"

"I called the neighbor who looks after my house this afternoon to say I'd be there tomorrow," I told her. "And I'm more than ready to settle into one that doesn't have wheels, so I'd better hit the road in the morning. But let me look at you."

I held her off at arm's length and she stood smiling—straight and tall. A thin ray of sunshine fell through the branches of one of the trees surrounding her yard to give the generous lashes framing her clear gray eyes a golden glow to match the short, honey-blond tumble of waves and curls of her hair. There was a settled look about her that having a new house in place of the one she had loved and lost to fire could have inspired. But I suspected it also had something to do with the return of Alex Jensen, Alaska state trooper, with whom she was once again sharing both house and affection. I looked forward to meeting him.

With a cacophony of sled dogs barking near at hand in the yard it had seemed wise to have Stretch on his leash. But they quieted at a word from Jessie. Tank, who had been in the house with her, had come bounding out to greet the smaller friend he had met on our earlier trip together, so I turned him loose. They circled each other, sniffing as dogs do in getting reacquainted, and trotted along companionably as we turned toward the house.

On my way south the preceding fall I had seen the new log structure, which had been constructed in the footprint of the old, but was larger, with a partial basement, a second story, and a broad, roofed porch that faced the road and sheltered several comfortable-looking chairs, including a rocker.

"I've finished moving in and replacing stuff that was lost in the fire," she told me. "So now it's as fine inside as out. You'll see in a minute."

"I like it even better than when I was here last, Jessie," I told her. Then, thinking of my own: "Isn't it a joy to have a house you love to come home to?"

"That sounds as if you're in need of some time spent in yours," she said, and raised a questioning eyebrow as she gave me a swift glance of assessment.

"Oh, yes, *I certainly am,*" I agreed heartily.

"You'll have to tell me about that."

She opened the door and waved me through with Stretch and Tank, where my first breath stopped me with the fragrance of something cooking—with an unidentifiable herbal, yeasty overtone.

"What *is* that wonderful smell?"

"*That,*" Jessie told me, with a grin, "is the drunk pot roast I promised you ages ago. There isn't any moose left from my neighbor's hunt last fall, so you'll have to put up with beef instead."

"You darlin' girl. That's the one you make with Killian's lager, right?"

"The very same—with carrots, potatoes, onions, et cetera. And Alex will be home shortly to make the biscuits— his chore. But I warn you that 'from scratch' is not a part of his vocabulary. His secret weapon is Bisquick. Sit down and make yourself comfortable. I'll get us a drink. I'm sure you're ready for one and I'll join you."

She stepped into the kitchen, and I watched as Stretch wandered off to explore the house with Tank, for all the world as if the larger dog were giving him a guided tour.

I stood for a minute looking around admiringly. The inside of the log walls of the house were a lovely honey color and the trim for the windows and doors was a soft medium blue that accentuated the color of the walls. I stepped across to look at an Iditarod print of a pair of wolves watching from the bank as a musher and his team of sled dogs pass on a wide curve of the frozen Yukon River. It hung prominently on one wall and had been signed by the artist: *Best wishes for good sledding, Jessie. Jon Van Zyle.*

"Was 1989 the first year you ran the Iditarod?"

"Yes," she said, coming back from the kitchen. "Which is why I love that print so much, I guess—and because I saw a similar pair in the same area in a later race. After the original burned in the fire, Jon gave me that one and signed it just like the other."

"The house is wonderful, Jessie. Even better than before," I said, moving back to the center of the room, where a large and colorful hand-braided rag rug lay in front of the sofa.

"Wherever did you get this marvelous rug? Did you make it?"

She smiled, shaking her head as she denied it. "Not a chance I should be so talented. My uncle sent it to me after the fire. My aunt—Mom's sister—made it long ago, before she died. Isn't it great? Can you imagine that neither of my cousins wanted it?"

Sitting down on the large, comfortable sofa draped

with a couple of afghans and heaped with colorful pillows, I gratefully accepted the Jameson over ice that Jessie handed me before kicking off her moccasins and curling her long legs under her in the opposite corner of the sofa.

"So, things are going well with you and your trooper?"

She gave me a smile of satisfaction. "Better than well," she told me. "But you'll see for yourself. Now—tell me all about your travels this winter and spring. I thought you were planning to stay Outside this summer."

For the next hour I told her about all my travels, the good and bad situations I had experienced in the Southwest, why and how I had decided to come home. In the middle of the part about New Mexico, I suddenly remembered that I had promised to carry a message from an old friend—a long-distance trucker we had met on our trip up the highway together.

"Who would you guess that I ran into in Taos?" I asked her.

"Butch Stringer, of course," she said, sitting up with a smile and reaching to refresh our drinks from the bottle she had set on the table in front of us by a bucket of ice. "I was waiting for you to mention it. He had lost the number and couldn't remember the name of my kennel, so he got in touch with Iditarod Trail Headquarters and they gave it to him. He called a couple of weeks ago and said he'd seen you. Told me about your adventures in crime down there. No wonder you want to go home for some peace and quiet. I was glad to hear that he recovered from that awful wreck. Is he really doing as well as it sounded?"

I was telling her that, except for a limp, he was, when she turned her head suddenly toward the door and I heard the sound of a vehicle approaching.

"There's Alex," Jessie said, setting down her glass and standing up. "Stay where you are. He'll see your rig and be right in."

Before she could reach the door, he was coming through it to catch her up with one arm for an affectionate hug and kiss.

I am about an inch shorter than Jessie, but he was taller still, lean and strong looking—definitely a man to look up to. I had expected an Alaska state trooper's uniform, but he wore jeans, a plaid shirt, and had hung a western hat on a hook by the door with one hand, as he swept Jessie up with the other. I caught a glimpse of clear blue eyes and a remarkable reddish-blond handlebar mustache that must have made the kiss interesting, though the rest of his face was clean-shaven. And from the look of it things were indeed going very well for them. He set her down, keeping his left arm around her waist to draw her with him as he came, right hand outstretched toward me.

"You have to be Maxie," he said with a grin and a firm handshake. "It's a pleasure to meet you, and about time I'd say. Glad you could make time for us on your way home."

Tank had trotted across the room to stand near him, with shorter-legged Stretch bringing up the rear, as usual.

"Hey," Alex said, hunkering down to rub the ears and chins of both dogs, but speaking to Stretch. "Who're you, short stuff?" Then to his housemate, "Hope you're not thinking of trading down, Jess. In harness this one wouldn't win you any races. You'd be six months getting to Nome."

We all smiled at the mental picture of a sled dog team of mini-dachshunds.

Stretch accepted the introductory attention as normal and rightfully his, but in a minute or two both dogs were lying together like a mismatched set, medium and small, on a rug under the table in front of the sofa.

Without sitting down, Alex went whistling to the kitchen to fish out a lager from the refrigerator and complete the dinner menu, from whence melodious strains of "She'll Be Comin' Round the Mountain" drifted out, accompanied by the rhythmic clatter of spoon against bowl that signified biscuit making in progress.

Half an hour later we were settled comfortably around the table, making an appreciative inroad into the pot roast and biscuits.

"Here's to a good summer," Jessie suggested, raising her glass of Merlot in my direction.

I lifted my own in agreement.

"And to less time between *longer* get-togethers," Alex added, clinking our glasses with his bottle of lager.

"You must all three come to Homer sometime this summer and stay with me for a few days," I suggested, with a nod to include Tank. "I intend to be home all summer, have plenty of space, and would love to have you anytime, for as long as—whatever."

"We'll do that," said Jessie enthusiastically.

"I was part of the way down that direction a couple of days ago," Alex said, laying down his fork with a thoughtful frown. "Had a meeting with the mother of a runaway I took home to Soldotna. Fifteen years old. She'd hitched a ride to Anchorage, then to Palmer, before we picked her up six miles east of town on the Glenn Highway with her thumb out. From her attitude I wouldn't be surprised if she tried it again the first chance she gets."

"What a dangerous thing for a teenager to do, especially a girl."

"Would she really try it again?"

"Why did she run?"

Alex shook his head at our questions and shrugged. "Who knows? She wouldn't tell us—stubbornly refused to answer. Her mother, a single parent, was relieved to have her back, of course. But she was pretty close-mouthed as well. I got the impression it wasn't the first time she'd taken off. A neighbor said she's a bit wild and a problem for her working mother. She had a black eye and a couple of other bruises that she wouldn't talk about—some fight with another kid, maybe—maybe not. There are other possibilities. I couldn't get a word out of either of them that I could do anything about short of a warning. I'd be surprised if she didn't take off again."

"Remind you of anyone?" Jessie asked, passing me the platter of pot roast and vegetables. "You said you stayed at Dutch Creek."

"Patrick," I told her, helping myself to another biscuit and the honey Alex had set temptingly near my plate. "His was a different situation entirely—and he was older. But what a trip up the highway that turned out to be. Have you heard anything from him?"

"He called late in January to tell me he was working as a handler for one of the mushers up there and was all excited about going to Whitehorse for the start of the Yukon Quest—the race between there and Fairbanks."

From that, the conversation ranged widely as I told them about my travels and heard about both their reunion during the Alaska State Fair and current busy lives. It was pleasant and satisfying to spend an evening with friends—made me feel even closer to home, where I would surely be the very next day.

Both Stretch and I slept well in the motor home in Jessie's yard that night, glad we had stopped, and that the next day would be the last on the road—for several months at least. We were up shortly after the sun, which comes very early in our northern latitudes near the summer solstice. Finishing breakfast, we said our good-byes, and I was soon making a left turn from the long driveway onto Knik Road shortly behind Alex, who had disappeared a few minutes earlier on his way to keep the public safe.

Four

A LITTLE OVER AN HOUR AFTER LEAVING JESSIE'S, STRETCH and I had passed through Anchorage to the Seward Highway and were headed along the north side of the long arm of ocean water that extends southeast from Cook Inlet, with its dangerous bore tides and the glacial silt that has been known to trap and drown the unwary. Framed by majestic peaks of both the Kenai and Chugach mountains, the highway loops around the arm onto the Kenai Peninsula followed half an hour later by the high sweeping valley of Turnagain Pass as it continues on to the city of Seward. One of the most beautiful roads in Alaska, it has wisely been given federal designation as a national scenic byway. I have always loved the names of places and things geographic. Turnagain speaks to me of an area that always deserves much more than a second look, though that was not how it came by the name.

On his quest for a northwest passage in June of 1778, the arm was named River Turnagain by Captain Cook because, arriving at its end, he found himself unable to proceed farther inland and was forced to turn around. He concluded, "These circumstances convinced me that no passage [from the Pacific Ocean to the Atlantic] was to be expected by this side river, any more than by the main branch [Cook Inlet]." Captain Vancouver adopted the name in 1794 as Turnagain Arm, and the Russian Captain Tebenkov in 1862 called it Zaliv Vozvratseniya, meaning "Return Bay."

Ninety miles from Anchorage I took the right-hand turnoff that would take me to Soldotna and, beyond it at the end of the road, Homer. It is 226 miles from Anchorage, through spectacular country, but in June traffic on that route is heavy with local as well as tourist travelers, some in motor homes similar to mine. Many are headed for some of the most accessible and famous fishing in the state. Early salmon runs tempt them to launch the boats they have towed behind their vehicles, or to simply pull on waders and join the long, curving lines of people bracing themselves hip deep against the current of the Russian and Kenai rivers, casting optimistic lines with the hope of not snagging another combat fisherman by mistake.

In Soldotna, I stopped at the big Fred Meyer store for some basic groceries, made myself a quick sandwich, then drove out on the last eighty-five miles of my protracted journey home.

One of the best parts of arriving in Homer is the very last couple of miles. The highway rises to a crest over which, suddenly, the breadth of both Cook Inlet and Kachemak Bay comes into view, along with the narrow spit that extends out into the bay with the sharp, rugged crags of the Kenai Range beyond, and Mount Augustine—one of our several active volcanoes—far across the waters of the inlet to the west. On that sunshiny day the sight gave

me a warm, *it's about time* sort of welcome feeling and I
quickly let the cab window all the way down for a deep
breath of the familiar clean, briny air that carried with it
just a hint of evergreen.

Slowing, we went down the long hill, made a left on
Pioneer Avenue, and passed through town until it became East End Road. Another two miles and just before four o'clock I was turning into my own driveway,
where I parked the Minnie Winnie in its designated
place next to the garage on the right, switched off the
engine, and sat looking at my house with a sense of complete pleasure and relief at being—nine months after I
had hit the road south to Colorado—*once again where
I belonged*.

Stretch reached from his basket to give my elbow a
remember me sort of lick, eager to be lifted out and put
down.

"Okay, buddy. We're home again, home again,
jiggety-jig."

Taking the keys and unfastening my seat belt, I tucked
him under one arm, opened the driver's door, and got
out, setting him down on the driveway. He trotted immediately across it to the lawn that wraps from there
around the east side of my house to become a wide,
gentle slope that faces the bay. Rolling over several
times, seemingly to rid himself of travel, he then began
a survey of the area and soon disappeared from sight
around the lilac bush in bloom at the corner. The grass,
I noticed, had been recently mowed—probably by the
son of my friend and neighbor Doris, who cares for and
keeps an eye on the place in my absence.

Straightening, I spread my arms wide to stretch and
alleviate the small ache in the middle of my back, then
went up the short walk to unlock the door, leaving it

open behind me for Stretch, who would soon be in to check out the inside of the house. Passing through the short entry hall, with its bathroom door on the left, I stopped in the large open living space to appreciate the view of the mountains beyond the bay, for Doris had opened the heavy drapes over my large south-facing windows and doors, with the thought, I was sure, of allowing afternoon sunshine to stream in and welcome me home. In addition, on the dining table she had left a vase of late yellow daffodils, a bright spot of cheerful color.

My home is of average size—more a snug and comfortable two-story cottage than a house, I guess. Except for an enclosed den in the northeast corner, most of the first floor is largely open space with a fireplace in the southeast corner, a comfortable sofa and easy chairs gathered companionably around it. My large dining table, with its eight chairs, sits at the west end, separated by a counter and four tall stools from the generous and otherwise open northwest corner kitchen. It all faces the bay through large windows that are centrally divided by a pair of glass doors that open onto a wide deck outside.

Upstairs along a hall are another bath, four bedrooms, two of which look out at the bay through dormer windows and two that face the driveway. At the end of the hall between is the steep, narrow stairway, which rises to a widow's walk on the roof, complete with a surrounding waist-high railing. This unusual feature was the inspiration of the man who built the house, my first husband, Joe Flanagan, who came from a Massachusetts family of several generations of fisher folk.

The house is the only one he ever planned and constructed. As he was a fisherman first, boat builder second,

the place has a few other interesting traces of his nauti-
cal bent—the porthole window in the front door, for instance, and the kitchen space that is as tidily arranged as
any floating galley, though significantly larger. My con-
tribution to the plan was several secret hidey-holes, the
result of a fascination I had shared since college days
with the friend I had recently lost in Colorado.

Between deep blue shadows, the white, snow-covered
peaks glistened in the bright afternoon sunlight, the
wide, wind-stirred waters of the bay sparkling below. A
familiar view in all seasons and degrees of weather, it
drew me, as always. Crossing to the French doors, I unlocked and opened them wide, allowing the breeze that
ruffled the bay to sweep in uninvited, but it easily found
its way out again through the door I had left open. Stepping out onto the deck, I took a long look at my yard,
already planning the gardening that needed to be done.

Back in the house, I took a deep breath and noticed
that even with Doris's care it held a slightly musty, un-
occupied smell—a reminder of a winter without me.
There was something else in it that I couldn't identify.
Under the odor that a house empty for some extended
period of time acquires there was a hint of some unfamiliar semifloral fragrance. It was not one of those truly
ugly pseudoscents; probably an air freshener of Doris's
choosing, I decided, pleasant, but not one I would have
chosen over my usual handful of spices simmered in
water or fruit juice on the kitchen stove.

As I started to go and make a quick search for the
source of the scent, the patter of Stretch's feet on the deck
attracted my attention as he came trotting in through the
open door and straight to his water bowl in its usual corner of the kitchen. Finding it empty, he gave me an astonished, inquiring look that was more than a hint.

"Okay, okay," I told him, scooping the bowl up on my way to the sink, where I filled it and set it back down. "Sorry, old thing."

So I forgot my search for the elusive foreign fragrance until much later in the evening, when, realizing I had not smelled it again, I determined to wait for a reemergence to make the search simpler. Instead, I moved the contents of the motor home's refrigerator into the kitchen and brought in the few odds and ends of laundry to take care of later. The file box that holds the necessary records and documents I need in my travels—the rig's license and registration, and the veterinary papers for Stretch, for instance—I took to the den. The rest, and giving the motor home a good cleaning, would wait a day—perhaps two, if I felt more inclined toward gardening. After all, I had the whole summer, didn't I?

At that particular moment, however, I was inclined toward a celebratory homecoming splash of Jameson, which I poured over a couple of cubes of ice—blessing Doris for filling the trays—and took to the deck, where I sat on the steps to drink it and appreciate one of the finest views the state has to offer, especially because it was precisely what I had expected and been yearning to see. Dorothy was right. There's no place like home.

The June days are long as Alaska approaches the summer solstice, so at almost five o'clock it was still the middle of the afternoon and the sunshine warm on my face. Stretch, thirst slaked, came padding out, lay down next to me, and went to sleep, chin on paws, ignoring the rasping ruckus of a magpie in a nearby birch, obviously considering us both intruders.

A sailboat made broad zigzags, tacking eastward against the breeze that disturbed the waters of the bay, slowly headed toward a small, rocky island that is always crowded with water birds. Among the gulls there are two of my favorites: fat, black puffins with their clownish white, yellow, and orange markings, which flap their wings in underwater flight as they dive for food, and larger, long-necked cormorants, which stand very straight and lift their slender beaks at an angle that appears to exhibit a superior attitude. They always make me smile as I am reminded of a tall, thin woman who attended our local church when I was a girl and whose nose was always lifted heavenward in a seeming search for the grace and patience to tolerate the remainder of the congregation.

I spent the better part of an hour on the deck that afternoon, thankfully appreciating being home and knowing I could be there as long as I liked. Then I went in and fried half a pound of bacon cut into small pieces, chopped an onion to sauté in a bit of the resulting oil, and peeled and chopped several Idaho russets, all to make a kettle of my mother's potato soup, a favorite that has become a homecoming tradition with me.

While it simmered, I went upstairs to make my bed, only to find it already done, thanks again to Doris. Fresh towels had been hung in the connecting bathroom and a bar of new soap occupied the dish at one corner of the sink. It was obvious that she had vacuumed and dusted the whole house, washed the windows, and set everything to rights. I would have a lot to thank her for the next day, when I intended to stop by her house just down the road. That she had made a special effort to welcome me home made me realize that I had actually been gone three-quarters of a year on my trip to the Southwest.

I took a quick shower, put on comfortable at-home clothes, and went back downstairs, where I gave Stretch his dinner and put some classical background music on the CD player. Pouring myself a glass of Merlot, I settled at the table with a bowl of soup and crusty French bread from the Soldotna grocery, facing the window so I could watch the blue-purple shadows lengthen on the mountains while I enjoyed my homecoming dinner.

Finished, I took my dishes to the kitchen sink and reached under it for the detergent. My hand met empty space where I always leave the bottle. Leaning to look, on the opposite side of the space I saw a bottle all right, but it was not my usual Palmolive green. Instead I found a different kind of yellow dishwashing soap that was strange to me. Thinking back nine months, I knew there had been at least half a bottle of Palmolive there when I left Homer for the winter. To use it all Doris would have had to wash every dish in the kitchen, several times, but perhaps she had used it for something else in her cleaning efforts—possible, I supposed. Shrugging it off, I used a squirt of the yellow dishwashing stuff for my few dishes and set them to dry themselves in the drainer beside the sink.

From the tall bookcases near the fireplace I searched out and retrieved Edith Pargeter's marvelous book *The Heaven Tree*—which was not in its usual place, for some reason—from the bookcase and settled into my favorite chair for an evening of reading, with a second glass of wine at my elbow and Stretch, tummy taut with dinner, snoozing nearby in his basket.

There are chairs you sit *on* and those you sit *in,* and those you sit *on*—the wooden ones around my dining table, for instance—though appropriate, are never as satisfactory in terms of ease and coziness as those near my fireplace and bookshelves, which are the cushy, sit *in* kind, with plenty of padding and pillows to sink into comfortably for reading or a nap. And there is always a handy footstool nearby.

Sitting *in* mine, I knew I was really and truly safe *at home* and better for it. But not far into the medieval tale of Harry Talvace, English master mason, and his building of a wondrous church during the reign of King John, I drifted off. I woke the better part of an hour later, but only enough to close up and lock the house and take myself upstairs to that freshly made bed, where I slept long and dreamlessly until the bright sun woke me early next morning for a day in my garden.

How could I have guessed that just over a week later a pleading request for assistance from an acquaintance would interrupt my idyllic vision of a restful summer at home and take me off in new, unexpected—and frightening—directions?

FIVE

I WOKE LATE IN HILO THE MORNING AFTER OUR ATTEMPTED break-in hearing a thump or two from Karen's crutch as she moved down the hall toward the kitchen.

Luckily I didn't stop to get dressed, but went after her in my pajamas, for I got there just in time to see that although she had filled the twelve-cup coffeemaker with water, she was carefully measuring out one and a half level scoops of coffee to put in the filter—enough in my estimation for colored water, but nothing I would care to call coffee. To make it worse, I could read the package in her hand and it was beyond me to allow her to waste 100 percent Kona, the wonderful coffee for which Hawaii is famous. I'm not totally fussy, but weak-as-dishwater coffee would rank rather high if I made a list of dislikes in order.

"Let me do that," I suggested, seeing her sway slightly as she leaned on the crutch awkwardly to use both hands at the chore. "You'll fall and hurt yourself. Can't have that now, can we?"

"Oh, thanks," she said, setting down both package and scoop and moving away. "I hope I didn't wake you."

"No, I was ready to get up," I told her—glad I had done so in time to rescue the coffee. I loaded the filter amply, slipped it into place, and flipped the switch. "Sit down and I'll bring you some as soon as it's brewed."

I made us a quick breakfast of bacon, scrambled eggs, and toast while the coffeemaker did its gurgling job, and in just a few minutes we were once again sitting across from each other at the table, full plates and *strong* coffee in front of us.

The sliding back door was open and a soft breeze slipped in along with the morning sun that shone brightly as if the rain had been nothing but a dream. Except for a shrinking puddle or two, the patio outside was already dry. Beyond it was a grassy space and at one end under some trees was a colorful variety of white and purple orchids and anthurium, the bright, waxy red flowers that look plastic, which I had always considered exotic, but that Karen told me were common in local gardens. On the other end was what looked like a large bush, but was actually a short tree with lemons all over it in varying states of ripeness. Tall slender palm trees rose above rooftops in the distance and I could smell a fragrance on the light breeze that came from the direction of a plumeria tree in the yard behind ours. I was definitely not any more in Kansas—or Alaska—than Dorothy had been when she found the poppy field.

"Okay," I said, when I had rinsed our dishes, put them in the dishwasher, and picked up a notepad and pen from beside the telephone as I returned to the table. "Now, help me make a list of everything that needs to be done so you can get out of here. First, the packing. I assume you want to ship your furniture and household goods back to Alaska."

"Yes—well, most of it. But there's a lot that needs to

be sorted and about a third of it either sold through the newspaper or maybe a yard sale. Before I decided not to stay here, I was buying furniture for the new house. It's out there as well." She waved her good hand toward the extra room that had been a garage, where she had taken her fall.

"So the furniture in this part of the house was here when you rented it and belongs to the landlord?"

"No, it's all mine, except for the appliances. I bought the ones that are in there for the new house."

I got up and went to the door to take a look and found that three-quarters of the space was depressingly crowded with stacks of shipping boxes, a few empty and tossed in a corner, but most full, with narrow aisles between. Some had been opened, but many were still sealed with labels that told me they were things she had shipped from Alaska and never touched.

I went down the steps and walked slowly between the piles of Karen's possessions, new and old. Along one wall there was, as she had indicated, a lot of new furniture, some in large cartons, some not. I could see two large living room chairs and a sofa, a pair of end tables and a coffee table, a file cabinet, a desk and chair, three chests of drawers, a queen-sized and two twin bed frames, their mattresses still in boxes. In other large boxes were appliances—refrigerator, stove, washing machine and dryer, even an entertainment center that included a large-screen television.

After that brief assessment I could tell that Karen had furniture enough for two houses and then some. From what she had told me the contractor had barely started work on the building site and, except for the foundation, her new house still existed only on paper.

"Good grief, Karen!" I couldn't help saying, going

back to stand at the table and look down at her. "What were you thinking to buy all this stuff before your new house was even built?"

Startled, she stared up at me with her eyes and mouth wide. The helpless little girl vanished as her expression became a scowl of resentment, her tone, annoyed indignation.

"Look, I don't need your criticism and I don't see that is any of your business anyway. You may do everything perfectly, but I've just been doing the best I could."

Well, she probably had. We just defined it differently.

She abruptly stood up, tucked the crutch under her arm, and started for the back of the house.

"I'm going to get cleaned up and dressed. Then we can talk about what needs to be done—if you can keep from enlightening me on how you'd do it."

I stood looking after her, sorry I had spoken so quickly and without thinking—not used to dealing with such a thin-skinned and defensive attitude.

"Good job, Maxine," I muttered to myself under my breath. "Tell her how you really feel!"

Still and all, in ten minutes and in my estimation, the size of the task I had anticipated had more than doubled, and it was pretty evident that most of it was going to be up to me. That is not even to mention that, because she couldn't drive with her casts on, I had taken a taxi from the airport the day before and, considering who had been capable of making breakfast and who had not, I would be taking care of Karen, as well as her packing and whatever else the job required. Yard sale?

As I stood there, mentally grasping for perspective, there was a sudden shriek from Karen in the bathroom. I hurried in that direction, hoping she hadn't fallen and hurt herself again, but met her at the door as she came hobbling out without her crutch, clinging to the door frame with the other hand to maintain her balance, toothbrush in hand, paste around her mouth.

"Are you alright? What is it?" I asked.

She tried to speak through the toothpaste, gurgled, leaned against the wall and spit it into the palm of her good hand.

"The drain," she said. "It's stopped up and the whole shower space is full of ugly water and rising."

I moved around her to get into the bathroom and found that she was right—and that she had left water running in the basin, which would compound the problem. Giving the faucet a crank to turn it off, I stood looking into the shower stall that, one step lower than the rest of the room, was now more of a wading pool, though the filthy, brownish water slowly filling it would not have tempted me to try. The effect was emphasized by what was still clean of the white ceramic tile that covered the floor and the walls ceiling high.

"What will we do?" Karen wailed from behind me.

"What we *won't* do is run any more water or flush the toilet," I told her, watching the level of the ugly shower pool slow and stop just short of escaping into the main part of the bathroom. "Then *we* do nothing. We have to get someone else to take care of this problem. Is the house on a sewer line or septic tank system?"

She gave me a blank look. "I have no idea," she said. "What's the difference?"

"Never mind. It's the landlord's responsibility. Where's his phone number? We'll call and find out what he wants done—who to call."

"Oh, he's not going to like it," Karen said, shaking her head as she backed away into the hall as if he were standing next to me. "Can't you just call someone else to fix it? He'll just yell that it's all my fault if you call *him*."

She had said *you*. Already she was assuming I would take control of the situation.

"Maybe it was someone else's," I told her. "*We* won't know until *we* find out what's plugging the line. If there's a septic tank, it could be full and need to be emptied."

She looked close to tears at the idea of a confrontation with the new landlord, to say nothing of the disaster at hand—or should I say at *foot*? It was obvious that whatever was going to happen—and something clearly had to happen—this was another disaster that would fall directly on my shoulders.

"Just—get me—his phone number, Karen," I said in weary resignation.

Perhaps it was time for me to meet this unreasonable, ill-tempered, uncompromising new landlord anyway. I like to know what to expect from an adversary, if he really was as disagreeable as Karen described him.

He was!

In half an hour, after pounding on the front door, then impatiently—and illegally, I might add—using his duplicate key to gain entry before I could answer it, Raymond Taylor was standing in the living room, glaring offensively at the two of us. Without a word he wheeled and disappeared into the bathroom to see the problem for himself.

Karen gave me a worried look and limped slowly across to sit down at the table.

He was a bantamweight man with—it soon became clear—a matching small, malicious mind and no lack of a nasty temper as well.

"What the hell did you put down the drain?" he

asked with a scowl, fists planted aggressively on hips as he leaned over Karen in her chair.

"Nothing but what is supposed to go down," Karen told him in a small strained voice that held a hint of inappropriate apology as she shrank as far from him as she could get.

"Hey!" I snapped. "Back off. There's no need to get hostile about this. It's a problem that needs to be fixed, that's all. We can talk it over sensibly and you can call someone to get it taken care of, since it's your property."

"And just who the hell are you?" he demanded, swinging my way. "If you're living here with her you'll have to get out. The place was rented to a single tenant, no more, and not even that for long."

I gripped the back of a chair hard enough to make my fingers ache and managed to keep as tight a rein on my rising temper.

"My name is Maxie McNabb. I'm a friend of Karen's from Alaska and I'm *not* living here. I'm a guest, here to help her pack. Considering her injuries, she needs my assistance. So if you want her to move out of here, as she says you've so unreasonably insisted, then I stay while the job is done. After that we're both gone. Satisfied?"

He sniffed. "Just be sure you are, or I will move whatever's left."

"Karen's rent is paid through the end of the month. That's two full weeks away. We'll be out by that time."

"She'd better be, or a minute after midnight on the first of July I'll evict you both—toss any of your stuff left inside out onto the street—legally."

I made no attempt to repress the *gotcha* smile that lifted just the corners of my mouth. I knew, from a description long ago provided by my Daniel, that it gave me a satisfied *I win* expression mixed with the cold promise of reprisal if I should be ignored. He had called it my look of "evil glee."

"Before you start making that kind of threat, you'd do well to consider your illegal entry to this house, with two of us to witness that you let yourself in without proper notification or invitation—and not for the first time, as I understand," I told Mr. Taylor.

In two minutes, he was gone with a parting shot: "I'll send you a plumber, but it's your problem. You caused it—you pay for it."

"I don't think so. Karen will send you the bill," I called after him.

Pretending he didn't hear, he slammed the door behind him and left us staring at each other.

Six

AN HOUR AND A HALF LATER, JUST AS I WAS GETTING READY to have another round with Taylor by telephone, two plumbers arrived in a yellow van full of tools, hoses, buckets, lengths of pipe, high-top rubber boots, and a general assortment of other items I didn't recognize, or need to.

The older one came to rap politely on the door and look up at me with a cheerful grin. "You the lady gotta drain problem?"

In contrast to our last visitor, this man's friendliness was obvious and welcome in the lines around his mouth and eyes that told me his grin was habitual. A native Hawaiian, he looked to be in his forties, was about my five foot seven in height, and had broad shoulders and muscular arms. What color his pants and sweatshirt had originally been was anyone's guess, as, though fairly clean, they had clearly been washed over and over, which had transformed them to a faded universal gray-brown.

His partner, a much younger Caucasian man, came to stand close behind with a watchful look on his serious face. He looked to be in his late teens, but it was hard to judge. Close to six feet tall and very slender, in overalls and a grubby T-shirt, in motion he gave the impression that he was still a bit awkwardly growing used to the height he had attained and to the size of his hands and feet. And I noticed that he had a couple of bruises on his left arm that reinforced the idea.

"I'm Adam," the older man told me, then waved a hand toward his helper. "And this is Jerry—plumber in training."

"And I am Maxie," I reciprocated, offering my hand.

He hesitated to take it, explaining, "My hands aren't very clean."

"Not a problem," I told him smiling, hand still extended. "Hands are washable. It's respectful to touch hands with new friends, clean or not."

The grin reappeared as we shook hands. With it he gave me a single courteous nod of the head and a bit of something more in the amusement that twinkled in his eyes.

"It is a pleasure to meet you, Maxie. Now," he requested, "show me this problem with the water that doesn't drain and goes where it is not wanted."

I introduced the two to Karen, then acquainted them with the ugly pool in the shower. Adam frowned at the sight of the backup.

"You on a septic tank?" he asked.

"This house is rented, so I don't know."

"Never mind," he said and, with another grin, gave me an interesting gesture with one hand, middle three fingers close to the palm, thumb and pinkie extended. "We'll take a look. If you have one, it'll be in the backyard."

They disappeared around the outside of the house

and I went through to the back door to see them set to work with a rod, which Adam had Jerry thrust repeatedly into various spots in the backyard in search of the tank.

"What does this mean?" I asked, repeating his gesture to Karen, who had not gone to the door, but was letting me, as expected, deal with the plumbers.

"It means 'hang loose,'" she told me with a shrug. "A careless Hawaiian sort of thing, I guess. You'd better keep an eye on him."

Her attitude annoyed me, but I remembered her exhibiting some of the same superiority toward Alaska Native people and was not too surprised. Where I find other cultures' customs richly interesting, some people still feel themselves better than others and don't hesitate to let it show. They are the losers for it, in my estimation.

In a short time Adam came to the back door and called me to see where they had found the septic tank, buried shallowly under the grass, and the main pipe that drained wastewater and sewage into it. Jerry was now at work cutting and lifting away blocks of sod to uncover its access lid. He glanced up and gave me a quick half smile, but went silently on with his work in distinct deference to his boss.

"This," Adam said, pointing to the heavy metal cap on the end of a pipe low on the side of the house, "is the access to the drain pipe that goes into the tank. I'll be able to let you know soon what is causing the problem, probably something blocking that line."

Leaving them to their discoveries, I suggested to Karen that we start sorting her belongings. Pulling a chair close to the doorway I recommended that she sit there, so she could tell me which items should be packed to ship to Alaska, and which somehow sold before we left Hawaii.

I pulled a small table up close and handed her paper and a pencil. "Keep one list of items for a yard sale and another for what you want to mention in an ad for the local paper. The rest I'll pack for shipping."

We had worked for just over half an hour when Adam called me to the backyard again, with Karen following slowly with her crutch to see what they had found.

Jerry looked up from where he was now laying the squares of sod back into place to re-cover the top of the septic tank ten feet away.

"The tank is not full, so that is not the problem," Adam told us. "Here is what was blocking the pipe." He pointed to a soggy, dark brown mess of water, sewage, and what looked like some kind of fabric that together half filled a bucket he had placed under the access to the drain. I could faintly hear what I assumed was the water on the shower floor now draining through the pipe on its way to the septic tank. With the rod he had used to locate the tank, he hooked the fabric and lifted it above the bucket, where it dripped dirty liquid. A pink spot or two were now visible on one side.

"That's one of *my* pink hand towels." Karen identified it in an injured tone, as if Adam were responsible for its condition. "I left it hanging on the line on the patio to dry yesterday and forgot to bring it in. But how did it get into the pipe?"

"Someone put it there," Adam said, giving her a long, questioning look. "It could not have gone down the drain from inside—too small. This pipe is the short arm of a Y that joins another, longer arm that is the underground line to the septic tank. Someone had to open the cap and shove the towel far enough in to block that part of the Y in order to stop up your drain. This was done on purpose."

He lowered the filthy towel back into the bucket and we stood looking down at its distasteful contents.

"But *why*?" Karen asked, frowning.

Adam and I looked up at each other for a silent, extended moment and I knew we were thinking the same thing: harassment. This was a nasty trick perpetuated by someone who wanted to cause trouble. But it was not necessary to say so. It would just anger and upset Karen with more suspicions in the landlord's direction.

My thoughts turned immediately, of course, to his intolerance. Then I took another mental step. Could last night's attempt at the front door have been no more than a distraction while Taylor, or one of his minions, took the cap off the pipe and shoved in the towel? If so, it could be an attempt to drive us out sooner than the end of the month, which, in my estimation, was possible, but would be counterproductive as it would only slow down the sorting and packing process.

Adam shrugged and turned to wave a hand at the cap, which he had screwed tightly back onto its threads at the end of the pipe.

"Everything is fine now," he told Karen. "The problem is solved, the drain is open, and you can run water again. Call me if you have further trouble, okay?"

I agreed. He wrote out a bill for Karen, who thanked him in her overly profuse, but slightly superior way and limped slowly into the house with it, hopefully intending to send it on to the landlord.

Jerry, who had been listening closely, finished replacing the sod, gathered their tools, and disappeared around the house to return them to the van. So I walked the same direction with Adam, not only feeling a wish to wordlessly atone for Karen's attitude, but that Adam had something more to say to me.

"What's on your mind, Adam?" I asked him. "There was something you almost said, but didn't, back there, wasn't there?"

"You are a wise and careful woman, I think," he said, stopping to give me a careful, but respectful look. "You and I, we see more than just an obstruction in the pipe. Yes?"

I nodded without speaking, waiting, as did Jerry, who had come back around the corner of the house.

"Maybe your friend would be frightened," he said. "I think you are not so easily alarmed, but are also careful. You know this problem was no accident. Someone made it happen for a reason. Do you have any idea who or why?"

"No." I shook my head, still listening, but thinking back again to the possible implications of that person at the door in the middle of the night. "Not really—just some suspicions that may not be accurate."

"There was something else, then?" he asked, interpreting my frown correctly.

I told him about the midnight incident in brief terms, but decided not to mention the landlord. He listened with a kind of thoughtful concern on his face.

"This is not good," he told me. "I think you should watch carefully. Don't be afraid to call the police if anything happens to worry you."

"Believe me, I will," I said, extending my hand as I had in meeting him. "Thank you, Adam—for everything."

The irrepressible grin once again transformed his face as he glanced down at his now truly soiled palm and gave it to me anyway, in a way that made it a considerate gesture, dirt and all.

"Thank *you,* Auntie," he returned. "You take good care now."

Then they were gone up the long driveway past the front house to disappear in a right turn onto the street beyond.

I stood looking after them, thinking hard for a minute or two, slowly becoming aware that over the sound of local traffic on that street I was hearing the voices of many birds in the nearby trees. A flock of sparrows, brown like those we have at home, took sudden wing and vanished over the roof, leaving their familiar chirping to the few that remained. Within it there was a sudden soft warble that I didn't recognize. I looked carefully into the branches and had just located what I thought was the singer when it too flew quickly away—a small gray bird with a white belly and white cheek patches on a black head. Its tail was also black and its bill yellow with a hint of rusty orange. *"Pik-pik-pik,"* it called, just before it flew and before I had a chance for a really good look.

I went in the front door to wash my hands, hoping that when we finished the job at hand, before I flew home to Alaska, this being my first visit to our fiftieth state I would have a little time to see some of the Big Island. There was a place there in Hilo that supposedly rented motor homes and I intended to find out more about it. Then, if I could, I might even spend a day or two driving one around the island, to Kailua-Kona on the opposite and sunny side.

Somewhere along that coast, east of Kona, there was a place I had read about years before that had always fascinated me. It had a long and, to me, unpronounceable Hawaiian name, Pu'uhonua o Honaunau, but was called in English the Place of Refuge. There, early Hawaiians who broke a taboo, or *kapu*—and there were many of them—could be sentenced to death. According to the guidebook I had purchased in the Honolulu airport, while waiting for my short hop to Hilo, if that person could elude pursuers and reach this place of refuge, he could then perform certain rituals and all would be forgiven. I would like very much to see that particular place, which was now a national historic park.

For the moment, however, there was more on my plate than I had anticipated in terms of getting Karen ready to leave, so it would be wise not only to get as much done as quickly as possible, but to *watch carefully,* as Adam had suggested.

I went in smiling to myself in amusement, as I remembered what Adam had called me.

"Auntie," I told Karen with a chuckle. "He called me 'auntie.' I know he's younger, but it seems . . ."

"He did?" she interrupted, in an amused, but slightly awed tone, eyes wide in astonishment. "You're *really* sure he called you 'auntie'?"

Her reaction halted what I had intended to say.

"Yes, he really did. Why?"

" 'Auntie' is a Hawaiian term of respect for an older woman, and it's not used lightly or often. You must have impressed him a lot somehow."

I didn't wonder at, or take personally, her incredulity that Adam had given me such a compliment. I was amazed myself and—to tell the truth—more than a little pleased.

SEVEN

I DID NOT SLEEP IN MY BED THAT NIGHT, BUT TOOK A PILLOW and blanket with me to the futon Karen used instead of a sofa, next to the front door in the living room. The stool I had knocked over the night before, I moved to the other side of the room. If there was to be a repeat of the break-in attempt, or any other kind of mischief, I intended to be where I had easy access to both front and back doors in order to catch the perpetrator without allowing him, or her—for, I suddenly realized, it could be a woman—the time to escape without my at least getting a good look at whoever.

Karen, evidently assuming I would be responsible for the safety of us both, had hobbled off to sleep in her own bed. I had hoped she wouldn't protest my change in sleeping location, or offer to join me, for having her out of the way would make things easier, if anything should occur.

Nothing did, though I woke several times during the night at sounds that were of no threat but were not familiar to me—a shrill sort of whistle somewhere in the distance, for instance, that went on and on until I fell asleep again listening to it. Other than that, the night passed quietly and without incident of any unwelcome kind.

I woke with the sun and had the coffee made—my way—before Karen came yawning and thumping down the hall on her single crutch.

"Good morning," she said, sitting down at the table. "Did you sleep well? I certainly did."

I told her I had, and asked about the shrill sound I had heard. "Is it some kind of night bird?"

"Oh, no. That's a frog."

"A *frog*? No frog makes a sound like that."

"This kind does and everyone hates it. You should hear them in the forest outside of town, where there are thousands—millions. It's a tiny one, about the size of a quarter, called a coqui, and somehow they got in from the Caribbean. Just be glad we don't have more in town."

I tried to imagine what *millions* of the frogs must sound like and was very glad to have heard only one, as I proceeded to make breakfast, scrambling the remaining three eggs and putting the last two slices of bread in the toaster.

"Unless you want some of the instant oatmeal I saw in your cupboard, we're out of breakfast food," I said, sitting down across from her and picking up my coffee cup. "Looks like a trip to the grocery store will be in order sometime today."

"Oatmeal? Ugh!" she said, frowning. "I can't drive with this cast on my leg, but you can take my car. The grocery isn't far away."

"Is there a liquor store near it?" I asked, with the idea of my favorite Jameson whiskey in mind for later in the day.

"Oh, they sell booze as well—right there in the store. Not separate like Alaska."

That was good news, for it would save scouting one out in the unfamiliar streets of Hilo.

Having scrubbed out the filthy shower stall after the plumbers left the day before, I used it to let warm water soothe away the small tired edges of my somewhat restless sleep. Then I put my graying dark hair up in the twist in which I most often wear it and dressed in a light denim skirt and sleeveless blouse. I had been going barefoot in the house, but had worn what I have always called flip-flops to go outside. Here, Karen told me, they should be called "slippers," or you would expose yourself as a tourist and be subject to tolerant smiles from the locals. For the trip to the grocery I put my leather sandals on bare feet. I had expected the temperature on this sunny day to be much warmer than it was in Alaska's June. It was, but not as much as I had anticipated. Instead of being hot, it was pleasantly hovering around eighty degrees, though it had been significantly cooler at night.

Backing Karen's small blue Honda out of the carport—trust Karen to have baby blue—I made a quarter turn and headed up the drive toward the street. The drive ran between the larger house on the right and the long back walls of what appeared to be two office buildings on the left. A walkway ran the length of it and halfway to the street a narrow passageway separated the single-story buildings. I gave the opening a quick glance as I went by and caught sight of someone standing there in the shadow, looking in my direction—a man, I thought, leaning a shoulder against a wall, one hand raised to the side of his head, wearing a black T-shirt and jeans, a blue backpack at his feet. Then I was past and, arriving at the street, turned left on Kilauea Avenue as traffic permit-

ted, but it left me wondering if I should have stopped
and backed the car up to take a closer look. *Get a grip,*
I told myself. *Now you're getting paranoid.* So I went on
and soon found the KTA Super Store in the Puainako
Town Center a little over a mile away, but the drive itself
was very interesting.

The houses I passed on the way, especially the older
ones, had a distinctly tropical look, many built in two
stories, with the front door at the top of a flight of stairs
that ended in a porch. The roofs of these were often
square or rectangular metal with extended eaves that
would allow rain to pour off a foot or more away from
the underlying structure. They rose gently to a central
peak that would also encourage runoff.

There were literally hundreds of palm trees rising
close, and visible in the distance because of their height,
some lining Kilauea Avenue, on which I drove south
that morning. Everywhere along it was an abundance of
tropical growth. Each yard and space that was not otherwise occupied or covered with blacktop, cement, or lawn
was full of an incredible assortment of greens, much of
it adorned with flowers of all kinds and colors: bright
hibiscus, anthurium, both white and red, large and small
orchids, like those in Karen's yard, plumeria blossoms on
trees, and many other plants and trees I couldn't identify. It
was a feast for the eyes and for the nose, as I found in lowering the windows to let in the gentle breeze. Some of the
shrubs were as tall as the houses and had leaves the shape
of my indoor split-leaf philodendron at home. But these
were enormous—large as serving platters.

Pay attention to the road, Maxie, I told myself, as
someone behind me honked when I ignored a green
light to take in a particularly colorful garden. *You can
take an exploratory walk later.*

But what would a walk be like without Stretch, I wondered, knowing I would very much miss the company of my dachshund pal. It had been a long time since I had gone anywhere without him and I was definitely feeling his absence. I understood that, free of rabies, Hawaii wanted to keep it that way, but it was sad anyway not to have him along and always interested in exploring or, at least, examining whatever was within his low-to-the-ground reach.

Well, I thought, *it won't be too much longer.*

The grocery was every bit as intriguing as the drive. I love places with new kinds of food, and it was a gastronomical delight, loaded with as many kinds of ethnic foods as there are different nationalities of people who live in Hawaii—Native Hawaiians, Pacific Islanders, Caucasians, African Americans, Asians from many countries, and other, or mixed, races. And they had all brought their food preferences with them, it seemed.

I bought much more than I anticipated, for there was also an abundance of tropical fruit for what seemed like pennies and would cost the earth at home. If you could even find them they would never be tree-ripened. Into my cart went golden papayas—ready to eat with the limes I picked up for that purpose—and a pineapple so ripe it was already dripping juice, and I could not resist a couple of yellow-skinned mangoes.

Besides the usual aisles of packaged food, along the back wall of the store were a couple of large glass cases, like ones in a meat department at home, where the butcher will cut or just package your selection of meat or seafood. These displayed a variety of what the clerk told me was called *poke*—pronounced "pokey"—chunks of raw or seared meats, seafood, even tofu, seasoned with soy sauce, garlic, seaweed, chile peppers, and local sea salt, which is eaten as an appetizer or snack. I looked, but didn't buy, intuitively knowing it was something Karen, who wouldn't even eat oatmeal, would hate. Instead, I selected a chicken to roast and a couple of pieces of fresh *ahi*—tuna—and some jasmine rice.

Wandering up and down, I picked up three cans of soup, a package of cookies, and some crackers, then found my way to a dozen eggs and a pound of bacon. The everyday items looked boring when compared to the rest of my cart's exotic contents. I was distracted once, by a display of seed packages in a garden aisle that offered some interesting gourds I thought I might try to grow at home, tossing two into the cart.

A few aisles later, I found my bottle of Jameson near the bakery, which was another irresistible temptation. Sweet rolls followed two loaves of freshly baked bread—French and wheat for toast—into my rapidly growing collection. A tub of soft cream cheese completed my shopping, I thought, so I started for the checkout counter before I could discover more. But another enticing choice of aisles lay between me and my goal and I wound up with two packages of Kona coffee to take back to Alaska with me, along with a large bag of chocolate-covered macadamia nuts.

If I hadn't time at the moment to see much of Hawaii, I could at least taste some of it.

When I suddenly turned the cart in midaisle to head toward the front of the store, a figure swung around, moved quickly away from me to the end, and vanished around it to the right without looking back. It stopped me cold. But this time my impression was more distinct: a young man with dark hair over a narrow face, short-legged and husky through the shoulders, he was wearing jeans, a black T-shirt, and a pair of dark glasses—with a dark blue backpack slung over one shoulder. I was almost certain it was the same man I had seen in the walkway between the buildings as I drove up the drive on leaving Karen's. Could it have been the same person, or someone who reminded me of him? Was he following me, or was it just a coincidence?

Whatever. He was nowhere to be seen when I reached the end of the aisle and took a careful look around. I went on to checkout with my groceries, searching the faces of everyone I could see, with no results. Pushing my cart out to Karen's car in the parking lot, I looked around the area with no more success. Whoever he was, he was gone, was not the person I suspected, or had concealed himself well.

I put the cart in the corral provided for returning them and drove back the way I had come, checking out the drivers of as many of the cars as I could that followed or passed me, but had no luck. Turning back into Karen's driveway, halfway along it I slowed to take a look at the walkway between the two buildings, but it was empty. Almost convinced I was imagining trouble, I forced myself to put away most of my concern. Still, a bit of it lingered and I knew I would continue to keep the close watch Adam the plumber had recommended.

Parking in the carport, I carried one sack of groceries to the front door, wide open behind its screen, which opened silently. As I stepped in and paused to remove my sandals, I could hear Karen's voice in the kitchen, evidently on the phone.

". . . be okay. Yes—tomorrow. No, don't call here. I'll call you again when it's safe—when she's . . ."

I froze to listen, still holding the grocery bag, but I had leaned too far to unfasten a sandal strap and the package of crackers I had balanced on top fell off and hit the floor with a thump and a crunch.

There was an immediately suspended silence from the kitchen. Then, quickly, more quietly, "She's here. I'll talk to you later." Then there was the click of the receiver being replaced in its cradle and she came crutching out of the kitchen.

"There you are," she said. "I thought you'd got lost."

Her face was a bit flushed as she stopped, leaned on the crutch, clasped her hands together in a gesture that seemed nervously self-protective, then continued hurriedly, as I stood saying nothing, staring at her over the box of crackers on the floor that I had not yet retrieved.

"I was—ah—talking to the shipping company. They wanted to know when to schedule the pickup for the things to go to Alaska. I told them that as soon as I talked to you I'd let them know what day next week to come. Monday. I think Monday would be about right." Abruptly, she changed the subject. "How was your shopping? Did you have any trouble finding the store?"

"It was fine," I told her shortly, picked up the crackers, took the bag to the kitchen, and, with my back to her, set the groceries on the counter, her words echoing in my mind: *Don't call here. I'll call you again . . . when it's safe.*

Safe? What wouldn't be safe to say to the shipping company with me there? Whoever she had been talking to, it had *not* been anyone connected with shipping her belongings. That was clear. Then who? And why the apparent secrecy?

Considering her defensive stance, I decided not to ask about it just then, but to think it over carefully first. That might have been a mistake.

"Why don't you put these away while I get the rest from the car?" I suggested, heading back to the front door.

I brought in the groceries and asked her no questions, letting her think I had accepted her unreliable and unnecessary explanation for the phone call. I also said nothing to her about the man I might have seen twice while I was away from the house, though I did ask her, "What are those two buildings to the left of the driveway?"

"A doctor or dentist, I think. Maybe an attorney," she told me. "Some kind of offices anyway."

It was pretty much what I had surmised. But that walkway between would make a good place for someone to keep an eye on her house, if someone wanted to, or was. So it couldn't hurt to be on guard, just as I would be watching and listening more closely to Karen in the near future.

Eight

For the next two days, though I kept that close watch and continued to sleep in the front room, nothing suspicious happened. I saw no more of the man with the backpack, the drains worked perfectly, and, thanks be, we neither saw nor heard anything from landlord Taylor, though I put the plumber's bill in an envelope and mailed it off to him when I noticed that Karen had neglected the chore.

I did not ask her about the phone call I had overheard, but I wondered about it uneasily. I had the distinct impression that if I questioned her, she would deny that anything odd was going on, so I let it ride, but paid closer attention, and considered calling the company that was to ship her goods to see what I could find out. Not doing so may have been another mistake, but how could I have known? Perhaps I should have demanded to know what was going on, just to see what kind of answer I would get, and to let her know that I am not so easily fooled.

We worked hard at getting Karen's belongings sorted,

packed, and ready to ship, or for sale. I did most of the sorting and packing, while Karen kept lists and tried to make decisions on what should be kept and what left behind.

Many of the boxes she had shipped from Alaska I refused to open; I just put them in the growing pile to be sent back, figuring they had already been through the selection process once and I wasn't going to give her another chance at them.

Packing the boxes was relatively easy. It was her indecisiveness over the sorting that made me half-crazy at times.

"Do you really want *all* these videotapes sent home?"

"Well, ah . . . I don't know. Maybe I should go through them and get rid of some."

She took two hours at it, and from 142 discarded three.

"How about the books in these twelve boxes?"

"Most of those belonged to Lewis."

Well, I knew Lewis had been a reader, but would he have been willing to pay for shipping them all? Remembering his practical outlook on life, I doubted some would ever have arrived in Hawaii in the first place.

I held up Volume A–B of a set of thirty-year-old encyclopedias. "These were his?"

"Yes."

"They're completely out of date. Will you ever use them?"

"Maybe not, but they were Lewis's."

"Karen! Are they really *worth* the cost of shipping? Save a few of his favorites and get rid of the rest, including these. You don't read much, do you?"

I knew the answer. Karen did needlework and

watched television—lots of television. Probably the last thing she had ever read was Nancy Drew.

"Well, no, but . . ."

The furniture and appliances she had bought for the new house were somewhat easier. She selected one chair, a sofa, the entertainment center, and the new refrigerator to ship. The rest she agreed to sell through an ad in the paper. Everything I could talk her out of I put in a yard sale pile, but I had to keep a close eye on it, as she tended to slip things out and move them back to the pile for shipping.

By the time we were finished with everything in that extra room, I was exhausted from lifting and sorting, but mostly from contending with her equivocation, and we still had the rest of the house to deal with.

Lying on my aching back in bed that night, listening to rain drip off the eaves again, I decided I needed a break—and not just an escape from the work at hand, but from Karen as well. I knew I would have to find a way to take it on my own, however, for having her along to—wherever—would be no break at all.

Maybe she would welcome some time on her own before we tackled what was still to be done. I could hope so, though I doubted it would be the case. Also, I suspected that with me gone there was the distinct possibility that she would relapse into old habits and take back half of everything now destined for sale.

I am generally a fairly patient person, not easily given to abandoning tasks I willingly let myself in for, like them or not. Though Lewis had clearly made most of the decisions for the two of them, it seemed to me her inclination to leave them to someone—anyone—else had not lessened as she grew older. I think one tends to overlook other people's foibles when one sees them not often and then only briefly, so, annoyed or not, it was my own fault for agreeing so readily to help out when asked.

As it turned out, arranging to take time for myself the next morning was easier than I anticipated, for Karen got up suddenly remembering that she had an appointment with the doctor at nine o'clock. She told me over papaya, toast, and coffee.

"I'll drive you," I volunteered before she could assume I would. "But could you take a taxi back?"

"Why?" she asked with a puzzled frown. "You could easily—"

I interrupted, deciding on the spur of the moment not to make excuses.

"I'd like to take a little time to see something besides the grocery store while I'm here. There's a botanical garden on the edge of town that sounds wonderful in the brochure I picked up at the airport."

"Oh," she said, as if I had invited her, and shook her head, "I couldn't do that. It's a lot of walking down a steep hill; a long ways—much more than I could do now. Besides, I've been there and it isn't much—just a lot of trees and weird tropical plants with flowers that look almost alive, some that eat bugs, I think. No, I don't think so."

The botanical garden was sounding more and more interesting to me as she said she couldn't come along, so I simply reiterated my request that she taxi home.

"Well . . . ," she said, unhappily. "I suppose . . ."

And so it happened.

I drove her across town to the doctor's office near the hospital, where she got out, turned to take her crutch and purse, and, still hoping I would change my mind, said, in a half-pleading tone, "You're sure you couldn't . . ."

"I'll see you back at the house sometime this afternoon," I told her firmly. "Good luck with the doctor."

Then I waved and drove off, leaving her on her own and perfectly capable of taking care of that particular appointment and the trip home from it.

The feeling of freedom and being on my own was delicious. But mixed into it was the knowledge that what I really wanted was to be back in my own house in Homer, with no one but my own good dog, Stretch. It was much the same desire that had brought me up the long road home to Alaska less than a month earlier. But this time there was also the weight of another person's eccentricity involved and for a minute I felt a little ashamed of my own intolerance.

It didn't last long. It was time Karen grew up and took charge of her own existence, and stopped depending on other people, wasn't it? So I didn't allow myself to dwell on it, but still wished I had stayed in my own safe refuge, where all is accepted, all forgiven, for nowhere else am I perfectly at home than in the one place I love most dearly.

A favorite quote from Kipling came suddenly to mind, expressing it perfectly:

> *God gave all men all earth to love,*
> *But, since our hearts are small,*
> *Ordained for each one spot should prove*
> *Beloved over all.*

It was time, I decided, to copy out that quote, frame it, and hang it on my wall, where I could see it often and remember to do a better job of appreciating my good fortune in having that beloved spot, however interesting the rest of the world might be.

Meanwhile, I would spend the next few hours gathering patience to finish the job for which I had volunteered, and try to do it generously, with sympathy, if not approval.

After that and, perhaps, another day or two of tropical freedom, I would go home, collect Stretch, stay there as long as I wanted, do no more sorting, and make no unnecessary decisions.

As I drove on I remembered another line that made me smile, for it fit the present situation well. Voltaire had said it first, but my Daniel had quoted it often over life's trials and tribulations: *"Life is a shipwreck, but we must not forget to sing in the lifeboats."*

Thank you, Daniel.

You're very welcome, my dear.

To reach the Bayfront Highway, which the map said would take me seven miles north to a turnoff that led to the botanical garden, I drove through part of downtown Hilo, an interesting place of historic buildings. On my way past, I could see they were full of tempting shops and galleries that I would save till later, along with a farmers' market and the Pacific Tsunami Museum I knew were somewhere among them.

The layout of the town is different from how it was originally, for more than one tidal wave has struck there with devastating force, taking many lives and reducing structures to rubble, then sweeping much of what was left out to sea along with an appalling number of its residents, few of whom were rescued. In the distant past Hilo was a trading place for Hawaiians, but with the unforgettable memory of ruin there have been no buildings set near the broad crescent of Hilo Bay, which has been left to beautiful public parks and a barrier built to help counteract future tsunamis.

It reminded me of the disastrous earthquake that hit south-central Alaska in March 1964. The most powerful in United States history, besides tearing apart downtown Anchorage—dropping some storefronts into what had or would have been their basements—it generated tsunamis that killed more than a hundred people and swept whole communities and parts of others off the map.

Luckily, my house in Homer did not yet exist, but its current location high above Kachemak Bay made it, thankfully, invulnerable to tsunami. Seeing another community that had suffered similarly made me remember that it is not *if* such disasters will happen again, but *when*. We do not own the earth—just occupy it at the whim of nature.

Turning left on Bayfront, I drove north out of town. In a few miles I saw a blue sign indicating the entrance to a four-mile scenic route and turned right onto a two-lane road that wound its way through what immediately became a tropical forest, crossing one-lane bridges below which clear streams splashed their way steeply down narrow, rocky valleys toward the sea.

It was a magical place, too tempting to simply drive through without stopping. So I pulled over into a wide spot just beyond one of the bridges and stepped out astonished at the tropical tangle of my surroundings. Without the sound of the engine I could hear that the incredible jungle of uncountable colors of green was full of birdcalls. They added grace notes to the gurgling laughter of falling water as it danced its sparkling way down toward the ocean, in and out of spots of sunshine and into the prevailing deep shadows of tall trees. Twisted vines climbed the tree trunks in search of light, and lower foliage was so thick it completely hid the ground, which I could tell fell sharply away beneath it.

I returned to the car and drove off feeling more

determined to see more of what the Big Island had to offer before leaving. There were two volcanoes, white and even black sand beaches, world-famous water-falls, and much more tropical splendor to appreciate—especially after spending so much time indoors in the middle of a town. And somewhere on the south side of the island was the Refuge that I very much wanted to visit. It was an opportunity too good not to take. Besides, I might never make it back again. With this in mind, I have adopted a do-it-now senior philosophy to match a determination to sing in my personal lifeboat.

A little farther along the road I came to the visitor center for the Hawaii Tropical Botanical Garden—as they described it: "A Garden in a Valley on the Ocean." Parking in the ample lot in front, I went inside what turned out to be a small museum and gift shop, empty except for a woman behind a counter, who turned with a welcome.

"Aloha," she said with a smile. "Can I help you?"

"I'd like to visit your garden," I told her simply. "I'm a new visitor and am rather missing my own."

In five minutes she had taken my registration fee, given me a map of the garden, and explained that the tour would be self-guided and I could take as much time as I liked.

"Here in the visitor center we are one hundred twenty feet above sea level. The walkway down into the garden is five hundred feet long and part of it is quite steep, but there are handrails to hold on to if you need them. Go slowly or you will miss some interesting plants and flowers on the way down. There are several benches on the way and in the lower part of the garden. If you are tired of walking, one of our golf cart drivers will bring you back up the hill—just flag one down."

Outside, I sat for a few minutes in one of the comfortable chairs provided for visitors, to look over the map she had handed me and to leaf through a book on flowers and tropical plants that I had found in the gift shop. Then I crossed the road to the garden's gate, where a volunteer directed me to the top of the walkway—an elevated boardwalk that wound away suspended over the rocks of a ravine much too steep for trails. Lush tropical growth of all kinds crowded up close to the walk and its handrails: tall trees, exotic ferns and vines that were new to me, along with some I recognized, like bamboo and banana plants—or were they trees? Many plants had blossoms, large and small. There were even a few orchids that looked down from the branches and trunks of trees. One or two plants looked like blossoms, but, upon closer examination, turned out to be deep red leaves. Others were striped with yellow or pale green. And there were flowers everywhere.

The information I had picked up in the visitor center had told me that this garden was "a plant sanctuary, a living seed bank, and a study center for trees and plants of the tropical world." The thousands of samples of tropical flora from all over the world that I saw around me confirmed it as I went down what they said was just the *access* to the rest of the garden. I could hardly wait for the rest, though I already felt somewhat overwhelmed with what surrounded me—it made my garden at home seem very small indeed. Then I reminded myself that the pleasure I took in mine, through many years of effort and careful selection of what would and would not survive and even, for a season, thrive in my cold-weather climate, must equate to the satisfaction these gardeners took in their tropical one. Size and exotic nature could make no real difference to a dedicated gardener, working with what was available and achievable, whatever the limitations.

So I went happily down the long wandering walkway, moving aside once to allow one of the golf carts to pass on its way up, stopping here and there to examine and appreciate, sitting down on a bench to look up in awe at some towering palms topped with fronds close to a hundred feet over my head.

Next to the rail in one place was a small, delicate heliconia, related to the bird of paradise for which Hawaii is well known. It charmed me with its long, waxy green leaves and unusual flowers in brilliant red and yellow. Red *bracts*—thin, narrow modified leaves—extended horizontally on alternate sides of a long, straight stem that zigzagged where each bract began; and where each joined the stem perched a delicate, canary yellow flower, like a tiny bird.

From the bottom of the boardwalk, I spent two hours wandering the maze of trails that rose and fell, winding away from and rejoining each other as the ground grew more level between the boardwalk and the eastern end of the ravine. In the dark shadow of trees ran Onomea Falls, a lovely three-tiered waterfall that burbled and splashed, filling the air with moisture that encouraged thick mosses on the surrounding rocks and tree trunks.

Nearby lay a myriad of different heliconias, large and small, with delicate and meaty blossoms, some of which even hung down from the largest of the plants, rather than growing up.

There was a whole garden of orchids and an interesting assortment of more than eighty varieties of bromeliads—air plants that in the crown of the plant collect rainwater, from which they draw nutrients.

Birds were everywhere. Seldom to be seen for more

than a momentary flash of bright feathers in the dense tangle of tropical foliage, they made themselves known with a continuous musical background as they flitted between trees and vines.

At one junction I found a small Asian man sitting next to the trail, hands busy expertly tying knots in an all but invisible thin line; he was making a circular fishing net that would be weighted on the edges when it was finished so it would spin wide when tossed into the surf, catching fish as it sank. I recognized what he was doing from watching fishermen like my first husband, Joe, make or mend nets out of larger line, and told him so. He smiled and we talked for a few minutes, sharing an appreciation of the craft, though his hands never stopped their talented work. Then I went on.

Arriving at last at the east end of the garden, I found the space where the map indicated there were benches where one could sit and watch the waves roll into Onomea Bay, but several people were already occupying them. Ready for a break, my head swimming with the exotic colors of what I had seen, and wanting to be by myself to think it over, I turned away, deciding to walk across to smaller Crab Cove, where the map promised another bench.

It was a short walk, with the sound of the incoming tide crashing against the rocky shore. Invisible from the trail, the briny scent of sea and a reflected sparkle of sun on water on some of the leaves overhead revealed its presence. The way wound around ironwood trees from Australia that whispered softly in the ocean breeze. I met no one at all as I strolled and was pleased to see an empty bench where the trail ended, intending to sit quietly by myself, take another look at the tropical plant book, and review what I had seen before heading back.

As I approached the bench, another came into view, and someone was sitting on this one—a slender young man in a blue shirt. One long leg extended in front of him, the other drawn up with his arms wrapped around it, he was leaning forward, staring at the cove. I couldn't see his face, but there was something vaguely familiar about him.

Not watching where I was stepping, I tripped over some unevenness in the path and my stumble made a small sound that attracted his attention. Startled, he turned his face in my direction, and I knew him as quickly as his expression revealed that he had also recognized me.

There at the far end of the botanical garden, in a place I would least have expected, I had encountered young Jerry, plumber in training, sitting by himself, watching the waves of the incoming tide break against the cliffs of the narrow inlet, and looking decidedly unhappy.

NINE

"HELLO, JERRY," I SAID.

Almost in one motion, he leaped to his feet, grabbed up a large green pack that had rested at his feet, and stood facing me with it clutched protectively to his chest with both hands, eyes wide in surprise, as if I were some kind of threat.

"Sorry. I didn't mean to startle you."

"Oh ... ah." He cleared his throat and tried again, frowning. "I didn't hear you coming. How did you find me? What do you want?"

What did I want? What an odd question. Why would I want anything in particular?

"Nothing," I told him. "I didn't know you were here. I came to see the garden. Not working with Adam today?"

"No!" he snapped, glowering. "I *quit*."

"Oh. I'm sorry to hear that. But if you didn't like it—"

"Did my stepfather send you after me?" he demanded, interrupting and still clutching the backpack defensively, which I could see was stuffed full of whatever it contained and had a sleeping bag strapped to the bottom.

"No, he did not," I told him quietly. "I didn't even know you had a stepfather."

As I spoke, I crossed to the empty bench I had been aiming for and sat on it, some ten feet from where he stood.

"Look, Jerry," I suggested, "why don't you relax and sit down? I'm not your enemy and I'm a pretty good listener. I don't carry tales, so if you'd like to tell me what's bothering you, maybe I can help."

As he jerked his head away to stare out at Crab Cove again, I caught a glimpse of sudden bright tears that escaped to run down the cheek I could see. It drew my attention to a fresh contusion on the cheekbone that would probably be a black eye soon. He swabbed at his face with the back of one hand, swung his pack onto the bench with the other, and folded himself down beside it with an audible sigh of discouragement, still not looking at me.

"How did you get hurt, Jerry? Did someone hit you?" I asked quietly, cautiously, remembering the bruises I had noticed on his arm when he and Adam had come to remedy our plumbing problem. The marks were now fading, I noticed, but from my angle of sight the two yellowish purple discolorations looked like finger marks—as if someone had grabbed him by the arm just below the elbow with a painful and detrimental grip. So the present injury might not have been the first.

Tossing a glance in my direction, he nodded.

"Who? Why?"

He turned suddenly toward me, a scowl of anger on his face. "My damn stepfather, Earl—that's who. When he found out I quit he was furious. So I took off. I never wanted to come here anyway. I want to go *home,* and I'm almost nineteen so he can't stop me. As soon as I can earn the money that's what I'm going to do."

It all tumbled out as fast as he could say it; as if he were ridding himself of resentment he had found little or no release for until I showed up and volunteered. Like most parents, having seen my own two children through their perilous teen years, it was not a totally unfamiliar sort of communication, but I kept my thoughts to myself as I asked, "Where *is* home?"

The frown faded as he told me, a little wistfully, "Fairbanks."

"So you're an Alaskan. I am too, but from Homer."

Wherever we meet, that connection almost always creates a bond of recognition and acceptance between those of us from the far north, and it seemed to make him feel a little more comfortable in talking to me. It even brought the hint of a smile to his lips.

"Yeah, I was born there," he told me. "We lived in Fairbanks until my mom died."

"Oh, I'm sorry. How long ago did she die?"

"Two years ago. After that *he* sold the house and made me come to live here with him. I was still underage then, so he was my official guardian and I had to move—and I hated it. The kids at school here called me *elelu kea* when I didn't want to 'hang loose' with them."

"What does that mean, Jerry?" I asked.

"I didn't know either, so I looked it up in the Hawaiian language dictionary. It's an insult that means 'dirty white man'—but I think what they meant was that I was stuck-up and thought I was better than them. But I didn't. I just didn't fit in there. All my friends are in Fairbanks, the kids I went through school with. And I missed my whole senior year, all thanks to Evil Earl."

It sounded to me that he must have had a pretty bad and lonely time that last year in high school. You can't reasonably judge anything, or anyone, from hearing only one side of a story, but it did seem that the relationship with Jerry's stepfather must be a troubled one at best. Who was responsible for that I had no idea. But I certainly didn't like the idea of an older man using physical force on a teenager, as Jerry's bruises seemed to indicate had been the case, even if at eighteen he was legally an adult. The abrupt move from Alaska when he had only a year to go before he could have finished high school with the rest of his classmates seemed insensitive on the part of the stepfather—especially considering that Jerry had just lost his mother. But, I supposed, it might have been work related and necessary. Still . . .

"Where is your real father, Jerry?"

"Oh, he died a long time ago, when I was only six— had a wreck in his truck. I hardly even remember him."

He stopped talking and stared down at his hands.

I thought about it for a minute, then asked the obvious thing. "If you've quit your job, Jerry, how are you going to make enough money to buy a plane ticket to Alaska?"

He looked up and gave me a lopsided grin.

"I already have half of it from working with Adam. I'm going to Kona on the other side of the island—where my stepfather can't find me—and get another job there until I make the rest."

"Do you have transportation?"

"No, but I'll get there with my thumb easily enough."

"Where will you live when you do?"

"Oh, I'll be okay. It doesn't rain so much in Kona— that's the sunny side of the island. I've got my sleeping bag, so I could just camp outside somewhere for a few weeks, while I work."

I supposed he could do that, but the idea of a homeless teen camping rough in a place where he knew no one sounded unwise to me. Young people can be such idealists, with no real concept that there are truly bad people in the world, even in Hawaii's tropical paradise. I remembered Alex Jensen telling me and Jessie about the runaway girl he had ferried back to Soldotna to her mother, and how she had ignored, or probably not even realized, the risk in heading for the Alaska Highway. Without transportation of his own, Jerry was planning to hitch rides to Kona. I wondered if his stepfather would go looking for him—notify the police? Even if he was of legal age, if he had no address they might pick him up.

I explained this to Jerry, who frowned.

"I hadn't thought of that," he said slowly, then straightened and gave me another crooked grin as he said, cheerfully, "Well, I'll just have to make sure I avoid them, because it would be just like him to send them out looking for me."

"Does he know where you're going?"

"*No!* After he went to work, I just took my stuff and left. He won't know till I don't come back tonight. I didn't leave him a note or anything, but he'll look in my room and see that my stuff is gone."

I didn't like his plans, but there was little I could do, and I was not about to try to contact the stepfather.

We talked a little longer, then he stood up and said he had better get going so he could be as far away as possible before evening. "I should be able to get at least to Waimea. That's more than halfway. Tomorrow I can make it on to Kona."

I remembered from a map that the town of Waimea was inland on the northern end of the island and that the highway from which I had turned off onto the scenic drive was the most direct route from Hilo. I couldn't stop him. He *was* of legal age, after all. So we said goodbye and I watched him until he was out of sight on the path that led back through the gardens to the top of the hill. Still, I was concerned. He was clearly a good boy. I liked him.

The last thing he had given me was a thank-you for listening to his problems and, "Maybe I'll see you in Alaska sometime."

"I hope so," I told him. Then I quickly wrote down my address and phone number in Homer and handed it to him, adding Karen's current phone number as well. "Let me know how it turns out, will you?"

He promised he would and was off, vanishing swiftly behind the lush tropical growth as the path took a turn, leaving me looking after him with an uneasy feeling.

For a little while I sat resting on the bench, listening to the birds in the trees over my head and watching the incoming tide break into foam like lace against the dark stones of the cove. When the voices of someone approaching joined the birdcalls, I got up and turned to follow Jerry back toward the boardwalk, but more slowly. It was rejuvenating to stop often and look more closely at the undergrowth that, without the bright tropical colors of flowers and even some leaves, was not so obvious and did not attract initial attention. The subtler plants were fascinating in their own way, with appealing shapes and hundreds of shades of green. It made me anxious to get home to my own garden, though it was very much different and smaller.

By the time I reached the boardwalk I wasn't really tired, so I didn't flag down one of the golf carts, but walked up it in stages, stopping to examine the vegetation that crowded close whenever it invited consideration, as it often did.

When I reached the visitor center I went back inside and straight to a display of plants packaged in plastic that were ready to grow, having been inspected and certified to meet *California's* quarantine requirements by the Hawaii Department of Agriculture. I had to smile to myself at the idea that no Alaskan was probably expected to buy and take plants home to our much less than tropical climate. There's an Alaskan saying, that freezing in the dark builds character. For me it builds determination to grow things, even in our short summer season.

Even indoors, the half dozen bamboo orchid plants I selected for Doris and myself would probably succumb to cold drafts next winter, or never reach the bloom stage in our dry air. But it was worth a try. People do grow orchids in specially heated and humidified spaces, and at least my optimism didn't extend to attempting pineapples.

Though I didn't take the time to explore downtown on my way back, I did stop at a small restaurant to pick up a sandwich, which I took across to the sweeping crescent of the park strip between Hilo Bay and the shopping district. There I sat on a bench to eat it and watch several fishermen casting lines into the water from the wall of the breakwater.

It was a beautiful sunny day and warm, but not too warm, so it was good to relax there, watching people come and go, while I finished recharging my personal batteries for the rest of the work Karen and I still had ahead of us. It felt a bit strange, however, to be anywhere without Stretch on his leash beside me, so I thought I might call Doris later to see how things were going with him.

Counting my time with Jerry, I had spent almost three hours in the botanical garden. It was now past time to go home and get back to work.

Jerry! Thinking of him suddenly gave me an idea I should have had earlier.

Putting away the uneaten half of my sandwich, I hurried back to the car and, instead of heading home, drove back out the highway I had taken to find the turnoff to the botanical garden. Passing it, I went on perhaps three miles, watching carefully, and finally saw him ahead, standing by the road as expected, with his thumb out, begging a ride.

Glad he had not found one quickly, I passed him and, pulling up in a wide space ahead, caught a glimpse of his surprise at my unexpected arrival. He came trotting to the window I lowered on the passenger side of the car.

"Hey, Maxie! Where are you off to?" he asked, bending to look in.

"Here. Right here," I told him. "I've had an idea that might appeal to you. Get in and we'll talk about it."

"Okay."

Putting his pack in the backseat, he climbed in and gave me his attention.

"You want a job, right?"

"Right."

"Somewhere your stepfather wouldn't think of looking for you?"

"Right again."

"So—when you and Adam came to fix the plumbing problem, you saw that I'm helping my friend pack everything she owns to move back to Homer. We could use someone to help clean the place, to pack, and to move the heavy boxes—books and stuff. There's room for you to stay with us, in a place your stepfather probably doesn't know exists. I'll hire you to help, which would work well for us, and for you. Two problems solved at once. What do you think?"

A grin had spread itself across his face. He gave me a look full of mischief. "What would you pay me?" he asked wickedly.

"What are you worth?" I countered, smiling back.

"Adam was paying me twelve dollars an hour."

"I'll match that. Plus I'll feed you and you'll have a free place to stay. Okay?"

He fastened his seat belt, settled back, laced his fingers together behind his head, and nodded.

"Home, James," he said, still grinning. "And don't spare the horses."

Did I happen to mention that I liked the boy?

TEN

I EXPECTED KAREN TO BE HOME WHEN WE ARRIVED, BUT THE
house was locked and empty.

Could she possibly have assumed that I would feel
guilty enough at leaving her to find her own way home
to change my mind and be there to pick her up after all?
It had been hours longer than I thought any medical appointment could have lasted, but there might have been
some emergency that delayed her doctor. It couldn't
hurt to check.

I poured some iced tea for Jerry and myself while I
considered it, then went to look on the list of names and
numbers she kept by the telephone for easy reference,
found a doctor's, and dialed it. A receptionist answered.

"Karen Bailey had an appointment with Dr. Hamilton
this morning at nine. Can you tell me if she's still there for
some reason?"

"Karen Bailey? Oh, no. She had no appointment for
today. Dr. Hamilton isn't even here. He went to Honolulu for a meeting yesterday and won't be back until
tomorrow."

"So you haven't seen her?"

"No, but she has an appointment for a week from today."

I thanked her and put down the phone, concerned, but not really alarmed. Annoyed would be a better word for my feelings—and perplexed. Could she have mistaken the date? I doubted that. But why would Karen have lied to me? She must have known there was no appointment. So where could she have been going that she needed to make one up? I remembered the phone call I had interrupted two days earlier on coming back from the grocery store: *Don't call here. I'll call you again ... when it's safe.* And she had said something about "tomorrow." What was going on?

"Something wrong?" Jerry asked when I turned my serious, thoughtful look toward him.

"Just a misunderstanding, I hope," I told him. "I expected my friend Karen to be back from a doctor's appointment by now. But she'll probably be along soon. How about some lunch?"

Remembering my son, Joe, at eighteen, I knew that a boy that age is always hungry. "I bet you haven't eaten since breakfast, right?"

"Right," he agreed. "Can I help?"

Together we made sandwiches and, ignoring the fact that I had already eaten part of a lunch, I had just settled at the table to eat again with him, when a taxi came down the long drive from the street and pulled up in front of the house. I watched through the window as Karen got out, stood back and waited for the driver to back away, then came slowly to the open front door with the aid of her single crutch.

"Oh," she said, seeing the two of us at the table and recognizing Jerry with a frown. "You have company. Is something wrong with the plumbing again?"

I assured her there was not and explained that I had hired Jerry to help us out with the cleaning and packing.

"I'm not sure about that," she said, shaking her head. "We don't really know—"

I interrupted what I could feel was a derogatory comment on the way and said, "I'll vouch for Jerry, Karen. He's a good boy. He isn't in the plumbing business anymore, if that matters, and needs a job and a place to stay. Did you know he's from Fairbanks and plans to go back there?"

"No, but— Do you mean he's going to stay *here*? I don't think that's a very good idea at all."

At that point I had really had enough of her attitude. Exasperated past tolerance level, I stood up and told her I had already promised him housing and if she didn't agree, there would be a real problem. "You said we needed help. I found some. He goes, I go," I said firmly.

She stared at me openmouthed for a long moment, then shrugged her shoulders. "Whatever," she muttered and started to turn away.

I caught her with my next question. "Where have you been?"

"You know where I've been," she said, without turning back to look at me. "I had an appointment with the doctor that took a long time. Then I had to call a taxi and wait for it to finally show up."

So she *had* lied to me.

"No, Karen. You didn't have an appointment. It's been hours and I was worried when you weren't here, so I called your doctor's office to be sure you were okay. The receptionist said Dr. Hamilton is in Honolulu and won't be back until tomorrow."

"I didn't go to see Dr. Hamilton," she countered quickly. "He referred me to a different doctor."

"What doctor?"

"That's none of your business, is it?"

And with that she headed off again toward her bedroom.

"I'm going to change clothes and take a nap. I'm exhausted with all that waiting. It would have been easier if you had been considerate enough to ... oh, never mind."

It was a rather pointed remark, but I let her go without another challenge that I knew would get me nowhere, just as I knew that she was not telling me the truth about where she had been and with whom. It was, after all, as she had said: none of my business. Or was it? Where *had* she been, and why?

I had one guess as I stood looking after her and remembering a time when my first husband, Joe, had come back from a fishing charter thoroughly disgusted with Karen's behavior. Driving home through town, he had seen her being more than neighborly with someone other than Lewis—who was out in his boat until the next day.

"Are you going to tell Lewis?" I had asked him.

He had scowled and shook his head unhappily.

"I think he knows. He just doesn't want to make it an issue by acknowledging it. You know Karen. She'd just deny it and somehow it would turn out being Lewis's fault."

I wondered if Karen had another someone now. It would be like her to want someone to make her feel cared for now that Lewis was gone. But was it my business or not? Could someone—if there was someone—be taking advantage of Karen's current circumstances? Possibly. Could this have anything to do with the man I had seen between the buildings next to the driveway?

Probably not. And was he actually watching the house as we came and went, or was it my own fantasy? Did it have anything to do with the attempted break-in? Or was I simply reaching too far in mentally connecting a series of unrelated things and making myself uneasy? Possibly.

I sat back down at the table and found Jerry looking at me with uncertainty. My appetite had taken leave of me, so I gave him the second half of my sandwich, which, after politely making sure I really didn't want it, he was more than willing to eat, along with a second glass of milk. But after the first bite he hesitated, frowning.

"If she doesn't want me here . . . ," he began.

"Don't worry about any of that, Jerry," I told him. "Karen will be fine with our arrangement when she's used to it and gets to know you better. She lost her husband not too long ago and it makes her edgy at times. Just ignore it and if you have questions or problems bring them to me, okay?"

"Sure," he agreed. "That's too bad about her husband. I know what it feels like, because of my mom."

"Yes, you would. Just be tolerant and don't let her attitude bother you. She's really not a bad person, just a bit . . . ah . . ."

"Unhappy?" he suggested.

"Yes."

I had been trying to figure out how to say *flake* without using that term. His word of choice was infinitely more sympathetic.

"Now," he said, getting up to take our dishes to the kitchen without being asked, "what needs doing? Where shall I start to earn my pay?"

Having watched him practically inhale his lunch, I could tell another trip to the grocery would be a priority and suggested we do that first, leaving the house quiet for Karen to take her nap in peace. Might as well take care of first things first.

So I left a note for her, and off we went. We came back a little over an hour later with groceries that included not only good healthy food, but also snacks and soft drinks that would be appreciated by a teenager.

Looking down the hall I could see that Karen's bedroom door was ajar, as had been the front door, but she was nowhere in sight. After putting away the groceries, I was about to put Jerry to work taping together some boxes in which to pack the contents of the house besides what we had sorted in the extra room—linens, dishes, pots and pans, and all the other things that would be moved back to Alaska—and look for Karen, but he stopped me with a question.

"Where should I put this so it's not in the way?" he asked, picking up the backpack he had left by the front door.

"There's a new mattress in that room with all the boxes," I told him, pointing that direction. "Why don't you move a few of them and make a space to lay it down. You'll be more comfortable in your sleeping bag if you have something under it. Just leave the plastic on it, so it doesn't pick up dust from the floor. You can put your backpack there and I'll get you a pillow later. Will that be all right?"

"Fine." He nodded.

I left him to that chore and went to find out what was keeping Karen. A glance into the bathroom as I passed told me it was empty, so I went on to her open bedroom door.

"Karen?" I called to let her know I was coming.

There was no answer.

Reaching the door, I pushed it open and stood looking in, puzzled.

The room was empty. Where was she?

I looked in the room where I had slept that first night, with the same result: no Karen. Then I made a quick tour of the whole house, inside and out, thinking maybe she was in the backyard. There was no sign of her. No note had replaced the one I had left on the table for her. So where was she?

Wondering if my insistence on having Jerry could have made her angry enough to leave so I would worry, I was about to look farther—out along the street, for instance—when the phone rang.

Assuming it would probably be the answer to my question, I picked it up. "Hello."

"Oh, good, Maxie, it's you. This is Doris."

Everyone always recognizes my voice—a lower tone than most women's—so I was not surprised. My Daniel used to say that my voice was more cello than violin— bless his humor and kindheartedness.

"How are things going over there in the tropics?"

"Quite well," I told my friend in Homer. "I think I'll be home pretty much as planned, though sorting Karen's things is . . . well . . . time-consuming at best."

"You don't have to tell me," she said. "As usual, she can't make up her mind by herself and is being a pill about what to bring back here and what to leave, isn't she? I don't envy you that job and you're a saint to take it on."

"Oh, it's really not *that* bad," I told her. "Now tell me, how's Stretch doing without me? I'm missing him—a lot."

"I'm sure you are," Doris agreed. "But he's being a perfect gentleman. My grandson Gary's here for the summer, you know, and likes to take him for walks, so he's doing just fine. He also mowed your lawn again yesterday—Gary, I mean, not Stretch. You know how fast it grows now that we've got such long days."

"Well, give him a pat or two for me—Stretch, I mean, not Gary. Tell Gary thanks for me. I'll make it right with him when I get back."

"I'll do that. But I called about something that's concerning me. Did you forget to tell me that someone would be staying in your house while you were gone?"

The question stopped me cold. *Someone in my house?* What was Doris talking about?

"No," I told her. "I decidedly did not. Has there been someone? Who is it?"

"Well, I don't know, but there was a light on when I went in to check yesterday. It wasn't on when you left, so I thought maybe . . ."

"Have you seen anyone coming or going? Is everything okay?"

"Yes, fine. And I checked everything carefully. But I thought there was a hint of unfamiliar perfume in the bathroom and one hand towel had been used and was slightly damp."

"A floral sort of scent?"

"Yes. Is it yours?"

"No, but I noticed it the day I got there—thought it was some kind of air freshener you used."

"Not me."

Then I remembered another unusual thing that I had noticed, but hadn't asked about. "Did you replace the dishwashing soap under the kitchen sink while I was gone?"

"No again. I noticed it, but figured that you had changed brands."

We were both quiet for a moment, thinking.

"What do you want me to do, Maxie? Shall I tell the police about it?"

"Well, as far as evidence goes it's pretty thin, isn't it—a light on, perfume in the air, and a bottle of soap? Wouldn't hurt to report it, but maybe I'd better do it, since it's my house."

"I think you've got enough on your plate, what with Karen and all. Bill plays poker with Jim Stall, so I don't mind calling him. They could keep an eye out—and so will I." There was a thoughtful pause and then she said, hesitantly, "You know, early one morning last week, just after you'd gone, there *was* a teenage girl I didn't recognize walking along the road toward town. I wonder if . . ."

"Have you seen her again?"

"No, but I haven't been out that early again either. Bill's truck was on the fritz, so I was taking him to work at just before seven o'clock. It might not even have been your uninvited houseguest—if there really is one—but I'll ask him if he's seen her. Is there anything else you want me to do?"

What I wanted to do was go home, immediately, if not sooner. The idea of anyone making themselves at home in my house—my place—my beloved refuge—was unacceptable in the extreme. It gave me an angry feeling of helplessness to be where I couldn't do anything about it. Or were we both imagining things? I had an apprehensive feeling that we weren't.

"You know, Doris, there was one other small, odd thing. I keep my books in my own sort of order, not alphabetical or anything, but some by favorite authors are shelved together, all my poetry in one place, that kind of thing. The evening I came home I reached for one of them and it wasn't where I expected it to be. I thought I must have put it back on the shelf in a hurry before I left, but now I doubt it. That's four things askew in my house. I don't like it—don't like it a bit."

After a little further discussion, we decided that Doris—or Bill—would speak to Jim Stall of the Homer police about the situation. If necessary, they could pass on my permission to inspect the property. She also suggested that Bill could check on my house late in the evening and very early in the morning to see if he could catch someone there. She would keep me posted on developments, or lack thereof, if they had anything to report.

It worried me, but given present circumstances, there was little I could do short of catching the next plane home, which was clearly not going to happen for at least another week.

Having driven all the way back to Alaska for the mental healing of a comforting, enjoyable summer in familiar surroundings, I now found myself with three different people-problems on my plate: someone who was evidently using my house as a rest stop—major problem—a runaway teenager who wanted to go home to Fairbanks—minor problem—and temperamental Karen with her huge moving and personal problems.

Was there some way to lessen this list?

Somehow it always seemed to come back to Karen. Where the hell had she disappeared to anyway?

Eleven

THE ANSWER TO THAT QUESTION ARRIVED SOONER THAN expected.

I had hardly put the phone down, when she came limping in the door, with landlord Raymond Taylor right behind her.

"Mr. Taylor says *that boy* can't stay here," Karen told me with a self-satisfied smirk. "He has to leave—*now*."

Where she had gone to gain his support in getting rid of Jerry, I had no idea, but she had obviously called and gone to meet him while we were grocery shopping.

"I told you this was a one-person rental," Taylor snapped, stepping forward to confront me like a banty rooster with feathers ruffled. "He'll have to go—and I probably should make you stay somewhere else as well."

Had I counted three problems on a mental list? He had just made it four—and that was the proverbial straw that broke my particular camel's back.

I wheeled toward Karen—tired of dealing with her and annoyed for more than one reason at this current state of affairs.

"I warned you that if Jerry goes, I will go as well," I reminded her tersely. "We'll both be out of here in less than ten minutes.

"*You,*" I cast at Taylor, "can wait and watch us leave."

"But—but—*you* can't—what will I do?" Karen sputtered. "I can't do ... all this ... *alone*."

"You'll just have to figure that out for yourself—for a change."

I very seldom lose my temper, but when I do people know I mean business. The tone of my already low voice drops to a pseudocalm flatness and there is absolutely no question that I should be taken seriously. My Daniel used to tease me about it, though I can't remember ever being really angry with him.

Karen blinked, mouth wide in surprise as she could think of nothing to say in response.

Taylor was silent as well at my reaction to his demand, but behind his startled frown I could tell that his mind was working overtime. He knew that Karen needed help and that I was evidently it. My leaving would make everything more difficult, if not impossible for Karen to take care of alone, and he wouldn't want that. It was obvious that neither of them had expected my reaction and he was thinking of mitigating his threats while trying to cling to what he saw as his position of authority.

"Look," he said, "you can't just take off and leave Mrs. Bailey with all this packing to do. It's just the boy who—"

"Watch me," I interrupted, and started for the bedroom where I had left my suitcase. "Jerry, get your backpack. I'll collect my things and we'll find another place to stay until we can catch a flight to Alaska."

"Oh, Maxie, I didn't mean for you to ...," and "Wait a minute, now, and we'll talk about ...," the two of them tried to say at once, as I passed them as if they didn't exist.

By the time I had tossed the few clothes I had brought into the suitcase, retrieved my toiletries from the bathroom, and brought it all to the front room, where I collected my purse, they had positioned themselves between me and the front door. Jerry, with his backpack, was waiting across the room by the table.

"Okay, okay—the boy can stay," Taylor gave in. "You, too, of course."

But Karen wasn't ready to accept that.

"I don't *want* him here," she reiterated. "We know nothing about him. He could steal—"

"Karen," I said impatiently, glancing at Jerry, whose glare was full of resentment at her implication. "He's fine. He's no thief—are you, Jerry?"

"No," he said heatedly. "I've never stolen anything in my life."

"I told you I'd vouch for him. Isn't that enough? If anything turns up missing I'll pay for it. But it won't, I promise you."

"That's that, then," said Taylor, who turned on his heel and walked out, leaving Karen to the problem she had created.

We all watched him walk back up the drive to wherever he had left his car.

"Well?" I asked, turning to Karen. "What is it? Do we stay, or go?"

"Oh, do as you like," she snapped. "You will anyway."

"What I'd like is to go home," I told her, fed up. "I just found out that someone I don't know has been staying uninvited in my house in Homer. So I'd much rather be there to take care of it than here."

"*Go,* then! You never did like me," she said, and burst into tears.

I turned my attention to Jerry, who was looking at me, eyes wide, and shrugged a disgusted *How should I know?* at him. Then with a tired sigh I set my suitcase down, dropped into a chair, leaned both elbows on the table, chin cupped in my palms, and waited for the flood to stop.

If all else fails—cry, I thought to myself. It could almost have been predicted.

Well, she does know how to stir the possum, doesn't she? I pictured my Daniel saying with a disgusted shake of his head. *Might as well let her get it out of her system. It won't help to get your dander up.*

He would have been right, of course. There was no sense in wading into any of it with Karen—who was seldom reasonable.

She simply stood there, tears running, swiping at her face with both hands, in what I suspected was a poor-pitiful-Pauline charade designed to get her own way, as she always had with Lewis. It was clear that she was angrily displeased at not winning this battle, but most of the display was histrionic.

"Oh, I just wa-want to g-go home," she blubbered.

That caught my attention and generated a sudden new idea. *Why not* send her on home and attain some peace and quiet for Jerry and me to get the job done? Without her dithering indecisiveness it would go much faster and easier. Besides, almost everything that needed decisions had been sorted already.

My mother did not raise dummies. So, when I suggested that Karen sit down to talk it over, and got her a damp towel to clean her face and some ice water to cool her off—it's difficult to cry and drink something at the same time—I did *not* tell her that packing and moving her household goods would be easier to accomplish without her. With all the pseudosympathy I could muster, I said I could tell that the whole process was causing her more stress than was worthwhile and that what she needed was peace and quiet.

I then recommended that she go back to Alaska as soon as possible, where she could rest, heal, and recuperate, and leave the rest of the packing, shipping, and details to me—with Jerry's help, of course.

And, wonder of wonders, it worked.

She agreed so quickly and with such relief that it crossed my mind to wonder if there was something she knew, that I did not, about her leaving Hilo ahead of time and with details left to complete. But, to my later frustration, I ignored it in my resolve to have her gone, along with the aggravation of her attitude and ineptitude. It wasn't my first, or only, mistake.

By that evening I had Karen booked in the last seat available on the next afternoon's plane to Honolulu, where soon thereafter, with assistance from the airline personnel, she could catch a direct flight to Alaska. I called and arranged for someone to meet and drive her to Homer, where she could stay in a hotel until her household goods arrived from Hawaii, to be moved back into the house she had shared with Lewis, and which, thankfully, had not been sold after she left, but was still on the market until I had her call the real estate agent.

We spent the rest of the afternoon getting Karen packed and ready to travel the next day. It turned out to be two large bags that weighed in at just under the allowed fifty pounds with all the clothes and personal things she wanted to take, and a small carry-on bag—reasonable, under the circumstances.

Then we all three sat down to a dinner that Jerry, who turned out to be an adept assistant chef, had helped to prepare.

"I like to cook. Probably because I like to eat," he told me with a grin as we shared the kitchen. "My mom taught me a lot."

He volunteered to do the dishes, so I left him to that chore while Karen and I made a tour of the house as she told me what else should be shipped—almost everything. As I could have guessed, there were several things she shilly-shallied over and there wasn't much she wanted to leave, but I didn't argue with her over any of it, just reminded her that weight would be a factor in the total of the shipping bill. She gave in on several items, but held firm on a tackle box that lay on the floor of her closet. It was old, dented, and firmly locked when I tried to open it. I shook it gently, but nothing rattled as I expected, though it seemed quite heavy.

"It was Lewis's," she said shortly, as usual.

"Will you ever use his fishing tackle?" I asked. "You could at least take out the contents and get rid of the heavy box."

"No. I want it just the way it is, locked."

So I agreed to make sure it was carefully packed as was, put it up on the shelf where I would remember to pack it, and forgot about it.

The arrangements she had already made for moving seemed pretty straightforward. The movers would arrive in a few days as scheduled, to pack the pictures on the walls and anything breakable, crate or cover furniture, and put everything to go to Alaska, including what we had already packed, into a shipping container.

Jerry and I would sort out the rest of the house,

including the kitchen—a major item. I would put an ad for the yard sale in the local paper and we would handle selling those items. Anything left unsold, Karen agreed, could go to a local charity. She assured me that the property on which the new house had been planned had been listed for sale with a local real estate agent and she could deal with it from Alaska. I made sure I had all the relevant phone numbers and we were done.

Karen's mood had done a complete one-eighty. Far from her storm of tears early that afternoon, she had turned, and remained, sunny—even to Jerry—excited to be leaving for home. This made sense considering how much better she liked it when someone else took responsibility for things she was disinclined to do but should have learned to handle long ago.

I was relieved, knowing that having her off my hands would allow what was left to do to be done more quickly and without quibbling. There was something, though, in the back of my mind that I couldn't get hold of that left me feeling a little uneasy for some reason. It had nothing to do with Karen's falsehoods over where she had been earlier that day, I knew I could deal with landlord Taylor, and Jerry was fitting in nicely. So what was it?

But there was enough to keep us busy in getting Karen onto a plane, and out of my hair, the next day, that I ignored it. Probably, I decided, it was just the half-conscious fear that she might change her mind at the last minute and decide to stay for some irrational reason of her own—always a possibility.

Happily, everything went smoothly the next day, with no reversals of intent.

I helped Karen get dressed and ready to travel, packed up the last few things she needed to take along, and moved her bags to the front room, while Jerry made us a hearty bacon, eggs, and toast breakfast. When we sat down to it Karen seemed to have abandoned all concern for her property. She chattered cheerfully about the people she wanted to see in Homer when she got there and what she wanted to do to get her house ready to move back into as soon as the furniture arrived.

She was still enthusiastically carrying on when we arrived at the airport, checked her in with her baggage, and said our good-byes.

"Thank you so much, Maxie," she said, giving me a hug, along with a clunk in the head from the cast on her arm.

"You're welcome. Have a good trip."

She smiled at Jerry, who glanced warily at that same chunk of plaster, clearly hoping she wouldn't aim it in his direction.

"Thank you, too," she told him. "And I apologize for thinking you might be a thief."

An airline person showed up with a wheelchair, so she wouldn't have to limp with her crutch all the way to the plane. She seated herself as if it were a throne and gave us a royal wave with her good hand until they disappeared around a corner and were gone.

In spite of the bustle of other passengers checking in for the flight, it seemed very quiet without her.

I drove us back to the house and we hardly said a word, enjoying the peaceful freedom that had descended upon us.

"You're sure she won't change her mind at the last minute and come back?" Jerry questioned tentatively.

"Yes, I'm sure."

But we had no more than parked the car and stepped into the house when the phone rang.

We looked at each other without speaking and Jerry's eyebrows rose.

I shook my head and went to pick it up.

"Oh, Maxie," said Karen in my ear. "I forgot to tell you about the car. It's leased till the end of the month. The company will pick it up, so just leave it in the driveway with the key in the glove compartment. And thanks again—for everything. We'll get together for lunch or something when you get back."

When pigs fly, I thought.

But I hung up the phone laughing with relief.

I should have anticipated that there would *have* to be one last word from Karen.

TWELVE

"Is there any more strapping tape?" Jerry called to me from the living room, where he was closing up the last of the boxes. It was afternoon and we had spent the last day and a half packing. He had worked like a Trojan, with enthusiasm and few breaks, more than earning what I was paying him.

Just finished with my work in the kitchen, I took him the single three-quarter roll, all that we had left, and stood looking at the large pile of cartons that were ready for the movers, each with a note of its contents written on the side. The rest was pictures in frames, decorative and kitchen items, all of which we had removed from cupboards and left on the counters for the movers to pack. We would use only what was necessary for simple meals until then, and I was thinking that eating take-away food or in restaurants might be easier.

After Karen left everything had gone smoothly and, with the packing done, we were ready for two days of yard sale to start the next morning. I had applied suggested-price stickers to most of the items for sale, but we would encourage bargaining, the object being to get rid of as much of it as possible. An ad in the local paper had carried the address and time, and Jerry had made a couple of large signs to put out next to the street with arrows that pointed to the driveway.

I had put in a separate ad for the new furniture and appliances Karen had purchased for her unbuilt house—all unnecessary now, except for the pieces she had decided to ship home. Several of these had already been sold: the queen-sized bed and mattress, the coffee table and end tables, and a chest of drawers to a couple who were moving into a condominium; the washing machine and dryer to a mother with two small children and a new baby. A man had called about the desk and file cabinet and was coming to see them late that afternoon. The rest—the stove, one chair, two chests of drawers, and the twin beds—I would put into the yard sale and hoped that, being brand-new, they would sell at two-thirds or at least half price.

As we stood looking over the result of our labor I put both hands on the small of my back and leaned to stretch the ache that told me I had done more than enough bending and lifting.

"Your back hurt?" Jerry asked, giving me a sympathetic glance.

"A bit. But it'll be better once I take a shower and let the hot water run on it for a while. Too bad this house doesn't have a bathtub; I'd climb in and soak out the kinks and aches. I'm just not as young as I used to be."

Younger than you'll be tomorrow, I recalled my Daniel reminding me from the past.

"Hey," Jerry said, "would you like to go to an outdoor hot spring? I know where there are ponds with all the hot water you need."

The idea was certainly appealing.

"Where is it?" I asked, thinking of phone calls about the sale that we would possibly miss.

"Not far—half an hour's drive, down in Puna." He waved an arm vaguely southeast.

It was too enticing to pass up, I decided. It was time to take a well-earned break from the work we had been doing. People seriously interested could either call back or leave a message, couldn't they? So, in ten minutes I was driving Karen's car past the airport with Jerry beside me, on our way to a park where, as Jerry explained to me, water that had been heated underground as it flowed over hot rocks made its way to the ocean, mixed with cold seawater, and created natural thermal pools.

Too bad, I thought, that our Alaskan volcanoes were too far away to create the same effect close to where I live in Homer. We who live in the cold of the far north for half the year would, without a doubt, appreciate such steaming hot pools more than the Hawaiians with their always-summer climate. It also reminded me that I would like to see an active volcano before leaving Hawaii.

As we traveled away from Hilo our surroundings grew more and more tropical until the road seemed to be a paved tunnel through an impenetrable jungle. Huge trees met overhead, covered with vines that had climbed them in a reach for the sun, and full of arboreal plants and roots that hung down overhead. The soil between them was invisible—covered thickly with the foliage, large and small, of hundreds of kinds of local flora, many with bright blossoms of various types and sizes. Next to the road I began to see single white blossoms half the size of my hand at the top of thin stems that were perhaps a foot to eighteen inches tall. The lower petals were a bright flash of magenta and the flowers looked almost like butterflies—which at first sight I almost thought they were.

"Chinese orchids," Jerry told me, as I slowed to take a closer look.

"And they grow wild?"

"Oh, yes. There's a wide spot. Pull over for a minute."

When I stopped, he hopped out and picked one that he brought back to show me.

It was lovely, clean and fresh, similar to some I had seen strung into garlands called leis that were worn around the necks of arriving or departing passengers at the airport—yet different and more attractive in its natural setting.

We drove on and soon pulled into the parking lot of the Ahalanui Park at the southeastern edge of the island. It was a pleasant grassy place full of trees, including many palms. I had to smile at a sign that warned visitors to "beware of falling coconuts and fronds," though I am sure the park service meant it seriously, for I could see several coconuts lying on the ground nearby and couldn't help glancing skyward as we walked through the trees toward the water I could see gleaming ahead of us.

I had worn my bathing suit under a pair of shorts and a T-shirt, so it took me only a minute when we reached the pool to slip off my outer clothes and step down into water that, as Jerry had said, was quite warm, but not really hot.

"It gets hotter and less salty if you go closer to that end, where the fresh water comes in," he told me, climbing in as well and pointing to our left. "Just move around till you find a spot that feels good."

I did as directed and was soon up to my neck in water the perfect temperature to soak the ache from my back.

Close to the surrounding rock wall, I found a place shallow enough to sit down and leaned back against it. The feeling was heavenly. I sighed and settled to let the hot water do its magic as I looked around.

The pond was as large as several swimming pools and at least partially enclosed on the seaward side. There were a number of people enjoying it, including children. Some were swimming and across from where I sat, two small boys, with shrieks and giggles, were splashing each other and an older sister. Closer to me, in a shallow area, several children in bright orange life jackets were being watched closely by their mother, who stayed nearby to be sure they didn't venture out into deeper water.

A stone and cement barrier in a series of steps separated the pool from the ocean. I could just see over it, stretching flat and level to the horizon beyond. Several adults and teenagers were sunbathing on sections of this wall and I saw two climb over, heading for the beach that evidently lay beyond.

Large trees, some of them palms leaning over it, shaded the pool. I wondered if their coconuts ever fell to startle swimmers with the resulting splash. If so, the nuts, even with their heavy shells, would probably bob in the water like corks.

Relaxing even more, I closed my eyes and, for over half an hour, enjoyed the heat of the water that was easing the ache from my lower back much more effectively than the shower I had been looking forward to earlier. It was thoughtful of Jerry to have suggested this short trip, and good to be away from the house, now full of packed boxes. Without him I would never have known it existed.

Now that the work was almost over, I was growing more eager to head home for the rest of the summer. I missed my traveling companion, Stretch, and decided it was time to call Doris to check on him again when we got back. I knew she would have called me if she had found out anything about the possible intruder in my house, but it seemed a long time since we had discussed it.

There was a splash very close to me and I opened my eyes to find Jerry, who had been swimming on the opposite side of the pool, now paddling up.

"Better?" he asked.

"Much."

"Want to swim a bit?"

"Sure."

We swam together to the beach side of the pool, which was deeper and, in the heavier concentration of seawater there, I remembered a high school science class that had taught me salt water is denser than fresh, making it easier to float in. I couldn't tell if it was true or not, but it was refreshingly cooler on that side, after my therapeutic thermal soak.

"Thank you, Jerry, for thinking of this," I told him. "It's just what I needed. I feel ten years younger."

He grinned and splashed off again. I breaststroked slowly back across, feeling the water grow warmer again, until I reached a place where the bottom sloped up and I could stand.

"Hungry?" I asked as he joined me.

"You must have figured out by now that I'm almost always hungry," he told me with his usual grin.

We drove back through the Puna jungle, past the airport and into Hilo, where we were soon parking again next to Karen's house.

Climbing out of the car, I was walking around it when Jerry, who had reached the front step first, turned suddenly to me with a confused frown.

"Did you leave the door open?" he asked.

"No. I'm sure I locked it."

Stepping up beside him I looked through the screen and could see that the door was now standing wide open, part of it and the frame splintered—obviously kicked open.

Without thinking better of it—that there might be someone inside—I opened the screen door and stepped in, Jerry right behind me.

"What the hell?" he said.

I agreed.

The space that we had left tidy and ready for moving was now in complete disarray. Most of the boxes we had packed, taped, and labeled had been ripped open, the contents dumped or dragged out onto the floor, the boxes tossed aside. A glass lamp lay in fragments and other fragile items lay crushed and broken where they had fallen and, evidently, been walked on. Towels, sheets, blankets, and some of Karen's clothing had been tossed into disordered heaps.

In the kitchen a serving platter and plates and bowls that had been removed from the cupboard seemed for no reason other than frustrated anger to have been purposely, senselessly thrown to smash into fragments on the floor.

I stepped into the lower room to check, but nothing there had been touched. It all stood where we had sorted, packed, and left it, along with the items for the yard sale.

Someone had been frantically, desperately searching for something they might or might not have found. It was impossible to tell. But the effort had been directed at our most recent packing. Why only that?

Next to the dining table, the sliding door to the backyard

stood open, as did its screen, as if whoever had kicked in the front door had found it easier, or less obvious, to exit from the rear.

I located the phone, which had been tossed under the dining table, and set it back on the counter. But before I could dial 911 it rang under my hand.

"Maxie? It's Karen," she crowed in my ear. "I just wanted to let you know I'm home okay and all is well. How's everything going there?"

Feeling the tension returning to my back, neck, and shoulders, I wasn't about to share with her the prospect of redoing the last two day's work—or the reason for it.

"Fine," I told her shortly. "Just fine. But I've got something on hold here. Can I call you later?"

"Of course," she agreed. "But what—"

"Later then," I said and hung up before she could finish that question.

First things first, I told myself.

And calling the police was clearly *first.*

THIRTEEN

A POLICE PATROL CAR SOON CAME CRUISING SLOWLY AND almost silently down the long drive to pull up and park behind Karen's car. Two officers got out and I met them in the carport where I had been waiting with Jerry.

"Mrs. McNabb?" asked the taller and larger of the two, who looked as if working out, not carbohydrates, caused the slight strain on the buttons on his uniform shirt. He identified himself as Officer Kennedy as he stepped into the shade, removed his dark glasses, and wrote a note on the clipboard he carried in one hand. "You have any idea who may be responsible for the break-in?" he asked me with a serious frown.

I told him I had none.

Officer Davis, a younger man with a pleasant smile and pale blue eyes, introduced himself and reached to shake the hand I offered. He gave Jerry a nod, then turned immediately to the house.

"Let's take a look."

We all trooped into the living room to stand amidst the chaos created by whoever had broken in.

Kennedy wandered about examining the extent of the damage and taking notes. "Does all this belong to you?" he asked.

I explained that it did not—that Karen, the renter, had taken her injuries back to Alaska, so Jerry and I were finishing her packing.

Davis had stopped to examine the condition of the door and its frame as he entered.

"Looks like this was kicked in, all right. Did you touch anything?"

"Nothing but the phone. It seemed better to just look and wait for you outside."

"Good. I'll get the print kit."

He turned and went back out to the patrol car, where I could see through the window as he opened the trunk and leaned in to retrieve the box that contained his brushes and black powder. Soon he was hard at work searching for, dusting, and collecting fingerprints, but first he took prints from Jerry and me, and I showed him a few in the bathroom that I knew were Karen's.

"Whoever it was must have worn gloves," he told me, when he had finished. "There are smudges, but nothing much that wasn't yours, the boy's, or Mrs. Bailey's. There weren't any others on the tape of the boxes you packed, or the kitchen items, broken or not. One or two near the front door are unidentifiable for now, but may turn out to belong to the landlord."

We answered all their questions and I told them that the landlord was anxious to have all of us gone, about the attempted break-in that had occurred on the night I arrived on the island, and the towel that had clogged the drain. Officer Kennedy wrote down all the information, but he was not encouraging about finding the perpetrator.

"From the type of damage it seems this person may have been looking for something specific in what you had just boxed up," he said, frowning. "Especially since nothing in that second room that you say was packed earlier has been touched. I think you may be right about the dishes in the kitchen having been smashed in anger—maybe because he was unsuccessful in finding what he was looking for. It's hard to say. But I have to tell you it will probably be impossible to identify your intruder from what little we've found."

That was no surprise to me. I had expected it, but you never know. Sometimes angry people who are desperate enough to break in can be careless. This one evidently had not been.

"You'd better get someone to repair the front door," Officer Davis suggested. "We'll send the night patrol by a few times in the next couple of days and you should call immediately if there's any further incident."

I promised I would, and the two policemen left as quietly as they had arrived. I watched the patrol car turn onto the street at the end of the drive and disappear, then turned to Jerry, who had slumped into a chair at the dining table with a frown on his face as he stared at the mess around him.

"You know," he said, "whoever did this may come back."

"There's no way to know," I told him. "But I think I'm going to nail shut the front door until we can get someone to repair it tomorrow. It's too late today."

"What about the back door?"

"We'll push the table and some heavy boxes up against it, so we'd hear if anyone tried to get back in tonight. There's also a bar that fits in the track when it's closed to keep it from sliding."

"Good."

Retrieving the tool kit from the pile of things destined for the yard sale, we proceeded to nail the front door solidly to its frame, Jerry doing the pounding as, one by one, I handed him the dozen long, heavy nails I found in it.

I had intended to take Jerry out to find dinner that evening, but now hesitated to leave the house empty again.

"We might as well get started on repacking this stuff," I suggested. "I thought we'd go out for dinner tonight, but I don't want to leave the house empty now. How about takeaway food?"

His answer was an enthusiastic nod.

"Okay. If you'll stay here on guard, I'll go pick something up. Any suggestions?"

"Do you like Thai food?"

I assured him I did.

"There's a place just a few blocks away that has great food."

Car keys and purse in hand, I was about to follow the map he had drawn for me to Sambats Thai restaurant, when the phone rang and, thinking it might be someone interested in the remaining stove or furniture, I went back to answer it.

"Hello."

There was a hesitation before a male voice asked cautiously, "Karen?"

"No. This is a friend of hers. Karen went back to Alaska a couple of days ago."

Another pause.

"She's *gone*?"

There was something abrupt and angry in the demand.

"Yes," I told the caller. "If it's about the yard sale tomorrow maybe I can help you. Who is calling, please?"

Without another word there was the click of the receiver being sharply put down to disconnect the line from the other end.

Lowering my receiver, I stared at it, frowning and irritated. What an odd reaction. Slowly, gently, I put it back in its cradle, wondering if it could have been the person who had broken in, calling to see if we were home. But how would he know Karen's name? I remembered I had heard Karen talking to someone on the phone when I returned from the grocery store several days earlier. Could this call have anything to do with that one? If so, she clearly hadn't contacted that person before she left for Alaska. Maybe her speedy departure had been something more than wanting to get back to Homer. More likely she had, as usual, simply left loose ends. How like her. I considered it with a bit of wry amusement as I locked the door and headed off to pick up our Thai dinner. Well, if it had been the person on the other end of the conversation I had overheard, now he knew. And it was none of my business anyway, was it?

Sambats restaurant was small, but busy, with every seat filled and several people waiting for spaces. Still my takeaway order was quickly filled and I was back home in just over half an hour.

Walking around the house to the back door—now our only entrance—I set the plastic bag of Styrofoam containers on the table and tempting smells filled the room. Thinking that was what had drawn Jerry so quickly from the living room, where he had already started repacking boxes, I was surprised at his serious face and that he all but ignored the food in front of him as he came to meet me.

He carried a small black cloth bag, holding it with both hands.

"What's wrong?" I asked in concern. "Did something else . . ."

Something in the bag thumped when he laid it on the table.

"While you were gone I remembered we were going to check those high shelves in the bedroom closets. You know—to make sure we hadn't left anything. So I took the small stepladder and found a tackle box and this— back in the corner of the one in Karen's room."

"What is it?" I asked, though I had a feeling I already knew.

"Take a look," he suggested, pushing it across to me.

The minute I touched it my suspicion was confirmed—a handgun.

I took it out, laid it down on top of its bag, and we stared at it for a long minute without a word.

Karen had to have known it was there. Who else could have put it on the shelf? Why hadn't she told me? Obviously, she hadn't wanted to declare it and couldn't have taken it on the plane with her. Perhaps she thought that up in the dark corner of the shelf it wouldn't be found and she could get rid of it that way. But why did she have it in the first place—concern at living alone in a new place, where she knew almost no one? Or so I had thought.

People keep all kinds of guns for protection. In Alaska you can pretty much expect anyone to have one or more—handguns, rifles, shotguns. I own a shotgun that travels with me in my motor home in a secret compartment, handy for use should I need it for protection.

In my house in Homer are three more: two hunting rifles that belonged to my first husband, Joe, and a handgun my second husband, Daniel, brought with him to our marriage.

But Karen had said nothing about having this one when someone had tried to break in that first night I was in the house. In the same situation, if I had one, I would have had a handgun out immediately, just in case.

"Maybe she forgot it," Jerry suggested.

"Maybe." But I didn't really think so. It was more like Karen to let slide things for which she didn't want to take responsibility. I put it on my mental list of things to ask her when I got home.

Replacing the handgun in its black bag, I put it away in the bottom of my suitcase in the room where I was sleeping. Might as well have it close at hand should I need it. When we were ready to leave I would turn it over to the police, but until then, considering the break-in we had just had and the other, earlier attempt, I felt justified in holding on to it for the time being—legal or not.

"Let's eat," I said, going back to where Jerry was already taking food containers from the plastic carrier bag. "I'm starving."

The food was delicious. We had a spicy coconut-based soup and some spring rolls first. Then I enjoyed a favorite, pad thai, and Jerry practically inhaled the spicy curry he had requested. Neither of us said much as we ate, except to appreciate the meal. When it was gone and we were finishing cups of tea he had made for us, I laid out a plan I had been turning over in my mind as we ate.

"It will be easier to repack the boxes this time, since we know it will all go to Alaska and how it was packed before. Let's clean up the broken dishes on the kitchen floor, get as much repacked as possible tonight, and go to bed early. I've got a feeling we'll be busy tomorrow and people may show up before eight o'clock. They usually do for this kind of sale."

So that is what we did and, amazingly, we managed to get it all done by nine o'clock—record time. Jerry had volunteered to do the kitchen and, with both of us packing and taping boxes, we soon had them stacked again, ready for the movers to haul away with the rest of the Alaska shipment.

We stood together, looking at the pile with satisfaction.

"That wasn't half as much work as I thought it would be," Jerry said.

I agreed and, tired, but pleased with our effort, we both took showers and went to bed—Jerry to the one in Karen's room, where he had moved after she left.

For a little while I lay in that drowsy state that precedes sleep, thinking how difficult it all would have been without Jerry and how lucky I was to have met him, then found him running away from home. I wondered what his stepfather could be thinking at his disappearance and if the man might be hunting for him, or if he had simply shrugged it off and decided he was better off without the boy. Who was the man anyway? What kind of work did he do? Was I aiding and abetting a runaway for the right reasons?

I recalled the runaway Alex Jensen had told us about on the evening I had spent visiting at Jessie Arnold's house on Knik Road, and wondered what the situation had been to make the girl he had mentioned decide to take off on her own.

Suddenly I remembered that I had not heard from Doris about the possibility of someone in my house. The idea once again worried and made me angry that someone might have invaded my personal space without permission or invitation. Wide-awake again, I rolled over and settled facing away from the window with its yellow curtain printed in tropical flowers. It shut out most of the outside light from the street, so I had not removed it, but planned to put it into a box at the last minute. I needed to call Doris to see how things were at my house and to check again on Stretch.

How I missed my long, low dachshund companion. In the Hawaiian nights there had been no familiar sound of him turning around in his basket next to my bed, his periodic snore, or the whines and whuffles he made at whatever he chased in his dreams. I wanted to go home—back where I belonged and could have his lively company padding along wherever I went, at home or on the road.

I would call Doris in the morning, first thing—before breakfast, even. I would call her and . . .

FOURTEEN

I WAS STARTLED AWAKE SOMETIME DEEP IN THE NIGHT BY the sudden feeling of someone taking hold of my foot.

"What . . ."

"Sh-h-h-h," said Jerry, whom I could see in shadow between the door and the foot of my bed.

Barefooted, wearing nothing but the pair of shorts he slept in, he came around to where I was now sitting up in confusion.

"I think there's somebody outside," he leaned close to whisper.

I swung my feet out onto the floor, crossed the room, and felt for the handgun in the bottom of my suitcase, where I had put it under the shirts and underwear I had left there when I hung the rest in the closet. Taking it out of its bag, I remembered that I hadn't checked earlier to see if it was loaded—too late now in the dark. Leaving the bag, I took the gun, wishing for my own trusty shotgun. I dislike handguns, but it was all I had.

"Did you hear, or see someone?" I asked, also in a whisper.

"Heard something in back and peeked out between the curtains, but couldn't see anything. It sounded like someone stepped off the grass onto the cement slab by the back door, then I thought I heard the screen rattle."

We had, as planned, pulled the table up against the glass door, and then piled several of the heaviest boxes we had repacked against it.

"Did you hear it slide open?"

We had locked both screen and door that led to the backyard, but neither lock was strong enough to repel a determined intruder.

"No—just a soft sort of rattle, like someone checking to see if it was locked."

I took a quick look out my window, but saw nothing. Listening carefully, I led the way down the hall to where it ended at the living room. There I hesitated. Jerry, following close behind, ran into me in the dark.

"Oh. Sorry," he said softly.

We both listened intently and heard nothing for a couple of very long minutes.

Then there was the sound of quiet footsteps outside the front door in the carport.

I walked quickly to the drape on the front window, which I had closed before we went to bed, and pulled it aside just enough to peer out.

"Turn on the light," I told Jerry in a normal voice, after a sigh of relief.

"Really?"

"Yes."

He obediently switched it on as, dropping the handgun onto the sofa that sat under the window, I opened the drape enough to allow the light to reveal Officer Davis moving quietly past Karen's car, on his way back to the police cruiser that was parked behind it. He stopped and turned to see me in the window.

"Sorry to wake you," he said, looking up into the light. "I was just checking to make sure everything was locked and you were okay. I tried the front door and it's solid—so's the back."

"We nailed the front one shut," I told him through the glass. "And half the packed boxes are piled in front of the back door."

"So I noticed," he said with a chuckle. "Good thinking."

"Are you still on duty?"

"Coming off," he told me. "Just thought I'd check on my way home."

I thanked him and he was gone in seconds.

"Well," I told Jerry, "that certainly rattled my cage."

"Me, too," he said, sitting down on the sofa and looking down at the handgun I had thought would be better not to show Officer Davis, since I had no license to carry it. "Would you really have used that?"

"Honestly?" I asked.

"Yeah."

"Well, honestly, I don't know. Depends on the circumstances, I guess. To tell you the truth, I don't even know if it's loaded."

For some reason that seemed funny and I couldn't help laughing. It started as a giggle and, with the relief of stress past, soon developed into hilarity that was contagious, for Jerry caught it from me and couldn't help laughter of his own. For a minute or two we couldn't even speak for our slightly hysterical laughter. The idea of me, with a shaking hand, pointing an unloaded handgun at a burglar seemed a kind of slapstick and much funnier that it actually would have been for real. Finally, slowly, we were both able to contain ourselves and take deep breaths without breaking into chuckles again.

"If someone had been trying to get in, he wouldn't have known it wasn't loaded," Jerry said, still grinning. "Good thing you didn't point it at the policeman."

"You've got that right," I said, sitting down to ascertain whether the gun was loaded. It was. I wondered again about Karen's leaving without telling me it was there, and wished I had somewhere to lock it up.

Laying it down in my lap, I gave him a serious look.

"Tell me about your stepfather, Jerry. What kind of work does he do? Why did he move here?"

Any hint of amusement immediately left the boy's face and a frown replaced it.

"He's a manager of the electric plant for Hilo," he said slowly. "They hired him because he had worked on the thermal generation of electricity once before somewhere else."

"Thermal generation?"

"Yeah. All the electricity for the Hilo area is generated by the volcano's heat. It makes steam that runs the generators—all underground."

"Fascinating. I never knew it was being done that way. Have you ever been down to see the plant?"

"Once. It's pretty interesting, but I didn't understand everything about it."

"I'm sure I wouldn't either. So he brought you along when he moved here?"

For a long few seconds he looked away thoughtfully, then spoke quietly.

"He had to. I was still underage and my mother had left him legally responsible for me. But if there'd been any way to get away with it, I'm sure he would have left me in Fairbanks. And you already know that I'd rather be there anyway."

I nodded sympathetically and decided to share an idea I had been turning over in my mind for the last two days.

"You know, Jerry, we've done everything that can be done here except for the yard sale tomorrow and Saturday, and some cleanup on Sunday. You've been wonderful help and I can't begin to thank you for it. But I've been thinking. The movers will show up Monday morning, take everything away, and we'll be out of here.

"I promised Karen I'd stay and supervise, and I will, but my plane reservation isn't until Friday next week and I'd like to see a little more of this island before leaving for home. You know it and I don't. How would you like to stay on my payroll as tour guide for those three days? If you will, I'll pay for your plane ticket back to Alaska as well."

His surprise was evident in the wide-eyed look he gave me.

"You wouldn't have to pay me to do that," he said. "It would be fun. I can earn the rest of a plane ticket doing some other kind of work after you leave."

"I know you could," I told him. "But it would really be a favor to me, as I don't know much about the best things to see and do here on the Big Island. Besides, I'd really like to know that you made it back home okay."

He thought about it for another long minute, looking down, then sat up very straight in his chair and lifted his eyes to me with a direct and serious expression.

"I'd be glad to show you around," he told me, "on two conditions."

"Yes?"

"The first is that what you hired me for—the packing—is enough. Those three days will be my thanks, okay?"

I could tell there was definitely a matter of pride involved in this alternative proposal, so I agreed. "Okay, if that's what you want. And the second condition?"

"That I will pay you back for the ticket when I've found a job in Fairbanks and earned the money—probably a little at a time. You know how much I want to go home, but a plane ticket is expensive and I couldn't accept that without an agreement to pay you back."

I didn't tell him how proud I was of him at making those conditions. It clearly had much to do with his dignity and was exactly what I would have expected from my own son, Joe.

"Deal," I told him, offering a hand. We shook and smiled at each other, both more than satisfied with the agreement. I found myself wishing the mother who had raised such a boy could have known how well he had turned out. Who knows? Maybe she did.

The yard sale turned out better than I had anticipated. Friday was bright and sunny, without a hint of rain—a good day to be outdoors.

People started arriving half an hour before the eight o'clock hour I had specified in the newspaper ad, so we started early as well, making toast and coffee do for breakfast.

By noon I had sold the two twin beds and chests of drawers to a mother with teenage girls, and a tall red-haired woman was coming back with her husband to carry off the stove in his pickup.

"It's really brand-new?" she had asked twice, writing me a check, still hardly believing, but delighted with the price on which we had agreed—a third less than it had cost Karen.

A plump young man in a startling orange, red, and green Hawaiian shirt had settled in the last chair with a book, totally ignoring the crowd that swirled around him—a dozen other volumes piled at his feet.

"That's a great chair to read in," he said half an hour later, finger marking his place in one of the books when he came to pay for the chosen additions to his library. "What do you want for it?"

While he carried his prize chair, Jerry lugged the box of books off up the drive to where he had parked his car.

"Does this clock work?" a woman asked.

"Yes, it keeps good time—just needs batteries."

"Will you take five dollars for all the flowerpots in that box?"

"Why not?"

"How long are these curtains—do you have a measuring tape?"

I turned to find and lend it to an Asian girl, who was holding one curtain up in front of her as if she intended to turn it into some article of clothing.

I didn't ask. I was too busy searching among the customers examining our sale for interesting items for one figure I thought I had seen before—a young, narrow-faced man with dark hair and a blue backpack over his shoulder. Either it was my mistake, or he had slipped away. I had no time to look further.

"You got any tools?" asked a man in carpenter's overalls, a well-worn pipe clenched tight between his teeth.

"Just the screwdrivers and hammer in that box with a few bits and pieces of hardware," I told him, pointing to a carton I had set under the living room window.

He hunkered down to go through it and soon departed with the hammer and a pair of hinges.

It was well into the afternoon and things had slowed for the time being when, like a thundercloud in a perfectly clear sky, landlord Raymond Taylor showed up with his usual attitude.

"Why wasn't I *told* that you intended to have this sale?" he demanded, glowering at me. "You didn't have *my permission*! Where is Mrs. Bailey? I need to speak to her about this."

"Then you'll have to do it long distance," I leaned back in my chair to inform him, more calmly than I felt, and with some satisfaction. "She's been back in Alaska for three days now."

"What?"

"You heard me."

"That's not possible. She *can't* leave until everything of hers is removed. And *you* can't be allowed to live here without her present."

So the old *you can't stay here* thing was to be gone through once again. What was this man's major problem anyway? A lack of self-confidence probably.

Don't let him make you lose your temper, lovie. I heard my Daniel's softly whispered advice, and took his counsel.

"Isn't this all a bit academic?" I asked in a pleasant tone.

"Academic?" he all but shouted, turning the heads of several prospective customers from their examination of what remained to be sold.

"Is this man causing a problem, Mrs. McNabb?" asked a familiar voice near at hand. I glanced around to see a uniformed Officer Davis just behind me, with a hand casually placed on his holstered sidearm.

Jerry stood close to him, eyes dancing with mischief.

With "the law" so clearly on my side, landlord Taylor, sputtering denials, was gone before another question could be raised.

My heroes!

They both stood smiling at me in triumph at their success in rescuing me from the ogre. What could I do but laugh?

"Don't you have other responsibilities?" I asked Davis.

"Oh, sure," he answered. "But every time I drive close by I'll probably stop in. You did a great job cleaning up the crime scene, by the way. When are the movers coming to take away all those boxes?"

I told him they were expected early Monday.

"Well, keep the coffee on. I'll probably be back," he said, then drained the mug Jerry had evidently given him while I was busy helping customers and not paying attention. He hiked off up the drive to wherever he had left his patrol car before I could thank him.

By six o'clock the number of people who came by on their way home from work had slowed, then stopped. So we moved the thinning remainder of unsold items inside and made ourselves a soup and tuna sandwich supper.

Over half the things for sale were gone and, hopefully, most of the rest would disappear the next day. A used-book salesman had taken all the books that were left when I made him a deal for the lot, carting off even Lewis's outdated set of encyclopedias.

"I can sell 'em on my buck-a-book table outside the front door," he said optimistically.

Jerry and I went to bed early, satisfied with our efforts. It was a quiet night with no interruptions.

If Officer Davis checked the premises on his way home from duty, neither of us heard him, though I doubt I would have heard a burglar either.

Fifteen

By just after noon the next day there was very little left to sell and the scattering of insignificant items wasn't really worth the trouble. So, while Jerry retrieved the signs from out along the street, I packed up the yard sale remainders in a few boxes that I left in the carport for a local charity van to collect on Monday, and the yard sale was officially over.

I was pleased with the tidy sum we had made for Karen by selling things she would never have used or, except for the furniture and stove, would have cost more to ship than they were worth. I hoped she would be happy, though she was seldom completely satisfied.

Thinking of her in Homer reminded me that I had forgotten, once again, to call Doris, but no one answered when I tried to reach her, so I put it off until later and went to the kitchen to see what I could find for lunch. I had also promised to call Karen, but found myself grasping for reasons not to do so, knowing she would want all the details of the yard sale.

I was assessing what little we had left in the refrigerator

when Officer Davis leaned in the open back door with a smile to say, "Hey, it looks like the sale went well."

"It did, but now we've got more money than food."

He thought for a moment and made a welcome suggestion.

"If you want to go for a few groceries and won't be long, I could stay for a while. It's been a slow day, but if I get a call and have to leave, Jerry could have dispatch contact me if there's a problem while I'm gone."

With thanks I took him up on his offer.

Perpetually hungry, Jerry, who had come to peer over my shoulder and was evaluating the all-but-empty refrigerator shelves with a concerned expression, brightened and agreed enthusiastically.

"Anything you want me to get?" I asked him.

He frowned, considering.

I reached for a pencil and wrote down the number of my cell phone. "If you think of something, call me."

It was a good solution, and I had another errand in mind as well.

"Would an hour be too long? There's one other stop I need to make today."

I left the two sitting at the table, getting to know each other better, and took Karen's car to the grocery, where I spent a quarter hour collecting necessities and a few snacks, and replenished the supply of sodas and milk. That accomplished, I headed out to Harper's Car and Truck Rental near the airport on Kalanianaole Street. From a friend who had visited the Big Island the previous winter, I knew they also rented motor homes and campers on the back of pickups, either of which I thought might do well for our planned sightseeing trip when the movers had come and gone with Karen's household goods.

The night before I had mentioned it to Jerry.

"With a motor home or a truck camper we could drive around the island without having to find a hotel, stop wherever we wanted, and have a bathroom and cold drinks along with us. What do you think?"

"Hey, that would be cool, but are you sure they really rent them here?"

"Yes, they really do."

"And you know how to drive one?"

I explained that I had driven my own large motor home, not only up and down the long Alaska Highway, but throughout the Southwest as well in the last two years.

"I'll see about renting one when we finish this sale and I have time," I had told him.

But now I thought it better not only to find out the details of renting such a rig, but also to take a look at one before deciding.

"I'm sorry, all our motor homes are rented or reserved," the pleasant woman behind the counter at Harper's told me. "But you only want one from Monday afternoon to Thursday—just three days? Let me check on something that might possibly work."

She disappeared into an interior office and, after a few minutes, came back with a smile.

"You're in luck," she told me. "We have one truck camper that was unexpectedly returned early and isn't due for another rental until next Saturday. We don't usually rent on such short notice, but you could have it Monday, if you could have it back by Friday. Would that work for you?"

I assured her it would and that I would be very grateful to have it.

"There are no RV parks on the island," she told me. "You can only camp in state parks and they require permits. If you go into the Parks and Recreation office in person on Monday morning, I think you could take care of that and see which of their campsites are available. They have ten of them, and the Volcanoes National Park has two campgrounds available on a first-come, first-served basis, if you decide to stay there."

I filled out the paperwork, showed her my Alaska driver's license, and gave her a deposit for the truck camper on my credit card.

"If you'd like to take a look at the camper, it's right out in front. It's just been cleaned and the camper door is open," she told me, pointing through the window to a white pickup with a camper on the back. "We'll expect you Monday, then."

I thanked her and went out to preview this new and smaller mode of transportation and camping than I was used to.

For starters, the door to the camper opened in the rear. I climbed in and was pleasantly surprised at what I saw. It had been years since I was inside a truck camper, and they had certainly changed—for the better. In a compact and well-planned layout was just about everything we would need, and most of what I had in my Winnebago Minnie Winnie. Space was, of course, limited, but arranged conveniently. There was a small kitchen area with a diminutive sink and counter, a surprisingly sizable refrigerator, a stove and oven, even a microwave in one of the cabinets at eye level. Near the rear door was a tiny bathroom that included a handheld shower. Across from it a dinette table with benches could be converted into a bed if needed. Over the pickup's cab was a larger bed, and every possible corner was taken up with storage cabinets and drawers of varying sizes cleverly designed to fit the spaces.

It would do very well for the two of us, and be a new adventure for me. Driving a truck would be no problem. I've driven trucks of one kind or another all my life—not the huge Peterbilt tractors that haul all kinds of things in containers on trailers around Alaska and the Alaska Highway, but pickups and a variety of somewhat larger trucks, including my thirty-two-foot motor home. One summer I even drove a step-van as a bookmobile for the local library. This vehicle would be easy and convenient.

With a trip to the office of Parks and Recreation on Monday morning we would be all set and could start our minivacation as soon as the movers had finished packing and loading Karen's things. I had a feeling that Jerry would enjoy it as much as I would.

I would let the airport rental company know they could pick Karen's car up Monday and that the keys would be in the glove compartment as she had arranged. We would take a taxi to pick up the truck camper.

I drove home feeling a pleasant expectation, as if being lucky in finding the camper were a reward for all the work of getting Karen and her possessions on the way to Homer. In just over an hour after leaving, I was pulling into the carport, to find Officer Davis had been called out, but Jerry was keeping good watch, with Karen's radio tuned to a rock station, volume cranked up enough to let anyone in the area know there was someone in residence.

"Good thing the landlord didn't show up again," I teased him, as he helped me carry the groceries around the house to the back door. "I doubt he's any kind of a music fan."

Then I gave him the good news about the truck camper I had rented for us.

The next day we slept in, cleaned the house, and

rested, having earned it in packing, repacking, and selling off what Karen had agreed to leave behind, with
more stress than I had anticipated. There wasn't much
real cleaning to do. Whatever Karen was that tested my
patience, she had always been a good housekeeper.

Jerry had kept back two of the sale books, a mystery
and a history of the Hawaiian Islands. He started on the
mystery, Robert Barnard's *The Skeleton in the Grass*. It
was obviously one of Lewis Bailey's, for while he read
voraciously, Karen would have considered it boring if it
didn't come with moving pictures and sound.

I've never understood people who don't appreciate
reading. My house is full of books, many of which I inherited from various members of my family; and both
my husbands were, and my two children are, readers. For
me it has never been a pastime like watching television,
but an education without commercials in every area you
can think of, especially how people think and behave—
good and bad.

My mother, a librarian, loved mysteries and introduced me to the Rabbi Small series when it was first
published. That was the start of a great friendship with
the genre. Though I read all kinds of other books as well,
there is something totally satisfying in settling in with a
new mystery by a favorite author, with a glass of good
wine, or cup of tea, beside a crackling fire, with some soft
music in the background—especially in the middle of an
Alaskan winter. You can't beat it.

So I was glad to see what Jerry had picked out, and
settled myself in Karen's recliner with Margaret Maron's
Rituals of the Season—a mystery I had unfortunately lost
half-read in Taos, New Mexico, and had been very glad
to find in Lewis's collection.

We enjoyed the relaxed afternoon, both with our own

books, radio station turned low to a classical station. For dinner I browned the pork chops I had picked up at the grocery and baked them on top of scalloped potatoes, which we ate with a green salad—our first real dinner in two days.

We went to bed early again and, with no midnight interruptions, were up Monday morning, breakfasted well, and had our belongings packed before the movers came knocking at eight. They backed their huge container truck down the driveway almost to the front door—from which Jerry had extracted the long nails so it would open.

There were three of them, cheerful, strong, and efficient. One of them packed the kitchen items, including the coffeepot, which I emptied into a thermos that I had set aside to take with us along with two mugs rescued from the yard sale.

The other two were busily loading Karen's furniture and the boxes that were packed and ready to go into the container.

While they worked, I made a quick trip to the office of Parks and Recreation, picked up camping permits for a place or two that Jerry had suggested, and was back to find the kitchen packed and the three of them competently taking care of everything that was left—pictures, lamps, decorative items, the television, and music system. Everything vanished into shipping boxes in short order.

By noon they were finished and the place so vacant of Karen's possessions that I was aware of a slight echo when I thanked them, handing the signed paperwork back on its clipboard. We watched them close up the doors of the container, clamber up into the cab, and head up the drive to make a right turn onto Kilauea Avenue.

"Whew!" said Jerry, retrieving a soda from the refrigerator and sitting down cross-legged on the floor of the empty living room. "That's that. They work fast, don't they? Now what?"

With some of the leftover coffee, I sat on the step leading down to the extra room that had been a garage.

"Well, considering that our beds have gone with the truck, and that there is nothing left to steal since the rest of the yard sale stuff was picked up two hours ago, I suggest that I call the landlord for an inspection. Then we'll go pick up the camper I rented and we can hit the road."

While we waited for landlord Taylor to show up I finally reached Doris on the phone.

"Maxie, at last! I'm so glad you called. I tried Friday and again Saturday morning, but nobody answered."

I explained that the yard sale had kept us both outside.

"How's my mutt?"

"Oh, he's fine. When I took him with me to check your house he spent ten minutes looking everywhere for you, upstairs and down, before he believed you weren't there and gave up. Other than that he's been a very good boy—he and Gary are good buddies now."

"Well, give him pats for me, and don't let him go up and down those stairs if you can help it. They're pretty steep so I'm always afraid he'll take a tumble, and the breed is notorious for weak backs."

"I know. He got away from me and went up before I could stop him, but I carried him down."

"Anything more about someone in my house?"

"Nothing really. I stopped this morning and caught what I thought was a whiff of that floral smell again, but so faint that it could have been my imagination working overtime. We've been keeping watch and Bill went over yesterday to check the whole house. Everything was fine—all the doors and windows closed and locked. Jim Stall's been driving by once or twice a day as well and hasn't noticed anything unusual. Maybe we really are imagining it."

"Or whoever it was is gone."

"Yes, well, that's possible—I guess."

"Maybe."

But somehow I doubted it and could tell from her voice that she did too.

"You think there *was* someone, don't you, Doris?"

There was a long, hesitant pause before she answered me.

"Well . . . if I had to go simply by feelings, without proof positive—yes, I guess I do," she said slowly.

"Let me think about it. I'll be home in less than a week and if there is someone, that should take care of it."

"I suppose so," she agreed. "But I still don't like it—at all."

I changed the subject.

"Have you seen Karen?"

"No, but I heard she was back and going to move into their house as soon as her things get here from Hawaii. She was so determined about moving over there. Can't the woman ever make up her mind?"

"Oh, you know Karen. She only learns by experience, and not always then."

"Bet it was good to have her gone and be able to finish packing without constant indecision."

"Well, don't tell her I said so, but yes, it certainly was."

I laughed, mentally estimating how much longer it

would have taken if I hadn't convinced Karen to go home for *her* own good.

"Oh, listen," Doris interrupted my calculations. "I almost forgot. A friend of yours, that Iditarod musher Jessie Arnold, called a couple of days ago and left a message on your answering machine. Said they were thinking of coming down sometime soon and would you be here?"

"Did she say when?"

"No, just sometime soon. Do you have her number?"

"Yes, and I'll call her. Thanks, Doris."

"Not a problem."

I told her that Jerry and I would be leaving, so she should use my cell phone number should she need to reach me. We chatted for another few minutes and I hung up, turning to see Raymond Taylor coming down the drive.

"Well," he said, walking in without knocking as usual, "so you're finally leaving. There's no refund on the last few days, you know."

"Have I asked for one?"

"Just so you know."

He turned and began to go through the house room by room, starting with the kitchen.

"The refrigerator's not clean," he said.

"It is. I cleaned it thoroughly yesterday. There are just a few things on that one shelf, and I will remove them shortly."

"See that you do."

"What the hell happened to the front door?" he asked, for the first time noticing the splintered frame caused by the intruder while we were gone to the hot springs. Why his eagle eye had not fallen on it earlier I had no idea.

I told him it was none of our doing and he could get the police report from Officer Davis.

"You had the *police*?"

"Wouldn't you?" I countered.

With a huff, he headed down the hall to the bedrooms.

"What's that?" he asked, peering up at the shelf in Karen's closet.

Lewis's tackle box sat where I had left—and forgotten—it.

"That will go with me," I told him. I reached and brought it down, distractedly thinking it seemed lighter than I remembered it being when I had put it up on the shelf before Karen left. Carrying it with me, I followed him around as he made the rest of his inspection. Having missed the movers, I would now have to take it home on the plane.

"Good."

There was hardly an inch he didn't examine and I half expected him to pull on a pair of white gloves to test for dust on every level surface.

"Well," he growled, frowning when he had finished, "it's acceptable—I guess."

"You know it is."

Had it been this clean when Karen moved in? Probably not, but I was in no mood to argue with him about it.

He signed the required papers, excepting the damage to the front door, and left. I had a feeling Karen would get a repair bill and hoped she would refuse to pay it.

Jerry and I looked at each other and smiled in relief.

"What's his big problem?" Jerry asked.

"I have no idea," I answered. "Nor do I care. But now he's no longer a problem of ours. Why don't you collect your things and transfer the sodas, bottled water, and any ice that's left from the refrigerator to that small ice chest we kept out of the sale. I'll get mine together and call a taxi. Then we'll go get the camper."

He took his backpack and the ice chest to the carport, and I brought my belongings, including the forgotten tackle box, and put them down by his. The box was still locked and seemed much lighter than I remembered, making me wonder if Karen had taken some of its contents with her on the plane. I wouldn't have put it past her to take along fishing tackle she would never use and that could just as well have been shipped with the rest of the household goods, but I shrugged off the idea and took the box along, wishing it had gone with the movers. The handgun I had returned to my suitcase, wondering if I should have given it to Officer Davis, but deciding I could turn it over to the police when we came back to Hilo. Given the security screening at airports these days, I had no intention of trying to take it back to Alaska. I could imagine the kind of hassle that would undoubtedly ensue when they found I was not the owner and had no license for it.

On the way back on Saturday I had stopped at an ATM, so I paid Jerry for the work he had done in the last few days. "I believe in paying people when a job's done and you've been a real help. I would have had real trouble doing it alone."

He accepted it with thanks and without argument over the small bonus I had added—"For your moral support considering our intruder, though it was worth much more than that."

I made one last circuit of the house, closed and locked the back door, left the keys on the kitchen counter, and closed the broken front door behind me as I left.

The preceding day I had made a reservation for Jerry on the same flight to Anchorage that I was taking, the job I had volunteered for was done, and we had over three days to explore the island before leaving. As the taxi took us up the long drive and out onto the street in the direction of Harper's, I sat back and sighed in the relief of the freedom.

The truck camper was ready and waiting for us. I had requested a package of linen, kitchen items, and dishes for our use, so all we needed was another quick trip to the grocery, which we could make on our way out of Hilo.

Reminding Jerry that he was the tour guide, I asked where he thought we should go first.

He turned to give me a shrug and a smile, as he fastened his seat belt securely.

"It really doesn't matter," he said. "Wherever you want."

I waited while he thought for a minute.

"Have you ever seen an active volcano? No? Then let's go there first," he decided. "Everybody who comes here wants to see that and it's on the way to Kona and that refuge you told me you wanted to see."

"Why not?" I agreed. "The volcano is high on my list and not far away. With this late-in-the-day start, we can probably stay in their campground tonight. We can visit the Refuge later."

With an infinite sense of relief to have completed what I had agreed to do and to be going on to somewhere else, I drove the truck camper south out of Hilo, anticipating the pleasure of being a tourist and leaving landlords, intruders, and break-ins behind.

Perhaps I should have been more careful about what I wished for.

Sixteen

I FELT A LITTLE LIKE A CHILD LET OUT OF SCHOOL FOR summer vacation as we left Hilo and drove south on Highway 11 toward the Volcanoes National Park. Being back on the road, but in another, much smaller RV than I was used to felt as if I had traded my Winnebago for a dollhouse, but it promised to be another adventure in a new and interesting place.

When we stopped briefly at the KTA Super Store for groceries, Jerry had examined the interior of the camper in detail—opening cupboards, checking out the small bathroom, trying out the faucets in the sink, asking how the refrigerator worked, and taking note of how the dinette converted to a bed—and was fascinated by its compact neatness.

"It's sort of like a turtle with its house on its back," he observed—an amusing connection I would not have made. Sharing space with Jerry was never boring.

In a short time we had left the residential area and were traveling between thick areas of jungle that clung close to both sides of the highway with tall trees and tangled vines and creepers. Even from inside a moving vehicle we could hear the calls and warbling of birds invisible in the lush growth.

"The birds are nothing compared to the coqui frogs out here after dark," Jerry told me. "I don't understand how anything that small can make such a racket, but out here there are so many that the high-pitched sound is constant."

Here and there the jungle was interspersed with cleared agricultural land—some with groves of macadamia trees or the greenhouses of commercial orchid growers—and the houses and businesses of small bedroom communities of many people who didn't want to live within the largest population center on the island and farmed, or commuted to their jobs.

The national park was only thirty miles from Hilo and as we neared it, evidence was clear that past lava flows had crossed and covered arable land, destroying everything in their fiery paths to the sea. Houses, roads, farms—anything caught by the greedy fingers of molten rock would have burned or melted, and been buried. As we passed tiny Volcano Village just outside the park, where gas and food were available, I wondered how the proprietors felt, cautiously perched on an old flow. The highway on which we drove had also been built over the cold, solidified lava. Even though I knew that it was usually years between large encroaching eruptions and the current flow now reached the coast underground, I couldn't imagine that the merchants had put down much in terms of foundations for the buildings they occupied, for who knew when the next destructive lava would arrive? I wondered if structures were ever built on skids, so they could be dragged out of the path of danger.

As we drove, Jerry read to me from a guidebook he had suggested that we pick up from a section of books and magazines at the grocery store. Though we have a number of volcanoes in Alaska—part of the Pacific Ring of Fire—I knew little about how those that make up the Hawaiian islands were formed in the middle of the sea. It was interesting to learn that somewhere deep in the ocean there is a weak, or "hot," spot that remains fixed while the Pacific plate moves northwest over it at approximately three to four inches a year. At this spot superheated magma has erupted many times through the earth's crust, depositing new lava on top of old so that it grew to eventually reach the surface of the ocean and became an island. One by one, the islands were formed as they slowly slid away with the motion of the plate, leaving the hot spot behind over which a new island would begin to rise.

I also learned that, though it is larger than all the rest combined, Hawaii, the Big Island, is the youngest of the chain, and has been created over millions of years. The northernmost island, Kauai, is the oldest. Between lie Oahu, Molokai, Lanai, and Maui, in the probable order they were formed. But the creation process continues, for twenty miles off the coast of the Big Island a new island, Loihi, is slowly growing on the underwater slope of Mauna Loa—one of the volcanoes that formed the Big Island. It will be a long time until Loihi becomes an island, however, for its summit is still over three thousand feet beneath the surface.

Though most easily accessible, Kilauea and Mauna Loa are not the only volcanoes on the Big Island. There are five, but only those two have been active lately—meaning in the last fifty years, most of my lifetime. I couldn't help measuring my age against that fact and it amused me to think that volcano time is relatively generous compared to that of aging humans. It was fascinating to me to learn that volcanic eruptions happen frequently enough, however, that each of them is given an identifying name. The Pu'u 'O'o Eruption, for instance, is often called by its name, rather than simply "the eruption of January 1983."

I had just seen a sign indicating that the park entrance was coming up on the left, when I glanced in the exterior rearview mirror and saw a battered gray pickup following too close behind me with left tires over the center line. Its hood had rusty splotches and the left front fender had been replaced with a yellow one.

Easing off the gas, I hit the brakes lightly enough to make the taillights flash, clicked on my turn signal, and began to slow, assuming the driver would fall back. Instead, just as I was about to make the turn, he swung into the oncoming lane and sped up to pass with a roar of the engine, so close that the extended mirrors on both trucks came within an inch or two of colliding, causing me to abruptly apply the brakes. He sped on down the road, a brown plastic tarp covering something in the bed and flapping in the wind.

Both Jerry and I were thrown forward against our seat belts and the guidebook and map flew from his lap onto the floor.

"What the hell?" he said, eyes wide, watching the truck speed off into the distance. "Where did that idiot come from? Did you see him?"

I took a deep breath, released my death grip on the steering wheel, eased up on the brake, and shook my head, having caught no more than an impression of the driver as he went by—a man in dark glasses.

He was an idiot indeed—impatient and dangerous. And I had thought residents of our fiftieth state were supposed to be laid-back.

Catching my breath as my heart rate slowed, I looked carefully to be sure the road was clear both ahead and behind me, then made the left turn into the park. Pulling up to the entrance kiosk, I was greeted by a friendly female park ranger who welcomed us "to Hawaii Volcanoes National Park" and handed me a brochure or two that I passed on to Jerry, who immediately unfolded one to take a look at a map, taking up a large part of his side of the cab in the process.

"Do you have a pass or passport for the park?" she asked me.

"Yes," I said, reaching for my purse to retrieve and hand her my Golden Age Passport, obtained when I was on a visit to the Black Canyon of the Gunnison in Colorado.

I always smile when I use it, remembering that the Hispanic ranger in that kiosk had been politely circumspect in asking if I might possibly be old enough to qualify for such a pass. "Though," he had been quick to tell me, I "didn't appear to be."

When I had laughed and told him I certainly *was* old enough and proud of it, he had relaxed and told me that many women took the question as an insult and would rather pay the entrance fee than admit their age, though some of them were obviously much older than my sixty-four.

The current park ranger checked the pass, handed it back, and waved us through with a smile and a genuine invitation to "Enjoy the park."

I appreciated her sincerity and choice of words.

For once a service person did not say, "Have a nice

day," which is such an overused phrase that it always sets my teeth on edge.

"I'll have whatever kind of day pleases me, thank you very much," I am tempted to reply to any empty-headed clerk who repeats it meaninglessly.

"So you get into any national park for free?" Jerry asked as I drove on into the park, following a sign that directed us to the right toward the visitor center.

"Any national park, monument, historic site, recreation area, or national wildlife refuge that charges an entrance fee," I told him. "And if the park has a fee for the whole vehicle, the passport is good for anyone in the car with me. So you get in free here as well."

"Cool!" He grinned. "No wonder you like to travel."

By just after six o'clock that evening we had found a space in the Kulanaokuaiki Campground and had settled in for the night. Familiar with the Hawaiian language, the name rolled easily off Jerry's tongue. I, on the other hand, made two attempts and gave it up as a lost cause, leaving my tour guide to tackle the names of anything with more than a couple of syllables. Volcano names—Kilauea and Mauna Loa—I could handle. My pronunciation of longer ones was a complete disaster and a source of some amusement to Jerry.

According to a helpful woman in the visitor center, the other campground in the park was close to the highway and, therefore, filled earlier. Imagining the sound of traffic might be unwelcome, I was happy to drive in the approximate twenty miles and find a more isolated and quiet spot.

The visitor center had been a wealth of information in print and we had arrived just in time to see a short hourly movie about the park that included several places I didn't want to miss: the Jaggar Museum, an area of petroglyphs, and a lava tube that could be walked through. The people working there were friendly and knowledgeably helpful—and not one of them suggested what kind of day we should have.

In the art gallery next door, for my bird-loving friend Doris, I found a lovely framed print of some colorful 'apapane—honeycreepers that are unique to the islands and sip nectar through their long beaks from the bright red lehua blossoms of the 'ohi'a lehua tree. I also bought a set of cards for myself that showed the stars in the Hawaiian night sky over the wide cone of a volcano. Both items would pack easily into my suitcase, so I wouldn't have to carry them onto the plane.

As we left the visitor center and started around a loop that encircles the Kilauea Caldera, through the open window of the truck I caught the smell of sulfur and noticed steam rising from several vents fairly close to the road. Water doesn't make that kind of steam unless it is boiling, so it was a reminder that underground, the volcano was actively heating, melting, and altering everything with which it came in contact, water included, a sobering caution that this was an area that should be respected as well as enjoyed.

It was no wonder that some Hawaiian people believe that Pele, the volcano goddess, is clearly alive and well—and living in the Kilauea Caldera, where Hawaiian legend says she chose to reside after coming to the island chain with the earliest Polynesians, who crossed hundreds of miles of ocean in their great double-hulled canoes.

We found the Jaggar Museum perched on the summit rim of the huge caldera, including an overlook above the deep depression. It was a spectacular crater, three miles long, eight miles around, and several hundred feet deep, that had been formed by the collapse of the volcano's cone after an eruption subsided and left unsupported space beneath the crust. But it was clearly not dead, for there were clouds of steam rising from a number of vents in the bottom, where hiking trails could be seen twisting among those active vents.

I pointed them out to Jerry.

"Want to go down?" he teased.

"Not a chance. This is as close as I get to something that could possibly cave in again and dump me into a pool of melted rock."

"I don't think they'd let anyone down there if it was dangerous," he said thoughtfully.

"Better safe than fried," I told him. "Let's go inside."

We wandered through the museum for half an hour, examining the interpretive displays and recording devices that allow scientists to monitor volcanic activity and explain in layman's terms just what they studied and why. I bought us each a Hawaii Volcanoes National Park pin with a distant volcano spewing a fountain of lava that ran down the side and, in the foreground, a couple of the red lehua blossoms favored by the honeycreepers in the print I was taking to Doris.

"Does this make us official?" Jerry asked, pinning it onto his shirt.

"Maybe not, but it's an attractive reminder that we've been here."

Both wearing our pins, we drove on around the Crater Rim Drive to Chain of Craters Road, where we turned right, toward the ocean, and soon found another turnoff onto Hilina Pali Road—a name I could handle. Halfway along it the map showed the Kulanaokuaiki Campground—one I could not. There I found an empty space, parked, and we settled in for the night.

For me, that meant a soothing shot of Jameson Irish over ice, which I poured and took with me outside. Once there I immediately missed the lawn chairs that I carry along in my Winnebago, or the more solid variety of chairs I have on my deck at home. So I half-sat on the rear bumper and took in the other campers who occupied the campground.

Nearby was a family, a couple with two children, traveling in a small motor home. Close to them were two tents where three young men and a woman—hikers, from the look of the clothes and boots they were wearing—were barbecuing steaks on a charcoal grill. The space next to us was empty and beyond it was an older man whose pickup also had a camper in the bed, though it was even smaller than ours. He had a folding lawn chair, in which he was relaxing as he read a newspaper, a root beer bottle in the other hand.

Our camper cast little shade, but the sun was low in the sky, so the heat was not oppressive, but drier than in Hilo. I would have welcomed a tree or two. Just after summer solstice, the sun now rose just before five in the morning and set about seven. Looking northwest, I could see the long, gradual line of Mauna Loa rising to its summit against the sky and suddenly realized that it was the volcano pictured on the cards I had found earlier at the gallery.

Living in Alaska, I have always thought of campgrounds as green places surrounded by birch and spruce trees, often with a lake, stream, or river nearby. It felt odd to be in one that lay on the edge of a vast arid area that the map labeled the Ka'u Desert, where lava had long ago consumed any living plant, or perhaps there had never been much vegetation, considering that the whole island had been formed by flow after flow, over centuries.

I stood looking out and marveling at the wide expanse of what was now stone, but had once been fluid, live and glowing, that had crawled or fallen, as gravity had encouraged it, to the sea, becoming new land and enlarging the island.

Jerry, eager to try out the tiny kitchen in the camper, had volunteered to cook dinner, so I left him making hamburgers and, curious, walked a little way to where I had caught a glimpse of a bit of color. It turned out to be a small 'ohi'a lehua tree with three bright red blossoms, like pom-poms among its fat green leaves, and pleased me with its courageous insistence on life in such a barren landscape. It was possible to imagine how such plants had bit by bit occupied the rest of the island, as lava slowly eroded to rich soil, until foliage like that I had seen in the botanical garden and the roadside jungles of the Puna district had ultimately developed.

It had been a satisfying day of completions and discoveries, but a long one. I was tired, hungry, and ready for—perhaps, after some time with my book—an early bedtime.

Jerry leaned out the door of the camper and called to let me know dinner was ready, so I went back and climbed in to find it already on the table—mine with a welcome cup of tea.

We sat across from each other at the dinette table, with the door open to let in a breeze that wandered through and found its way out through the windows that he had slid open in their tracks.

"You're a good cook, Jerry," I told him, meaning every word of it. "Maybe you should consider becoming a chef."

"I like to cook," he said, after swallowing a large bite of his hamburger, fat with cheese, lettuce, onion, and tomato. Then a smile widened his mouth—a streak of mustard on the upper lip. "Maybe I'll find a job doing it."

"Not a bad idea. I'd give you a reference."

Enjoying his company and sense of humor, I wondered how even a stepfather could find such a young man valueless and deserving of abuse.

It reminded me, once again, that I should also use my cell phone to contact my own, much valued, son, Joe, in Seattle sometime soon.

SEVENTEEN

IT WAS DURING THAT NIGHT, IN HAWAII VOLCANOES NATIONAL Park's Kulanaokuaiki Campground, that things began to take a completely unexpected turn, though I didn't realize that it was anything more than an unpleasant coincidence at first.

By sending Karen back early to Alaska, finishing the job of packing and shipping her possessions, and turning the clean house and the rental car over to their respective owners, I had assumed that my part of the moving effort was done and I was free to take the next three days for sightseeing. This, I had also assumed, would include taking Jerry along, then on home to Fairbanks, where he had told me he wanted to be, and which, as a legal adult, was a decision he could make for himself without anyone else's approval or consent.

He was as fine a traveling companion as he had been a helper with the work we had just completed. Having someone with whom to share the pleasures of adventure often doubles them. Though at times Jerry had seemed a little too careful to defer to me when choices were to be made, he had relaxed considerably over the past few days and was now comfortable enough to express his own preferences at times.

After dinner we cleaned up the kitchen—I washed and Jerry dried the dishes and put them away. Then I showed him how the dinette converted into a bed—as he had insisted that I should sleep in the larger bed over the cab of the pickup.

It was while I was assisting in this conversion that a vehicle pulled into the empty space between our rig and the one belonging to the man who had been reading his newspaper. I was dismayed to recognize the yellow fender on the old gray pickup as belonging to the *idiot* who had roared dangerously past us outside the park entrance. Whatever lay in the truck's bed was still covered with the brown plastic tarp.

"Damn!" I said, half under my breath.

"What?" Jerry asked, looking up from where he was fitting a seat cushion into place that finished making a bed out of the dinette. "Did I put this in wrong?"

"No," I told him. "It's fine. But you remember that guy that almost hit us—the pickup that went past just before we turned off the highway?"

"Oh, yeah!" he said, sitting up in order to look out the open window.

"Well, he just parked next to us."

"Oh, shit!" swore Jerry. Then, "Sorry."

"It's okay. I feel the same way—especially if he's as inconsiderate a camper as he is a driver."

As I made this comment, the driver climbed out of the cab and walked past the window, close enough to overhear.

From under a red baseball cap with a bill, he looked

up with a scowl and made a rude gesture in our direction as he moved to the rear of the truck.

"Hey!" Jerry began angrily.

"Let it go," I advised softly. "He's not worth it."

As we watched, he pulled back the tarp and retrieved a sleeping bag and a foam pad, both of which he proceeded to unroll in the bed of the truck. Evidently, he intended to sleep there, right under our window.

Frowning, Jerry reached up, slid the window shut, locked it, and closed the blind.

"There. Now he can't see or hear us."

And we can't see him—or what he's doing, I thought—then asked myself if I cared and decided I really didn't. We would simply ignore him.

Closing the window and blind seemed a good idea, so I went to do the same with the ones on both sides of my upper bed. Thinking about it again, to let in some air I left the blind closed, but reopened the window on the side away from the truck. As there was no space on that side for anyone to park beside us, I also left the window open over the kitchen sink.

"Couldn't we move somewhere else?" Jerry questioned.

"All the other spaces are full," I told him, having noticed someone pull into the next-to-last one just before I came in for dinner. "We'll get an early night and just pretend he's not there."

"Can I leave the back door open a little too? It could get warm in here."

"Yes, but make sure to lock the screen door. It'll cool off when the sun goes down."

Before climbing into my bed I made a trip to the campground restroom, then stood outside it for a few minutes to appreciate a spectacular sunset that was staining the clouds a whole spectrum of shades in reds and purples, edging each one with gold so bright it almost hurt the eyes. Even the air seemed to take on a hint of the magnificent hues, and I wished we were near enough to see them reflected on the silvery waters of the ocean that I knew would be visible from the western side of the island. Hopefully, we would be somewhere that would be possible in the next two days.

Disregarding the man next door, I climbed back into our camper to find Jerry already curled up comfortably on his bed, a couple of pillows stacked behind his head and Robert Barnard's book open on his chest.

"Like that book?" I asked him as I went by.

"Yeah. I usually read thrillers, but this is great. Makes me want to go to England."

"Sometime I think you should. When you do, let me know, so I can give you a list of some great things to see."

"Like what?"

"Oh, the Ceremony of the Keys at the Tower of London, for instance. It's the oldest continuous military ceremony in the world. They lock up the Tower gates every night with the same ritual—haven't missed one for several hundred years. They even did it during World War II, with the Blitz and all."

"Someday I'd like to see that."

Usually I can read for an hour or so before going to sleep, but I must have been more tired than I realized because I kept drifting off. It was full dark when I woke for the third time the better part of an hour later, having read the same page of *Rituals of the Season* three times. So I put the book away, turned off the light over my head, and said good night to Jerry, whose nose was still buried in his whodunit.

I was asleep again in minutes.

I slept more deeply than usual, woke tired and groggy, with a bit of a headache lurking behind my eyes, and was, for a few seconds, disoriented. It was light enough to clearly see the interior of the camper and, recognizing my surroundings and remembering, I sat up and reached to open the blind and see what kind of a day we were about to have.

Early light brightened the inside space considerably, allowing me to see that the door at the rear of the camper was wide open and the screen door ajar and swinging slightly in a soft morning breeze. Frowning, I tossed back the blanket and climbed down the steps provided for reaching the upper bed. I distinctly recalled telling Jerry he could leave the door slightly open, but to make sure the screen was securely locked. It was unlike him to forget something I had made a point of suggesting.

As I passed the reconfigured dinette bed in which he had been sleeping, I glanced his direction. All I could see was one end of a pillow and a heap of bedding under which I assumed he had buried himself.

I closed the screen, locked it, and turned back toward the kitchen space, intending to get some coffee going—knowing that, once awake and in motion, there was no sense in going back to bed.

Nothing moved in Jerry's bed and, taking another look as I passed, I thought it seemed remarkably flat to hold a young man his size. Hesitating, I gently laid one hand on the spot where I thought his shoulder should be and felt—nothing.

The bed was empty.

My immediate thought was that he had slipped out on a trip to the restroom and hadn't noticed that the screen had not closed properly. However quiet he had been in leaving the camper, though, someone moving inside always rocks an unstabilized vehicle slightly. His getting out of bed had likely been what slowly roused me from sleep.

Sure he would be back soon, I went ahead with my coffee making and it was only when it had finished brewing and I had poured myself a cup that I began to wonder what could be keeping him.

Going back to the door I looked out toward the restrooms on the other side of the campground. The family man I had noticed the evening before was walking toward it hand in hand with his small son, but Jerry was nowhere in sight.

In my robe and slippers, coffee in one hand, I opened the screen and stepped out to take a wider look, thinking he might have wandered off to look at something that had attracted his attention, like the red blossoms on the ʻohiʻa lehua tree I had gone to see the night before.

It was only then that I noticed that the gray pickup that had pulled in beside us the evening before was no longer parked next door. It seemed odd that the sound of its noisy engine had not disturbed me as it left, but somehow I must have slept through it.

Had it waked Jerry? How long had he been gone anyway? Did the two things have anything to do with each other?

I was now beginning to grow concerned at the whole situation, but was halfway convinced I was imagining trouble. What possible relationship could Jerry have with that obnoxious man in the beat-up truck? If he had, wouldn't he have said so the night before? It made no sense, but the idea made me uneasy. Would he have confronted the man? Could something have happened to him?

Don't rush your fences, Maxine! I imagined my Daniel saying. *He probably woke up early and has just gone for a bit of a walkabout.*

He was probably right, of course.

Thank you, Daniel, I thought, as usual, as I climbed back into the camper and got dressed for the day in my denim travel skirt and a light blouse that would be cool, putting on a pair of tennis shoes in case we needed to walk over sharp pieces of lava that lay on most of the trails I had seen.

I made my bed, then took Jerry's apart and reassembled the dinette, where I sat down with a second cup of coffee, facing the door. His book had been under his pillow, so I laid it on the table.

Surely he would show up soon and my worries prove groundless. I wouldn't tell him I had been anxious, of course. He was not a chick to need a mother hen.

I retrieved my book and attempted rather halfheartedly to read, refusing to make breakfast until I could make it for us both.

An hour later Jerry was still missing and I was well and truly disturbed, apprehensive, and a couple of other things as well.

A growing and confused suspicion had become part of the situation when I found that he had taken his backpack and the attached sleeping bag with him, wherever he had gone. Looking around the camper I realized, now that I had turned the bed back into a dinette, there wasn't a single thing that proved Jerry had been with me at all. Even the book he had been reading and had left behind could just as well have been mine.

Several people at Karen's house in Hilo—dozens, in fact—had seen us together, if people who had come to a yard sale could be counted. Karen, the landlord, Officers Kennedy and Davis, the woman at Harper's rental office, all had seen and talked to him—knew he existed and was helping me with the work. Even the park ranger at the entrance kiosk had seen us both when we arrived the day before.

But in this campground Jerry had stayed inside, so no one could say he was ever there with me—except the man in the battered truck beside us, who had seen him through the window, but had now disappeared as well. And I didn't even have the license number, though I could describe the truck in some detail.

But who, I wondered, would I tell? And what *could* I tell?

I realized that I didn't even know Jerry's last name. How could he never have told me, or I never asked such a simple thing? If I had written him a check I would have known, but I had paid him in cash for the work he had done.

The things I knew about his stepfather were that the man's first name was Earl and he worked for an underground operation that provided Hilo with electricity. That might be enough to track him down and, through him, Jerry—maybe. But considering that what little I had been told and guessed about the man was decidedly unpleasant, it would probably be my last choice of action, if I resorted to it at all.

The only other person I could think of who could possibly tell me anything about the boy was Adam, the plumber, with whom Jerry had come to Karen's house to fix our drain problem. I had paid no attention to the bill Adam had handed to Karen, and I had sent it on to the landlord. That piece of paper had probably had the name of the plumbing company on it, but all I knew was that the company van was yellow. Adam could possibly be tracked by calling company listings until I found one that employed him, but what could he tell me if I did?

I became conscious that I was worrying about Jerry almost as if he were my own son, and he was not.

What if he had just decided that he would rather take off on his own than play tour guide for a senior citizen? Could he have just walked away, taking his possessions with him?

It was possible, I supposed, but didn't feel at all right. I think you know when someone is enjoying your company and when they are not. I had had no hint that he was unhappy or dissatisfied—quite the opposite. But could he simply have stayed because of the plane ticket I had promised him? It was the kind of thing that some people could have seen as a bribe, but that didn't work for me either. All I thought I knew about Jerry was positive and honest.

So for another hour I stayed in the campground, waiting hopefully for him to come back, though I had my doubts that he would. He was, after all, an adult who could make his own choices and, evidently, he had made this one and gone.

Unless . . .

Unless . . .

I decided I wasn't going to go there just yet.

Instead I called Jessie Arnold.

Eighteen

"Jessie? This is Maxie. Sorry I didn't get back to you sooner. It's been a busy couple of weeks here in Hilo."

"What in the world are you doing in Hawaii, of all places?" Jessie Arnold's cheerful voice came back at me over the phone. "I thought you were going to stay home for a summer of no traveling."

"Well, I was. But I guess I'll have to be more careful in making definitive plans," I told her, and proceeded to explain what had taken me so unexpectedly to rescue Karen Bailey.

"My friend Doris—who takes care of my house when I'm on the road—found your message on the answering machine and told me you'd called. She said you and Alex were coming to Homer soon."

"Yes, but not until Wednesday next week. Alex has a meeting, but I thought I'd ride along and would love to see you. When are you coming home?"

"I'll be home on Saturday. You'll both come and stay with me I hope."

"We'd love to, but are you sure you'll be ready for company that soon?"

"Of course. I can hardly wait," I told her enthusiastically, meaning every word. "But here's another idea. My flight gets into Anchorage late Friday night, so I'll stay overnight in a hotel and drive to Homer on Saturday. Why don't you have Alex bring you into town that morning and ride down with me? I'd love the company and you'll bring Tank, yes? I know Stretch will assume that if you are there Tank should be there too."

Jessie agreed, amused with the idea that my Stretch would be disappointed if his buddy, Tank, were not included in the visit.

"I'll work out the details with Alex and get back to you on your cell phone."

When we had both hung up, I sat for a minute, considering how good it would be to have the two of them in my house, at my table.

It raised my spirits considerably to have the visit to look forward to, along with a chance for further acquaintance with Alex on more than an overnight stop. I would have to stock up on Killian's red lager for him and a few bottles of good Merlot.

Restless, as my mind turned once again to Jerry's disappearance, I got up from the table and went to look out the door.

It was almost eight o'clock and the campground was already half empty. The family I had noticed the evening before was gone. As I stood there, a car towing a popup camper drove by. The woman in the passenger seat gave me a smile and a wave as she passed. It reminded me that most RV people tend to be friendly folk. I have only met a few in my motor home travels that are unsociable. The man in the gray pickup the day before certainly qualified as one.

Turning back into the camper I decided that it was time to do something proactive instead of just waiting. It made me uneasy again to leave the only place Jerry would know where to find me, if he tried. But being stuck in one place didn't solve anything, especially if he had gone of his own volition. If so, there was only one way out of the park and I might find him hiking along the road somewhere between there and where I was. I could also ask the park ranger at the kiosk if he had been seen on his way out.

And what will you do if you learn nothing? my Daniel asked, as I poured the remaining coffee into the thermos, rinsed my coffee cup, and tidied the camper, putting things away and getting ready for travel.

"I will go ahead and see the rest of this park today," I answered aloud, spreading some butter and jam on the piece of bread I intended to call breakfast. "Then I'll spend the next two days as planned, seeing some of this island. There's no sense letting two whole days in paradise go to waste. I'll go at least as far as that refuge I want to see and, maybe, Kona."

That's my sheila!

Closing the windows and locking the rear door of the rig, bread and jam half eaten in my hand, I walked around to the cab of the pickup, tossed my purse and the thermos across the seat to rest by the guidebook Jerry had left there, and climbed in, selecting the key for the ignition. As I reached to insert it, chewing the last bite of bread, a small spot of color and something white on the dashboard caught my eye.

There, where he must have known I could not miss it, lay the Hawaii Volcanoes National Park pin I had given Jerry the day before—bright red lehua blossoms and glowing lava on a black volcano, framed in a circle of green.

My hand flew to the collar of my blouse, where I had fastened on my own pin—checking, just to be sure. Then I reached to pick up Jerry's and a piece of paper came with it. The pin had been fastened to a page ripped from the guidebook that lay on the seat beside me—page 99. It had a header: "Volcano Sights."

There are two kinds of lava: 'a'a lava, a rough, clinkery sort, and pahoehoe lava, which is smooth and ropy, more like pancake batter. A photograph of a smooth piece of pahoehoe lava was under the header on the torn guidebook page. It showed heavily carved petroglyphs—two figures side by side, one holding something circular. Surrounding them were several other symbols that must have had meaning for whoever had carved them long ago. But I didn't think it was just the photo that Jerry had wanted me to see.

In red lettering that stood out in the black text below the picture, were the words *Pu'u Loa Petroglyph Trail*.

Holding his pin in one hand, guidebook page in the other, I considered them thoughtfully. There seemed only two reasons he would have taken the trouble to leave those particular things for me to find. One, the pin—to let me know that he had put them there. And, two, that, for whatever reason, he was headed for the petroglyph trail.

It was one of the places we had meant to see before leaving the park. But why had he gone alone?

On second thought, perhaps he hadn't *been* alone.

The man in the gray truck was also absent, wasn't he? Could Jerry have gone with him? It seemed unlikely,

considering the disagreeable nature the man had exhib-
ited, not once, but twice. Still . . .

And I couldn't help wondering why he would have
taken his backpack.

Giving myself a mental shake, I laid both items on the
seat beside me next to the book and turned the key to
start the engine.

There was no sense in speculating with no more to
go on than the clues I had held in my hands. If the Pu'u
Loa—a name I *could* for once pronounce—Petroglyph
Trail was Jerry's intended destination and he had wanted
me to know it, then that was where I should go. Probably I had wasted valuable time by waiting around in
the campground and should be on my way there, where
I imagined he would be expecting and perhaps needing
me.

Taking time for a quick look at the map of the park
to be sure I knew where I was going, I backed out of the
camping space and headed back up Hilina Pali Road,
which connected to Chain of Craters Road, which would
lead me down to where, hopefully, I would find Jerry and
get some answers to my questions.

It was a fascinating drive down Chain of Craters Road,
which ran through a part of the park that, unlike the
Ka'u Desert, was interspersed with lush tropical foliage
and included several small craters where magma—lava
before it reaches and hardens on the surface—had been
forced through deep cracks or rifts in the below-the-
surface sides of the Kilauea Caldera and moved underground for miles before breaking out at the surface in
flank eruptions. Slowly the vegetation thinned and more
and more lava was exposed.

The map had showed only two short side roads, so I

made no stops, but followed the main one, knowing that in around fifteen miles it would eventually take me to where I wanted to be.

Somehow I had expected it to descend gradually, but almost without warning I came to an overlook on the crest of a steep escarpment, a line of ragged cliffs that formed a wall that fell off dramatically, forcing the road to zigzag down along it to reach the ocean I could see in the distance.

Off to the left, I could also see huge, spectacular clouds of white steam boiling up from where the current underground flow from Kilauea pours out of a vent and into the sea at the shoreline. The fiery red-orange of the molten lava was completely obscured by the steam, but there was clearly a lot of it in the process of forming new land, as it had over and over again in the past.

At the foot of the escarpment the road appeared to level out. So down the zigzags I went, hoping, somewhere on the flats at the bottom, in what looked like endless, irregular fields of both kinds of lava, I would find Jerry waiting for me.

The trail to the petroglyphs began on one side of a straight stretch of road. On the other side was space for parking that was not large, but could hold, perhaps, a dozen vehicles. Three—two cars and a small motor home—were parked there, neatly, side by side in a line. I pulled the truck camper off the road and backed in to park across from, rather than next to them, for the rest of that space was taken, but anything but neatly.

There I sat for a long, disconcerted minute, staring at the vehicle that had been carelessly parked half-sideways, as if its driver had pulled in, climbed out in a hurry, and left it taking up all the space that was left—a gray pickup, with a yellow fender.

From my vantage point in the truck's cab, I looked around carefully to see if I could spot either the driver or Jerry—for my concern was all for him and growing.

Neither of them was anywhere in sight. But some distance away, across the rough landscape on the other side of the road, where I could see that a part of the trail wound like a snake through the rough, uneven surface of cold lava, I could see four figures cautiously wending their way toward me: a man in a blue shirt, a woman wearing a tan hat, and, between them, two children. It was, without a doubt, the family I had noticed at the campground the previous evening.

If Jerry was not there to meet me at the road, he might have gone on out the trail and these people might have seen him.

The morning sun was warm on my shoulders as I climbed down out of the truck and carefully locked it. Unlocking the camper door, I climbed in and found my own wide-brimmed hat, took a bottle of water from the refrigerator, and got out again, double-checking to be sure the camper door was securely locked. Crossing the road to where the trail began, I started along it to meet the quartet that was moving slowly in my direction.

It was work to walk that trail. It rose and fell, went around and over knots of lava that had piled up as it flowed across from the escarpment to the seashore. At times it almost doubled back on itself. I must have gone two hundred feet for what would have been a hundred if measured in a direct line between two points. Knowing it was approximately a one-mile hike to the place where hundreds of ancient petroglyphs covered the rocks, I was glad I had remembered to bring water along.

By the time the family reached me I had stopped to

rest beside the track on a flat, smooth bump of pahoe-hoe lava, picked because it had no sharp, rough edges.

The younger of the two small boys was clinging tightly to his mother's hand, worn out with the exertion of climbing up and down on short legs, but too big to be carried over such irregular terrain. The other, five or six years old, was walking by himself, but staying close to his father.

"Hi, there," the man greeted me, stopping beside my stone throne. "Going out?"

"Yes, I think so," I told him. "But I'm looking for someone. Have you seen a tall young man, very slender and friendly? He may have been carrying a green backpack."

"Oh," said the woman, "you must mean Jerry. We offered him a ride, if he wanted to go on to see the lava vent at the end of the road, but he said you would be coming to pick him up—at least I think it must have been you he meant, right?"

"That's right. Where did you see him?"

"Out there," she said, waving a hand in the direction from which they had come. "There are six or seven other people out there and a park ranger who was telling us all about the petroglyphs. He was walking with her and introduced himself to us because we were standing together as we listened. He was very good at telling our boys about the pictures on the rocks so they could understand. There are thousands of them."

"I saw a funny boat," the older boy told me suddenly.

"Did Jerry show it to you?" I asked, giving him my attention for a moment.

He nodded. "Jerry said it was a sailboat, but it didn't look like ours."

His father smiled.

"But he told you it was made differently than ours and a long time ago, didn't he?"

The boy nodded again.

"He must still be there," I said, getting to my feet. "I'll go on out and—"

"I didn't see him there when we left," the man interrupted me. "I assumed he had probably come back ahead of us. He's not in the parking lot?"

"No."

"Well, you're supposed to stay on the trail or the boardwalk out there, so the pictures aren't damaged. But he might have wandered off to take a look at something farther out, don't you think?" his wife asked him.

"I guess he could have."

He turned back to me. "Was that other man who showed up soon after Jerry came with the ranger a friend of his?"

"What other man?"

"There was another, but he's gone now too. Maybe they left together. Was he someone you know?"

I had a sinking feeling that I knew exactly who he meant, though I had no wish to know him.

"I don't think so," I told them. "But thanks for your help. I want to take a look at the petroglyphs anyway. So I'll hike on out and ask the park ranger if she knows where he went."

I watched them walk away toward the parking lot and, as they went, the older of the two boys looked back and waved at me.

NINETEEN

IT TOOK ME ANOTHER TWENTY MINUTES TO REACH THE boardwalk they had mentioned and on the way I met three other people headed back to the road. As I walked I began to notice that some of the rocks I passed had carvings on them. I could identify few, but was sure of a turtle I found on one and the human figures on several others that were similar to the ones in the picture Jerry had torn from the guidebook and left for me. Many of the stones, with and without carvings, were pocked with holes about an inch or so in diameter. It seemed odd that anyone would go to the work of carving a hole and not a picture. Perhaps, I thought, it was some kind of record of the number of times a person visited the place.

That was not a bad theory. But, as I joined three other people standing next to the park ranger, who was explaining the petroglyphs to them, I soon learned that it had missed the mark by a mile.

One of the two men in the group asked about those holes before I could.

"They are piko holes," she told him. "The early

Hawaiians had a custom of bringing a new baby's umbilical stump, called a piko, to this place. It was considered good luck to carve a hole, put the piko in, and cover it with a stone. If the piko was still there the next morning the child would have a long life."

"They must have had a lot of children," the man who had asked the question commented with a smile, waving a hand at the hundreds of holes visible from where we stood.

"Oh, it wasn't just a custom on this island. Whole families came here from the other islands as well." She pointed to a large flat stone close to the boardwalk. "See those piko holes with the circle carved around them?"

We all looked and saw that it was a large circle that enclosed more than a dozen holes.

"That was an extended family. They would save the piko of their children and bring them all at once, sometimes years after they were born. It was a long and significant journey to make by canoe all the way to Pu'u Loa from, say, Kauai or Oahu."

As she talked, I looked around as far as I could see for any sign of Jerry, but he was nowhere in sight.

"I really don't know where he went," the ranger told me, when the others had drifted off to see more carvings along the boardwalk, which made a loop and returned to where we were standing, close to where it joined the trail. "He was here for maybe half an hour, then I got talking to an interesting ethnographer from Minnesota and when I thought to look for Jerry he was gone—probably back along the trail to the road. It's been the better part of an hour since I saw him. Sorry."

Would he have wandered off the boardwalk?

She didn't think so. "I tell everyone to stay on it for preservation reasons. But off the walk there are some steep, hazardous places and a few serious depressions where a person could easily fall. Some of the lava is thinner than it looks and can break. Just beyond that hill, for instance"—she waved a hand eastward at a large bump that could be called a hill—"there are some fascinating petroglyphs, but a dangerous pit that would be difficult to climb out of as well."

Her best guess? That Jerry had hiked back to the road and, if he was not hitchhiking along the road, had caught a ride with someone going either to the end of it, where it was possible to walk close enough to see the lava that was pouring into the sea from the Kilauea vent, or back up the way I had come down, to the top of the escarpment and the rest of the park.

The park ranger went off to answer a question about a carving at the other end of the circle made by the boardwalk. I made another, smaller circle in turning to look carefully in all directions for any hint of Jerry. I was somehow sure he would not quickly or easily leave the place where he would be expecting, or at least hoping, for us to meet, as he had indicated by the clue he had left.

As I turned, it occurred to me that I had no idea where the unpleasant man from the gray truck had gone either. From what the family I had met on the trail had told me, they thought he had arrived at the boardwalk shortly after Jerry and might have been a friend.

A friend? I didn't think so—not from Jerry's reaction to his appearance in the campground the night before. What he had said was not what one would have said about an acquaintance one was glad to see. If he knew the man wouldn't he have said so?

I had seen nothing of the fellow on the mile of trail I had walked, or anywhere in sight of the boardwalk. But his truck had been empty and, evidently, at least from the careless parking I had seen, he had left it in a hurry. On the other hand, I wouldn't have put it past him—with his disagreeable attitude—to park it as inconsiderately as he had with no regard for the inconvenience it would cause other people.

So where was he?

I decided I would wait for a while and see if either of them showed up.

Concentrating on possible solutions to Jerry's disappearance, I started slowly around the loop made by the boardwalk, still searching the surrounding area, but also taking a look at the carvings that had been made in the rocks below.

Many were a kind of simple stick-figure representation of humans with round heads, some with triangular bodies—one short side forming the shoulders to which arms were attached and the other, longer two narrowing to meet where the legs extended. Around these were other shapes and symbols for which I could discern no meaning, but which must have had significance for the people who took the time to pound them out of solid stone with whatever tools they had—another stone, I imagined, smaller, the size for holding.

"I saw a funny boat," the small boy had told me, and I found what must have been that very one. It *was* a funny-*looking* boat, but the real ones the image portrayed must have been remarkably seaworthy; for those intrepid Pacific travelers to have made the long journey from Polynesia to the middle of the Pacific Ocean would have needed good strong ones, considering that they sailed for thousands of miles in them.

I had completed half the loop when I heard the park ranger say, "I'm sorry, sir, but you shouldn't be out there. Please come back to the boardwalk."

Turning to see to whom she was speaking, I recognized the man from the gray truck, looking straight at me with a frown. Where he had appeared from I had no idea. But he was standing about ten yards off the end of the walk, near the section of lava that had piled up to form the hill she had pointed out to me earlier, beyond which there lay what she had called a "dangerous pit" of some kind, as if he had come from that direction.

Evidently intending to ignore her request, he wheeled around, turned his back to her, and took several steps away.

"Please, sir," she called out, "you could get hurt out there. Also some of the petroglyphs are very fragile and easily broken, so you must come back, or I will be forced to write you a citation."

Angrily, he swung around to face her. "Go ahead, lady," he snapped. "I'll just tear it up. I'm not hurting any of your precious petro-whatevers."

"Hey, fella," one of the tourists on the boardwalk told him in a loud challenging voice. "You're out of line there. Do what the lady says and get your—ah, get yourself back on the walkway. I'd be glad to help you—if you make that necessary."

He was a large man, who looked entirely capable of enforcing what he was saying and would.

The man from the gray truck hesitated, glaring back at those of us minding our manners by staying on the walk, shrugged, and came slowly back. Stepping up onto the boardwalk, he stomped past the park ranger, ignoring her thank-you, and headed around the loop to where the trail to the parking lot began.

"Bitch!" I heard him say under his breath as he passed her.

I moved aside to allow him room to go by me, which

he did without a glance—as if I wasn't even there—and I saw that he had a trickle of blood from a cut at the hairline that was running down the side of his face to stain the collar of his shirt.

It was as I watched him move furiously away that I also noticed that in one hand he was carrying a blue water bottle with a strip of adhesive stuck to the side—one I recognized. Before we left Karen's house, I had watched Jerry fill that bottle with ice and water at the kitchen sink and knew that the strip of adhesive had his name written on it.

The man's determination to go, without permission, off the boardwalk and around that hill of lava had given me a good idea where Jerry might possibly be found. That there was blood involved worried me considerably.

The park ranger remembered him, of course.

"I wondered how he had disappeared so quickly," she said with concern. "But I was busy answering questions, so I thought I had just missed seeing him go."

"You probably did, but I don't think he took the trail back to the road," I told her, and explained where I thought he might be.

"I'll take you around there to look" was her immediate response, and she asked the strong-looking man to accompany us in our search. "We might need your help if we find the boy hurt."

We found him—not injured—but apparently anxious and relieved to see us.

When we reached the other side of the hill, after carefully following the ranger through a minefield of petroglyphs that could be damaged, I called out Jerry's name.

Hearing my voice, he stood up so we could see him—

not in the pit, as I had feared, but from where he had been crouched behind an outcropping of black lava stone to one side of it.

"Here," he said. "I'm here, Maxie."

"Thanks be," I breathed. "Are you all right?"

"Fine. I'm fine," he assured me.

"Stay where you are," the park ranger told him. "We'll come out and help you back."

The three of us went cautiously toward him, the strong man and I following the park ranger, conscious of the history beneath our feet and stepping where she stepped. Jerry stood still and waited until, skirting the edge of the deep pit in the ground that lay between, we reached the place he was standing.

"I was worried," I said, and reached out to lay my hand on his arm. "How did—"

"What happened out here?" the ranger asked with concern before I could finish my question. "Was that guy giving you a bad time?"

"Yeah," he told her, "he sure was."

He gave me a quick glance that told me there would be more to the explanation than he was willing to tell her, so I respected his reticence and asked no questions. We could talk about it later.

"Do you know why?"

"No. I don't know him, but he seemed angry at me for some reason, so I went looking for a place to hide until he went away, but he found me. He demanded that I give him my backpack. I told him I'd throw it down that hole if he came after me. When he came on, I threw my water bottle at him, but he caught it. When he kept coming I tossed the backpack down there, like I said I would."

We all looked into the hole where the green backpack

lay at the bottom, about ten feet down. Something else caught my attention. Lying next to it was the red baseball cap I had seen the man wearing when he parked next to us at the campground the night before.

"He was furious," Jerry continued. "But when I started throwing rocks at him, he gave up and went back toward the boardwalk area. I used to pitch baseball, so I connected a few times with some fair-sized lumps of lava—none with petroglyphs on them," he assured the park ranger seriously.

A smile spread itself across her face.

"Jerry," she said, "I think you must be one of only a few people who would have the presence of mind to be careful what they selected to use for defense. But I do appreciate the thought."

Between them, Jerry and the man who had joined our search managed to retrieve both the backpack and hat from the bottom of the pit. We then trooped single file back to the boardwalk, Jerry wearing the red cap as if it were his own.

"He stole my backpack," Jerry told me, when we were safely back in the camper I had left in the parking lot.

It had still been locked and, as far as I could tell, nothing had been tampered with.

The small motor home, with its family of four, was gone. Three additional cars had parked neatly in the space the now-absent gray truck had crookedly occupied when I arrived.

"I went to the restroom and left the camper door unlocked because I was only going to be gone a minute or two. When I came out I saw him walk away from the camper and put my pack into the back of his pickup. I yelled and ran, but he came at me with a tire iron from the back of the truck. All I could do was get into the cab of our truck and lock the door."

"Didn't I lock it last night?" I asked.

He frowned, thinking about it. "I think you locked the driver's door, but the passenger side was open, because I got in there."

"Then what happened?"

"He suddenly got all reasonable and *asked* me to get out, that he just wanted to talk to me. He said that if I did he would drive us down to the petroglyphs and we could have a conversation—that if I wouldn't, he would go inside after you. That scared me enough so that I agreed to go with him. But I ripped that page from the book and left it with my pin before I got out, hoping you'd understand that was where I thought we were headed."

"Oh, Jerry—and I slept through all that?"

He gave me an odd look before saying, "He was pretty quiet about it, but he was angry and I knew he meant it. He made me get into the back of his truck, told me to stay there, and drove off—didn't stop till we got to this parking lot or I would have jumped out.

"But when he turned in I was ready. I jumped with my pack and ran to catch up with a family that was just starting along the trail. I walked with them, but he stayed right behind us. When we got to that wooden walkway around the petroglyphs, I kept close to them, talked to the kids and waited till he had his back turned at the other end of the loop. Then I ran, but he saw me, so I found that place to hide on the other side of the hill, where you found me."

"Why didn't you run back toward the road?"

"Ah, I was closer to the other end of the walk."

That made perfect sense.

"So you didn't find out what he really wanted?"

"Nope. But I don't think it was anything pleasant, whatever it was."

I didn't either, but didn't say it, wondering what he could have thought Jerry would have in his backpack that was worth his threats.

"He had your water bottle. That's how I knew for sure that you must be out here somewhere."

"Yeah, he took it with him—too bad, too. It was a good bottle. But it was a fair trade, I guess"—he grinned—"since I got his hat."

"His truck isn't here. I wonder where he's gone," I said, concerned we hadn't seen the last of him. "There's a lot of road between here and the entrance. I hope he's not somewhere between here and there, waiting for us to come along."

"Me, too. Do you still have that gun?"

"Jerry," I told him with a serious look, "that gun isn't an option. It's going to the police as soon as we get back to Hilo. I'll call Officer Davis and give it to him."

"Okay. What do *you* think he wanted?"

"I have no idea at all," I told him and we both agreed that, whatever it was, it couldn't have been anything good.

"Have you any idea at all *who* this guy is?" I asked Jerry. "From what happened this morning, he seems to be after something from you, not me."

"The only thing I can think of is that my stepfather may have somehow found out where I am and sent him out after me."

"Would he do that?"

"I guess he might—just to let me know who he thinks is the boss of me. But he doesn't really care. It would be easier for him all the way around if I was gone. Really."

"He may show up again. We'd better think about what we should do if he does."

We were both quiet for a minute or two, considering our options.

Having left Karen's, I had no place to go back to and had no desire to have anything more to do with landlord Raymond Taylor. We still had three days until we were to return the camper to Harper's and catch the plane from Hilo to Honolulu, then Anchorage.

"When he cut us off on the highway, the guy was coming away from Hilo, right?"

"Right."

"So I think we shouldn't go back there till Friday morning, when it's close to time to catch our flight."

Jerry nodded.

"Maybe he went back there," he said hopefully. "I think we should go ahead as we planned. But we should keep watch, in case he shows up again."

I agreed, then asked him a question.

"You've never told me your last name. What is it?"

"Monahan," he told me. "It's Jerrod Craig Monahan. Now, let's go see that lava tube you wanted to walk through. Then we can drive on toward Kona to that refuge place you mentioned."

He hesitated and a grin once again made an appearance on his face. "Maybe we can find a Refuge at the Refuge."

Irrepressible, optimistic Jerry.

TWENTY

WE DROVE UP THE CHAIN OF CRATERS ROAD TO WHERE IT met Crater Rim Drive and turned right. Not far along it was a parking lot for the Thurston Lava Tube.

Parking the truck camper between another similar rig and a motor home in the hope it would not be recognized, we crossed the road and I found myself looking down into a crater, much smaller than the giant Kilauea Caldera, that had been created when part of the lava tube collapsed. It was densely crowded with a jungle of trees and huge ferns.

It was incredible to come upon such a contrast to the stark desert beyond the campground where we had spent the previous night.

A trail went down the side in switchbacks with steps at the turns, and as we went down to where it wound off into the thick vegetation I noticed a distinct increase in the humidity. This was real rain forest and evidently home to a multitude of birds, for I could hear their chirps and warbles all around me in the foliage.

"Oh, look, Jerry."

Overhead there was a sudden flash of red and a bird with a long curved beak perched above us on a branch of a tree next to the trail.

"I think that's a honeycreeper bird like the ones in the picture I bought for Doris. It feeds on the nectar of those fluffy red 'ohi'a blossoms."

"Hey," he said, with a grin, watching the bird. "You pronounced that right."

"Well, it's a very short word."

"Still—you're getting better at it."

I watched until the bird flew away.

"The two are sort of a matched pair," I said thoughtfully. "Red flower and red bird."

"Yes, but some of them are other colors, I think."

As I watched it disappear, two small bright yellow birds darted overhead in the treetop canopy. I wondered if they had matching flowers as well, but decided probably they were hunting insects in the air over our heads.

We followed the trail as it twisted and turned through a forest that was very different from anything in the north I was used to, with its birch and spruce. Giant ferns were everywhere, some taller than Jerry, others close to eye level for me. Every foot of the ground seemed covered with something green and growing. It reminded me of scenes from the movie *Jurassic Park*.

"You almost expect to have a velociraptor come charging out onto the path at any moment," I said to Jerry.

"Rather a velociraptor than that guy in the gray truck," he returned.

At the end of a short—perhaps ten-minute—walk we came to the lava tube, a dark cavelike opening in the side of the crater we had crossed to reach it.

"Don't we need a flashlight?" I asked, noticing that

the two people walking ahead of us were each carrying one.

"Naw . . . it's got lights in this part. We won't go on into the other half. There it *is* dark—*really* dark. You need a good one there."

We crossed a short bridge over a small chasm at the entrance and walked into the darkness of the tube. It was huge, big enough to echo, though the guidebook had said there were many larger ones. Roughly circular, it rose high over our heads and, from the lights that had been installed on the walls, I could see that it continued on and turned a corner some distance ahead. The floor was damp, with puddles here and there. Water ran from the walls and dripped a little from tree roots that grew down from above and hung from the ceiling.

"When it rains it drips a lot more in here," Jerry told me.

As we started through the tube that, incredibly, had been formed by a red-hot river of lava as it poured through on its way toward the ocean, I turned, as I had been doing periodically, to look back. We had seen nothing of the gray truck, or its owner, but it seemed wise to remain aware that he could turn up again. Behind us, there was no one but a woman with a blue sweater over her print dress and a couple of teenage girls in hiking shorts chatting to each other.

"*Spiders?* Ugh—I *hate* spiders," I heard one of them say.

"Oh, they won't hurt you. They're blind from living in the dark," her friend told her. "They just eat the other bugs that live in here."

"Doesn't mean they can't bite."

"They won't bite *you*."

It grew darker as we walked and, as the tube made a

curve to the right, the entrance disappeared behind us. I could imagine that without the lights provided by the park service it would be very dark.

We were catching up with a small group of people who had stopped ahead of us to look at something on the wall.

"Oooh, look at it run," a youngster's voice crowed.

"That's the Martins," Jerry said, recognizing the family of four from the petroglyph trail.

The woman heard him and turned as we joined them.

"Jerry!" she said, greeting him warmly. "So you found your friend."

"Hi," he said, nodding at her and the father, who had turned at the sound of Jerry's name. "This is Maxie McNabb."

"Lloyd Martin," the man said, extending his hand with a smile. "And this is Shelly"—he indicated his wife. "These two rug rats are David and Michael, who is the oldest."

Michael had come and was tugging at Jerry's hand.

"There's a white spider on the wall. Come and see."

With a grin, Jerry allowed himself to be pulled around past the grown-ups and crouched down at the boy's level to examine the spider that was indeed on the wall of the tube.

"Cool," he said. "Do you know why it's white?"

"My dad says that's because it lives in the dark all the time," Michael told him.

"Right. And . . ."

The smaller boy had been clinging once again to his mother's hand as we joined the family. But, interested in what was going on with Jerry and his brother, he now let go and went to be with them.

"Jerry's really good with kids," Shelly said to me. "Bet he'd make a good teacher."

The teenage girls passed us—with another "Ugh" and a shudder from the one who had said she hated spiders. The other gave Jerry an interested look as she went by, then hurried to catch up with her companion.

Well—I smiled to myself at the thought of what my Daniel would say—*he's an attractive young man, after all*.

We soon followed them, walking together through the rest of the lava tube, coming to a place where the roof had collapsed sometime in the past, allowing a flight of stairs to lead us up to the rain forest jungle again. A different and longer path took us back through it to the parking lot where we parted.

"Where are you headed now?" Lloyd Martin asked.

"To the Kona side," I told him. "There's a place I've always wanted to see there: the Place of Refuge. I can't pronounce its Hawaiian name, but I'm working on it."

"Pu'uhonua o Honaunau," Jerry said easily. Then more slowly and phonetically, "Poo-oo-ho-nooa o Ho-now-now."

"If you say so," agreed Lloyd, and we all laughed.

"A teacher—definitely," Shelly said aside to me, as she turned to assist her husband in helping the boys into their seat belts at the table in the motor home.

We watched them drive off, both youngsters enthusiastically returning our waves from a side window.

We saw no more of them, the gray pickup, or the man who recklessly drove it, as we left Hawaii Volcanoes National Park, turning left onto the highway that would take us farther south.

About a mile from the park entrance I noticed two large birds by the side of the road.

"Look." I pointed. "I didn't know there were geese in Hawaii."

"They're the Hawaiian state bird. Nene—like *n-a-y n-a-y,*" he told me, spelling it out. "You can say that one."

I could, and did.

"A goose is the state bird?"

"Yeah. They've been here a long time and have adapted so they don't have webbed feet anymore. Theirs are like chicken's feet, so they don't swim like ours, but have an easier time on uneven lava."

"Jerry, Jerry. You're a walking encyclopedia of Hawaiian facts. What would I do without you? And you're sure you don't want to stay here?"

"Nope. I know a lot about Alaska too, and that's where I want to be."

"Then that's where you should and will be soon."

According to a mileage chart I had picked up somewhere in Hilo, it was about a hundred miles from Hilo to Kailua-Kona, which locals seemed to call simply Kona. Not quite halfway between we passed through Na'alehu, where Jerry suggested that we stop at a local fruit stand. It wasn't fruit he had in mind, however, but some macadamia nut shortbread that was worth the stop, especially considering it was after noon and we hadn't had lunch. It was terrific. We drove on, both munching happily.

Beyond Na'alehu a few miles we came to a turnoff on the left.

"That," he told me, "is South Point Road. It leads to the most southern point in the islands, which means that it is also the most southern point in the whole United States—if you'd like to say you've been there."

I took a pass, suggesting that we drive on to Kona instead.

"It's getting late in the day to take a good look at the Refuge and it's less than an hour from Kona. How would it be if we came back to it tomorrow? We can find a place to park in or near Kona, and I'll treat you to dinner tonight."

"Hey, food is good. That works for me."

After the stark lava-covered area of the Volcanoes park, the landscape on the west side of the island seemed very green, even though we passed a number of lava-covered areas between the tropical foliage.

"The lava from old flows in the past breaks down pretty fast," Jerry explained when I commented. "The soil is rich with the stuff that makes plants grow well. It's why the coffee they grow over here is so good."

The road ran up and down low hills and around curves that followed the shape of the land we crossed. Far below the road the ocean was visible, sometimes far in the distance, sometimes closer, with deep blue water against the sweeping crescents of a sandy beach now and then.

"Great kayaking down there," Jerry said. "Snorkeling too. There are places full of hundreds of colored tropical fish—bright yellow tangs, orange ones, striped black-and-white ones—lots of colors. I even saw a red one with white polka dots once. And there are sea turtles, really big ones."

Along the way, houses and small businesses began to appear, some of them farms with dense stands of coffee trees ten or twelve feet high—much larger than I had imagined they would be. I reminded myself that I should buy several more pounds of Kona coffee to take home to Alaska with me, for myself and as gifts for friends.

The window on my side of the truck was open to let

in the warm breeze. As we came around a curve, over the sound of our engine I heard another that a glance in the rearview mirror told me was a motorcycle following close behind, evidently waiting for a gap in oncoming traffic in order to pass. He must have thought he had one as the pavement straightened, for he came roaring up in helmet and goggles, crouched low over his machine. But he had misjudged the distance and, to avoid an oncoming car, was forced to swerve quickly back into the right-hand lane too close in front of me. I applied the brakes gently to slow us down and he sped away with one quick glance back over his shoulder.

"Another idiot," said Jerry, frowning.

I didn't answer, frowning myself. The driver had been wearing jeans and a black T-shirt—but half the island dressed in similar, casual fashion. What had attracted my attention was the blue pack on his back, reminding me of the man I had seen between the buildings along Karen's driveway, as I drove out on my way to the grocery store.

"What's wrong?" Jerry asked.

"Nothing," I told him. "Just for a minute he looked like someone I remember seeing somewhere else."

"Not the guy . . ."

"No—not him, or anyone I know. Just a momentary reminder of someone else—but it wasn't him." Or, at least, I hoped it wasn't.

But it had been one too many coincidences for my liking and I began to wonder if we were actually being followed for some reason. Could it be somehow related to the break-in at Karen's—or the attempted one the first night after my arrival? The idea disturbed my peace of mind and I resented it. Once again I had been made wary and would remain more watchful of those around me.

A few miles farther, we passed the road that would take us down to the Puʻuhonua o Honaunau National Historical Park—the refuge I planned to visit the next day, when we had plenty of time.

Little did I know that, as Jerry had suggested, we might need to find our own refuge there.

TWENTY-ONE

KAILUA-KONA, FAMOUS FOR ITS GORGEOUS SUNSETS, IN the afternoon was a town full of markets, historic buildings, large hotels, a myriad of shops, restaurants, and, of course, tourists—much more so than Hilo, though Hilo was larger. North of Hilo steep cliffs formed the coast, falling sharply for hundreds of feet to the sea, with very few accessible beaches. The Kona side, in contrast, was the sun coast that occupied the lower part of long volcanic slopes that fell gently to the ocean. From one end to the other it had wonderful beaches—some white sand, others black or even green—and plenty of people to take advantage of them.

The town, Jerry read to me from the guidebook, was originally a small fishing village named Kailua. It was renamed Kailua-Kona by the post office because there were Kailua towns on other islands. Kona being the name of a local wind, they added that. The airport, however, was named Kona, adding to the confusion. So most people seem to call it simply Kona, but Kailua is still in use by others.

I was glad that I was not driving my much larger motor home, for the streets were narrowed by parked vehicles and busy with traffic between them. It was difficult to find a place to park near the downtown area and I drove around several blocks a number of times before finding a spot within walking distance of the main part of town.

Going down the hill, we soon found ourselves on Alii Drive, the main street, crowded with shops and restaurants, that ran through town. At its northern end we came first to King Kamehameha's Kona Beach Hotel and turned left to walk along the sidewalk next to the seawall that followed the curve of the bay. Several small boys sat on it with fishing lines dangling into the water and I could see a couple of swimmers out a bit farther.

Two huge cruise ships at anchor were running small boats back and forth to ferry their passengers to the Kailua Pier next door to the hotel. At the far end of that pier was a vessel the like of which I had never seen and which caught my attention immediately, with its three bright orange triangular sails above what looked more like a barge than a sailboat.

Walking to the end of the pier, we found it was a large double-hulled catamaran named the *Tamure*. A sign advertised it as the vessel for "Captain Beans' Dinner Cruise," which sailed every evening but Monday and featured Polynesian entertainment along with your meal.

"You'll have a good view of Kona in the daylight as you go out, the sunset over water, and the city with all its lights when you come back several hours later," we were told by a member of the crew who was there to take reservations—and to let us know that there was still room for two that evening if we wanted to make one. When I found that they featured island music and Tahitian dancing, I was sold.

"Oh, Jerry, let's go, shall we? It sounds terrific."

Reservations made, we walked slowly along the street, feeling like the tourists we were, enjoying the sunny day, and taking in the afternoon sights, though I noticed that Jerry was also casually examining the faces of people who passed us for anyone he recognized, as was I—still somewhat nervous.

On our side of the street we soon came to Hulihe'e Palace, which had been the vacation residence of Hawaiian royalty, but was now a museum. And across the street was the Mokuaikaua Church, the oldest Christian church in Hawaii, built by missionaries in 1820. Both had been constructed out of blocks of lava rock, but the palace had at some point been plastered over and was now a sandy tan color.

A little farther on I was pleased to find a large shopping area with a number of shops and galleries. Jerry's interest was caught by a place that sold surfing and scuba gear, so we arranged a place to meet and I spent an hour drifting in and out of shops, looking a lot and buying little of what I saw. Much of it was the usual tourist T-shirts, key chains, and other articles that had *Kona* or *Hawaii* printed on them somewhere. We have the same kind of things at home, but ours read *Alaska* instead.

When I rejoined Jerry, he was sitting at a small round table that had an umbrella to provide shade.

He leaped up with a grin.

"Sit down," he said, pulling over a second white plastic deck chair. "I'll be right back."

He returned almost immediately, proudly bearing two large ice cream cones and a handful of paper napkins.

"Here," he said, handing one to me. "I hope you like

this. It's my favorite ice cream—coconut. See if it isn't the greatest stuff ever."

In the warmth of the day, it was, and I told him so, with thanks.

As I enjoyed the treat, catching drips with a couple of the paper napkins, at a table near us I was amused to see a couple of retirement-aged tourists—he in a billed cap, loose Hawaiian shirt, and knee-length shorts, while she wore a brimmed straw hat and a long, orange, wraparound skirt that was oddly topped with a black long-sleeved knit shirt—an outfit that looked to me uncomfortably warm for the weather. They were busily writing notes on a handful of postcards—clearly the obligatory *wish you were here* messages to send home. It was almost worth a picture, but I had left my camera in the RV.

Finishing our ice cream, we walked a little farther and came upon an open-air market taking up half a parking lot on the other side of the street. Carefully crossing the lines of slow traffic heading each direction, we wandered in and found a wealth of interesting things for sale that were much more appealing than the commercial offerings in the shops I had seen.

The market was arranged with aisles between tables of goods under canvas awnings to keep off the sun. Bright, colorful items were everywhere, most home-made or homegrown.

There were several displays of local flowers, both on long stems and just the blossoms strung into leis. A familiar sweet scent encouraged me to follow my nose and, instead of passing, I turned to see several creamy white leis hanging together, but the blossoms were much larger than the tiny ones I remembered seeing.

"Jasmine," I said and bent to take a deep breath of

the fragrance, with a pleased smile to the woman behind the table, who was stringing another lei from a pile in her lap. "Wonderful!"

She nodded and gave me the Hawaiian word. "Pikake, a relative of jasmine—with a similar smell."

Of course the sale had been made as I homed in on the heady scent, and I continued market exploration with my purchase around my neck.

"The flowers won't last long in this heat," Jerry observed.

"Probably not. But some of life's most significant pleasures are fleeting, aren't they?"

Several vendors had fresh fruit and vegetables for sale, so I picked out some bananas and a papaya for the next day's breakfast.

At another table piled high with fabric in Hawaiian prints I bought enough of a beautiful red one to make a tablecloth when I got home.

I looked long and covetously at some wonderful quilts in traditional Hawaiian patterns, but decided the size I liked best would be difficult to carry home and, regretfully, did not buy it, though I was severely tempted.

"Mail it," Jerry suggested.

But I had had enough of packing and shipping for the time being. Anything bound for my home in Alaska, I told him, that would not go with me on the plane, would not go at all.

"Can't say I blame you after the past week or two," he laughed. "It's almost four thirty anyway. We should take the things you've bought back to the camper, so we can make it to the pier for the cruise at five fifteen."

So we passed up close examination of traditional ukuleles, attractive baskets and woodcarvings, several tables of jewelry, including some created of coral and shell, and drums made of large gourds, among other temptations, and hiked back to where we had parked.

It had been a pleasant day full of interesting sights and surprises. How could I know that before the day was over *surprise* would be one of the more operative words in my vocabulary?

I started to use the key on the door in the rear of the camper, but found it already unlocked. Trying to remember if I had, or had not, locked it, I opened it and stepped up into what was becoming a familiar sort of chaos.

Karen's household goods had been packed in the container and shipped, so we had aboard only the personal items that would go with us on the plane to Anchorage.

Everything else in the camper, the basic packages of dishes, pots and pans, and linens, belonged to the rental company and would go back with the vehicle when we returned it to them. None of it, however, was now neatly stowed as we had left it. All had been torn out and tossed wherever it landed. The contents of my suitcase and Jerry's pack had been dumped out onto the floor and pawed through. The book I had been reading lay facedown in the sink. The cupboards had been emptied and the storage spaces below as well. A bottle of my lotion was a puddle around shards of glass on the bathroom floor, where it had fallen or been dropped. Even the refrigerator had been emptied and its contents dragged out onto the floor in front of it, but nothing else broken.

The interior had been thoroughly searched, though I couldn't tell if anything had been stolen.

"What the hell . . . ?" Jerry exclaimed, peering in over my shoulder. "Not *again*!"

I stood looking at the mess around me, shoved the

tangle of his clothing out of the way to sit down on the dinette bench closest to the door, and sighed, wearily close to tears.

"I'm afraid so."

"What do they want?"

"I just don't know."

He stood taking it all in for a long minute, then shook his head and turned to me, holding out his hand to help me up.

"Come on," he said suddenly and, for the first time, taking charge. "Let's go to dinner. Lock the door and we'll take care of it when we come back."

"Oh, no," I began. "I can't just leave it like this. I should call the police and—"

"It'll all still be here after dinner. What if we hadn't come back, but gone straight to the boat? You couldn't have done anything till then. What difference will it make? It's not fair for you to miss doing something you really want to do and we have to have dinner anyway, don't we? What difference is a couple of hours going to make, as opposed to doing anything about it now?"

As I listened to this argument, I began slowly to agree and a spark of anger replaced my initial shock and dismay. Enough was, after all, *enough*.

He was right, of course. I was perhaps too used to taking care of other people and problems when they arose. It felt good, I realized, to have someone else— even someone as young as Jerry—take the initiative for a change.

"All right," I impetuously agreed. "Put whatever needs to stay cold back in the refrigerator, while I clean up the broken bottle in the bathroom, and we're *out of here*!"

A grin was his answer, as he bent to comply.

In five minutes we were hurrying back down the hill, the camper locked securely once again, and the chaos left behind.

Sometimes it is absolutely the best thing to simply refuse to respond to a situation.

"Jerry," I told him, after we had walked the length of Kailua Pier and handed our tickets to Captain Beans' crewman, stood together to have a picture taken, and crossed the gangway onto the catamaran *Tamure,* "like everyone else, sometimes I need a good kick in the pants. Thank you for giving it to me tonight."

There would be a cleanup job to be done when we got back later, but it could wait. So I refused to consider it further, intending instead to enjoy the evening and let someone else do the cooking for a change.

Twenty-two

The configuration of the interior of Captain Beans' double-hulled catamaran, *Tamure,* was interesting and unique. A generous walkway ran around the port and starboard sides, a narrower one down the center. Between the three walkways and level with them were six large built-in platform tables with benches, three on each side. We had to step down to seat ourselves at the portside table that we selected to be near a stage that was located toward the forward end.

Immediately, we were offered a drink from the bar by a waitress who astonished us by stepping from the center walkway directly onto the tabletop to take our order and, when she returned, to serve the drinks we ordered—an old-fashioned for me, a Coke for Jerry. We sat sipping them as we watched the last of the passengers come aboard.

As soon as all were seated, the gangway was removed, the lines cast off, and the vessel moved slowly away from the pier, turning so our port side was parallel to the shoreline. Remembering that we had been promised a good view of Kona in the daylight as we went out, I took my digital camera to the rail for several pictures of the sunlit buildings that lined the sweeping curve of the harbor. Then I turned and took a few of the interior of the boat from one end to the other, with people sitting around the sunken tables and waitresses serving drinks from the tabletops.

The sea was calm, with only the hint of a light breeze whispering in off the water. Though it would be daylight for some time yet, the late afternoon sun was well on its way toward the horizon—a perfectly straight and level horizontal line where the ocean met a sky that held a few billowy clouds with edges just beginning to turn a faint rose. Jerry brought our drinks up from the table and for a while we sat on tall stools at the narrow bar attached to the rail, watching Kona slide away and the afternoon turn slowly into evening as we headed for open water outside the bay.

Soon the waitresses scrubbed down the tables they had been walking on, then served a family-style dinner and we passed around the dishes of roast beef, salad, potatoes—a delicious meal, if not exotic. Beside us at the table was an older couple that reminded me a little of the pair I had seen writing postcards at the table in the shopping area that afternoon. Hawaii is a popular vacation destination for Alaskans, retired or not, so I was not surprised to find that Mel and Julie Peterson were from Anchorage, but had a small house in Kona where they spent winters, returning home in the spring.

"My seventy-six-year-old arthritic knees are less painful down here," Mel confessed. "I get pretty crippled in the cold up there."

"We migrate north like the birds, usually in May. But we're late going back this year," Julie told me. "Our granddaughter had her wedding here a couple of weeks ago, so of course we stayed for that."

"Then you've done this cruise before?" I asked.

She smiled and shook her head. "We should have, I guess, but I think wherever you live you put off the local things you mean to do because they're always there to be done. So it's a first for us, too, though we've meant to take it for several years." She leaned forward to smile at Jerry and hand him the platter of roast beef. "Is this your grandson?"

"No, Jerry's a friend from Fairbanks who's being my tour guide for a couple of days."

"So you live there?" she asked him.

"Well—I guess . . . ," he began, frowning thoughtfully. Then an anticipatory smile turned up the corners of his mouth as he glanced at me and with an emphatic nod told her, "Yes. Yes, I *do*. And I'm going home on Friday."

What little it takes sometimes—the price of a one-way plane ticket this time—to change a life for the better. I was once again proud of Jerry and glad for him.

As we were enjoying our dinner, a band had appeared on the stage to play pleasant background music, not all island music, but also familiar tunes that were very danceable. Finished eating, we pushed back our plates, which were collected, along with the serving dishes, from the table, and Mel turned to Julie.

"Ready?" he asked.

"You bet," she told him and stood up.

They moved to the open space provided by the port-side walkway and began to dance. It was a pleasure to watch, for they had obviously danced together for many years and loved what they were doing in a very professional manner. Clearly, Mel's seventy-six-year-old arthritic knees were bothering him not at all. No wonder they enjoyed living in a tropical climate.

"Hey," observed Jerry, "they're really *good*."

"They certainly are."

Two other couples, encouraged by the Petersons' example, soon joined them. Both were younger, but neither was half as talented or enthusiastic about it.

I enjoyed watching them and found myself missing both my absent husbands. Both of them had liked to dance, but my first, Joe, had been the one to take every opportunity offered—and, if it wasn't offered, to take it anyway. Finding some music on the radio, he would come to sweep me out of the kitchen and dance me around the dining table without a care that the pork chops burned. I learned early to watch out for him and turn off the heat under the pan when I heard the music start.

Daniel, on the other hand, liked his music and dancing slower, but would make an attempt at almost anything that sounded like Aussie music. By the time we married we were both approaching senior citizen status and slow dancing was more our style and preference anyway. It had been a long time since I danced, but I wasn't about to climb on a table to try it now.

By the time dinner was over and the tables once again washed clean, the band began to play the island music promised in the advertising and several young dancers in bright Polynesian costumes were standing to one side, ready for it. They scattered along the walkways and each stepped into the center of a table as the beat of the drums started them all swaying to the rhythm of the music.

The women's costumes, most of them a bikini top and short sarong tied to one side, were a bright red and yellow print, and they wore yellow flowers in their hair. Each woman carried a rattle made of a gourd and red feathers. The men wore grass skirts of the same brilliant red slung low on their hips, but their upper bodies were bare and their tan skin lightly oiled. Their headdresses were an impressive design of opalescent shell with black and white feathers reaching tall above it.

All were barefoot and very physically fit, probably from the fantastic way they moved their bodies to the music, particularly the hips, sometimes so fast it was a blur of motion. These dances were not the slow traditional hula, but Polynesian in origin and wonderful to watch, though impossible to imagine doing. And these dancers did them six days a week. No wonder they were in great shape.

For most of an hour we enjoyed the dances, interspersed with songs from a heavyset man wearing a red-and-black-print costume. In a beautifully mellow voice, he sang island songs and some more familiar popular numbers.

The sun had gone down in a splendorous display, turning the clouds red, orange, and purple, all of which, including the gilded gold edges of the clouds, was reflected in the ocean waters, in combination with its own blues and greens. When it was just light enough to see them, a couple of flying fish broke the surface and glided along a few yards in the air before vanishing once again into the deep. Never having seen one before, I was fascinated.

By the time we were cruising back close enough to see, as promised, the lights of Kona along the shore, some of the younger customers were dancing with the entertainers on the tables. Just before they stopped playing, the band, with a sense of humor, tossed in a western

Boot-Scootin' Boogie, just for fun, and entertainers and customers alike all danced to that too.

What a delightful evening it had been.

As soon as the boat arrived at the pier, people began to collect near the exit, anxious now to disembark, but forced to wait while the gangway was fitted into place. In the shuffle of the crowd I lost Jerry, but saw him wave a hand back in my direction and knew he would wait for me once off the boat, so I didn't try to push forward, but stepped back to take my time while the congestion cleared.

The Petersons stopped next to me to say good-bye and we chatted for a minute before they moved on.

"Call us sometime when you're in Anchorage, won't you?" Julie invited me. "We're in the phone book and will be home—May till October at least."

As the way cleared ahead, I started forward, only to be shoved out of line by a man who suddenly pushed past me, causing me to stumble and drop my purse. Bending to pick it up, hoping my camera had not been damaged, I was regaining my balance when he swung back around to face me, leaned uncomfortably close, and half-whispered, half-growled: "We have your friend. If you want him back alive, give us the deed and the money and we'll consider a trade."

"What?" I asked, shocked, confused, and thinking I must have heard him wrong.

But I found myself speaking to air, as he had turned his back and lunged ahead to push past two people on the gangway. Reaching the pier he turned away toward the lights of Alii Drive, and trotted off into the shadows. I got a brief look at his profile as he fled, but it did me little good. He was wearing a cap and a large pair of sunglasses, though it was completely dark outside.

As I stepped off the gangway onto the pier, I saw him get into a dark sedan that immediately sped away and vanished around a corner.

Looking around for Jerry, I didn't see him waiting for me, as I had expected, assuming he wouldn't leave without me for the walk up the hill. My heart in my throat, I remembered what I had been told: *We have your friend.* Jerry was the only friend he could have been referring to, wasn't he? He had evidently been taken away in the car that I had watched disappear, right? What else could it have meant? Nothing I could think of, with concern and fear for the rest of what he had said to me: *If you want him back* alive …

I looked carefully, fearfully, around the nearly empty pier, and saw no one watching me, or seeming to be waiting to follow me. Going up to one of the crew members, I asked if he had seen Jerry, and described him.

He shook his head. "No. Everyone but you has already gone. There was a young man like that went off with two other men as soon as he was off the boat, though."

My heart skipped a beat. Could the man in the gray truck be back and after Jerry again?

"What did they look like?"

"There wasn't much light, so I couldn't really see. They walked close together, arm in arm, quickly toward a car at the other end of the pier. The young man looked back over his shoulder, but went along with the others. That's all I saw."

I thanked him and turned to walk myself off the pier, somehow sure it was Jerry he had described—and that they had taken him unwillingly.

"Oh," the crewman called after me, "one of the men was wearing sunglasses. It seemed odd to wear them at night."

Then I thought again of the man on the boat who had crowded past and had worn dark glasses so large they covered a third of his face.

With a sinking, helpless feeling, I went hesitantly a little way toward the end of the pier that ended at the main street, watching carefully for anyone suspicious on the way, staying in lighted spaces as well as I could and avoiding the shadows, and paused, trying to think through my alarm and dread.

Apparently, they thought I would know what they wanted, but I had no clue. And, if I didn't know, I couldn't give them what they wanted, could I? And where had they taken Jerry? What should I do? What could I do?

TWENTY-THREE

DEED? MONEY? WHAT WAS THIS ALL ABOUT?

The only thing that made any sense to me about it was that their demand evidently made perfect sense to them—whoever *they* were—enough sense to snatch Jerry to use as a bargaining chip in whatever game they were playing. I doubted he had gone willingly.

The way the demand mentioned "the money" sounded as if they had some specific money in mind and had assumed I would know what they meant.

And a *deed*? To what?

I had no knowledge of either a deed or some unknown quantity of money. Could they possibly have mistaken me—and Jerry—for someone else? But how many senior citizens in their midsixties would there be playing tourist in Hawaii with a young man who could be their grandson?

As I hesitated, the crewman from the *Tamure* called out helpfully, "Could I call a taxi for you, ma'am?"

"Oh, no, thank you," I told him, turning toward the

town lights at the end of the pier. "I've only a block or two to walk. Thanks for a great evening."

It was time to stop spinning wheels of confusion and do something, even if it was only to get myself in motion.

As I left the pier and crossed the street to start up the hill toward the camper, I looked around at the buildings and vehicles that I passed with the feeling one of them might hold someone covertly watching me to see what I would do, but saw no one. I felt very alone and vulnerable in an unfamiliar town where the only person I knew had disappeared. With all the shops closed it was quiet and few people were on the streets. A block away along Alii Drive, someone called out and someone else answered with a laugh as they separated after leaving a bar and restaurant. A couple crossed the street ahead of me, walking slowly hand in hand toward King Kamehameha's Hotel, absorbed in each other—honeymooners perhaps.

Once beyond that main street it was darker and I found myself casting cautious glances around me, but still saw nothing.

I could not imagine what could possibly have inspired this unsettling chain of events, though somehow I had a feeling that the man in the gray truck must somehow be involved—that much seemed possible at least. Then, thinking back, I expanded my considerations. The mess we had found in the camper could have been the result of its being torn apart in a search for either or both of the things demanded in the note. It seemed likely that break-in was somehow connected and that possibly the other intrusion that had occurred at Karen's rental house before we left Hilo might be as well. Or was I clutching at straws and taking too much together—put-

ting everything that had concerned me lately in one basket, so to speak?

I stepped out smartly, impelled by a glowing coal of
anger that was growing hotter in my mind, in contrast to
the lurking cold and fearful concern for Jerry that had
emerged as soon as I learned he had been forced away
by someone I didn't know—or want to know, for that
matter.

I knew what I would do at home—go directly to the
police, who were, in my small community, well known to
me both as neighbors and as keepers of the law. There I
would have known how they would handle such a situation. Law enforcement in Hawaii, and Kona in particular, was an unknown resource—except for Officer Davis,
who was now, of course, a hundred miles away on the
other side of the island and of no help to me now.

By the time I reached the rented truck camper I was
out of breath from having climbed the hill too fast and
had grown angrier and more resentful with every hurried step I had taken. The situation was intolerable and
the only possibility of assistance I could think of lay
with the police, so, knowing that I could not deal with
the problem alone, I used my cell phone and called
them.

It must have been a slow night for crime in Kona, for
in ten minutes a squad car was pulling in at the curb
behind my vehicle. I stood up from where I had been
sitting on the rear step and—glad Jerry had talked me
out of an immediate cleanup of the camper, so the law
could see the break-in damage the way we had originally found it—walked to meet the two officers who got
out and came toward me.

"Mrs. McNabb?" asked the one on my right.

"Yes," I replied, looking back and forth between the

men who stood before me in the light that spilled out the camper door from inside. The two were as alike as the proverbial peas in a pod and, especially in matching uniforms, were totally indistinguishable.

"You two must be . . ."

"Twins? Yeah." He grinned. "Identical, obviously. Officers William and Robert Holt at your service. You might as well just call us Bill and Bob. Everyone does, because 'Officer Holt' just gets a response from both of us when we're together. I'm Bill."

"Dispatch said you reported a break-in," Bob chimed in. "You just find it?"

I had already decided to forgo Jerry's idea of pretending we had not found out about the break-in until after Captain Beans' cruise. I told the truth.

"No. We found it late this afternoon, close to five o'clock."

I then told them what we had found, explained why we hadn't called at that time and where we had been in the interim.

"You keep saying 'we,' " said Officer Bob. "Who's traveling with you?"

Now the rest of the story had to be told and I did it as briefly and concisely as possible, knowing they would ask questions about anything they wanted to know more about as it related to the break-in or Jerry's seeming abduction on the pier. It all poured out: how I had hired Jerry to help pack and play tour guide for me, where we had been, the Hilo break-in and Officer Davis, the man in the gray truck, the other in dark glasses, and that there must have been two or three men who took Jerry away in the dark car, leaving me with nothing but anxiety and a growled threat.

"But you didn't get a plate number."

"It was too far away."

"And you locked and left this camper just before five o'clock and it was still locked when you came back."

"Yes, it was."

"Let's take a look inside," Officer Bill suggested to brother Bob. "You want to get the print kit?"

"I'd be willing to bet you won't find anything but prints of mine and Jerry's. The guy on the boat wore dark glasses so I couldn't identify him," I confessed.

"You're probably right, but I'll give it a try. Who knows? And down the road if we catch these guys . . ." He shrugged and frowned at the likelihood.

The two officers did a thorough and competent job of examining the chaos of the interior of the camper.

"Is there anywhere that you are sure would have the boy's fingerprints?" Officer Bob asked me. "If we have some you can identify, we can compare them to others."

So I showed him the window that Jerry had closed the night at the Volcanoes campground against the man in the gray pickup who had pulled in beside us. Soon he had lots of my prints and what we could assume were Jerry's, but he found no new others.

"You were right," he said, shaking his head. "They must have worn gloves. There are a few here and there, but most are under yours and were probably made by someone else who rented this camper."

When they had finished their examination and search for clues, we sat at the dinette table and discussed what could be done to find Jerry.

"You're sure he didn't take off on his own?" asked Officer Bob.

I assured him I was very sure.

"There's very little chance we'll have any joy there," Officer Bill told me. "Without a description of the guys and the car there's not enough to even start looking. Besides, they could be halfway to anywhere on the island by now. But from the tone of that message it's most likely they're somewhere close and will be back in touch with you soon."

"But I don't even know what it is they mean by a deed. And they didn't give an amount on the money they demanded as ransom."

"They will. Technically you're not supposed to park overnight where you are now, but I'd suggest that you stay right here anyway. We won't ticket you and it seems to be the one place where both these guys *and* Jerry know where to contact you, right?"

"Yes, I think so."

"Then just wait and see what happens. We'll be on patrol all night and will slip by every so often to check on you. If they contact you again, call dispatch and we'll be here right away. Give me your cell phone number. It's a weeknight and will probably be slow, but if we get really busy with something else I can at least call you to check in. Okay?"

It seemed like the only workable plan to me. They had taken it all in stride, but I had a suspicion that, without saying so, they were wondering if Jerry might have taken off on his own. I did not tell them all about his runaway status and his stepfather's resentment, seeing no reason to tangle that story with the current situation as the two seemed to have nothing to do with each other.

In five minutes they were gone, with matching grins and salutes, and it grew very quiet in the rig. So I closed and locked the door, cleaned up most of the mess, made myself a cup of tea, and sat down to think it over again, feeling oddly singular without my travel buddy, Jerry.

I ached to know where he was and how he was being

treated and it was totally frustrating to be able to do nothing but wait. I could not sit still for long and was soon on my feet pacing back and forth in the limited space within the camper. There was no prospect of going to bed. I couldn't have slept had I wanted to, and I did not. There was also the chance that one or more of them would show up in person, for who knew what they intended, and I wanted to remain dressed. It could be a long night indeed should they leave me alone to wait and worry as a way to wear down any resistance I might offer in handing over what they had demanded. They might have been watching, seen the police come and go, and could, as vindictive punishment, hurt Jerry or stay away until the twin officers had gone off duty in the morning. I hoped not, especially the former, but anything was possible, so I tried to stop imagining what they *might* do.

It was Jerry's welfare that occupied most of my thoughts, making me almost sorry I had met him and, thereby, drawn him into this tangled net of intrigue— whatever it was made of.

I was also missing Stretch, my other and more permanent traveling companion. When things upset me, he is always a dependable comfort. *Well,* I thought, *two more nights and I'll be back in Alaska—three and I'll be home again, thanks be.*

But first something must be done to retrieve Jerry from the hands of his captors. And I had no idea how to proceed, other than what I was doing—nothing.

As I thought back through the situation over and over again, my mind fastened on the deed they had asked for. The demand for money I could comprehend, but what deed could they want—to what?

The first thing a deed called to mind was, of course,

property of some kind. The only property I knew anything about on this island was the land that Lewis and Karen had bought and which was now up for sale with only the foundation of a house built on it. I assumed she had taken the deed with her, or left it with the real estate agent who had the property listing, and whom I did not know. If not, what would Karen have done with it—pack it in one of the boxes to be shipped? I certainly hoped she hadn't been careless enough to do that, but had taken it with her along with the other kinds of personal papers one collects as proof of ownership or, in case the worst happens, to delineate those to inherit possessions of real or sentimental value.

I did not remember seeing any such papers among the items we had shipped, or that I had helped her pack to take back to Alaska with her on the plane.

My own important papers were kept in a bank vault that my Daniel had insisted we obtain. "What if the house should burn down?" he had asked. "We'd at least need to know the worth of what we'd lost, yes?" So off to the bank they had gone, though we had kept copies at home in a file box that lived in the lockable lower drawer of a cabinet in our small office.

A file box—a *box*! The realization popped into my mind that in the confusion created by those who had broken into the camper, I had not seen the tackle box Karen had supposedly forgotten and left on the shelf of her bedroom closet. I remembered that I had put it into the taxi that had taken us to the rental agency where we picked up the truck camper and had taken it out along with my suitcase when we arrived there. I had tucked it away somewhere and had not thought of it since. Nor had I found it in cleaning up the jumble of items in the camper.

Often I left things in my suitcase that I did not intend to use or would not need until sometime later. I went to the closet where I had put it away and unzipped and looked in it for the tackle box. It was not there, but the handgun was. I had forgotten it as well, but now I took it out and stood looking down at it, the metal cold in my hand.

I have lived all my life with guns and the knowledge of how to use them, but few of them had been handguns. My father had had several hunting rifles, a regular shotgun, and a short-barrel with twelve-gauge slugs that he packed along on family hikes and camping trips in case we tangled with a bear. As he taught us all how to use his guns, he instilled proper caution and respect for them in us as well. To me a rifle or a shotgun was a tool like any other, with definite purposes. In my mind a handgun is more often than not a tool for killing humans, and not to my liking. In my Winnebago motor home I carry one of the shotguns that I inherited from my father in a well-hidden secret compartment built for me by a carpenter before I ever drove out of Alaska. I feel more secure with it than any kind of handgun.

I had considered leaving this handgun with Officer Davis in Hilo, and I did mean to turn it over to him as soon we returned there. But for now the handgun I was holding was the only protection I had available, so I wasn't about to put it away again, and I would use it if I had to—registered to me or not—and deal with the legal results later, if necessary.

Checking to make doubly sure it was loaded, I tucked it into my purse, which I set on the counter in the galley, then stood blindly staring out the window at the shadow of a tree cast onto the pavement by a streetlight, as I tried to remember what I had done with Karen's tackle box. Sometimes I swear that with age my memory is failing me so steadily that I will be an utter empty-headed idiot by the time I am really old. But it never helps to struggle with it, so, frustrated, I put it by—let it go, sat down again at the table, and thought about how much I longed to be at home instead of where I was at the moment.

Then, as I was reminding myself that it would soon be time for Stretch's regular visit to the vet, the location of the tackle box fell into my head as if someone had whispered a hint in my ear.

The camper shell extended perhaps a foot beyond and below the bed of the pickup on which it rested and was secured. Outside, on the passenger side of that lower rear section was the door to a storage space that, flush with the wall, had no handle, but opened with a key that kept company with the ignition key on its ring. I had put the tackle box out of the way into that space, knowing there would be no reason to take it out until I returned the camper to the rental agency on Friday, before catching the plane to Alaska.

Could that box, which Karen had refused to open or leave behind, have contained her important papers, including the property deed? "It was Lewis's," she had said. "I want it just the way it is, locked." I had assumed it held what it had originally been used for—fishing tackle. But could it enclose the deed that Jerry's abductors were demanding? If so, was that the right deed?

Without further ado, I took the keys, went out the back of the camper and around its corner to the storage compartment, and opened it. Under a fanny pack that Jerry had taken from his larger pack and asked me to store, I found and lifted out the remembered tackle box, along with a tire iron that I found there as well.

Putting back Jerry's fanny pack, I closed and locked the compartment again, and took both items back into the camper, locked the door firmly behind me, and set to work to open the box by force.

But there was more to this than just finding the deed, if it was there, as I suspected. I thought there would have to be additional steps to transferring property, and the deed without her signature would not be sufficient alone to reassign ownership. There had to be more to it than simple possession of a piece of legal paper, and that, I was afraid, was somehow where the demand for money came into the picture. If Karen knew that her property was at risk, she certainly had not told me everything I needed to know about the situation, had she? Now I would have to find out for myself.

Angry and suspicious of her probable part in our current state of affairs, I was tempted to try to reach her by phone for some answers, but decided against it. If she was somehow involved, one of two things would probably happen: she would claim to know nothing at all about any of it or she would refuse to take any responsibility, as usual—neither of which would be of any help or satisfaction to me.

But the time for secrets was over. With or without her permission, I had to know. If it held nothing but hooks and line, I would owe Karen an abject apology for ruining Lewis's tackle box.

If not, and the deed was there, she would certainly owe me one—not that I expected to ever get it.

TWENTY-FOUR

IT WAS THERE.

Lying on top, with Karen's birth certificate and Lewis's, was a now-outdated will that had been current until Lewis died, and a few other papers having nothing to do with the Hawaiian property. But the deed *was* there—and it bore both her signature and Lewis's.

Though I was almost certain that piece of paper was what Jerry's abductors were demanding, somehow I felt it must take more than just having a deed in your possession to claim ownership of a property. At that rate, with that piece of paper in my hand, perhaps even I could claim to own it. Signed or not, it might put forward a significant claim on the property if handled carefully and ingeniously enough by an attorney who knew the twists and turns of the law, but there must be more to it than that, legal steps to be taken, registration of a transfer of ownership at least. If it were mine, it was not something I would want to have fall into the hands of an unscrupulous attorney working for these men who for some reason seemed to want it so badly.

But the most curious and troublesome thing that confronted me, when I had finally broken the lock and pried open the lid of that metal box, lifted out the papers, and stood staring down into it, was not that there was still fishing tackle in the bottom—though there was—but something else. Snagged under one of the triple hooks of a lure was a page folded in half that seemed to be a record of assets and expenditures concerning the house building project. Evidently the work was to be paid in installments as it was accomplished. I picked the page up and found that an invoice for the foundation work was fastened to it, marked "PAID" and the same amount had been subtracted in the debit column of figures. Beneath it, in the bottom of the tackle box, I was surprised to find a small pile of bills—small in the size of the pile, not the amount. According to the amount of money listed in the asset column, there must have once been much more. But what I found left in the box was a pile of hundred-dollar bills—twenty-seven of them that I counted out onto the tabletop. Two thousand seven hundred dollars.

I stood staring down at them with now-familiar suspicion, remembering how Karen had insisted on leaving the box locked. Before she left, however, she must have opened it surreptitiously just long enough to remove the rest of the money that would have brought the total up to the well over a hundred thousand dollars in assets that were listed on the records page.

She had left me with the deed, but she must have been in a hurry to leave, for I was sure that had she noticed the small amount of cash I had uncovered at the bottom of the box she would have taken that as well.

Fishing tackle it was not! Bait—maybe! But not for anything with fins or scales that lived and swam in water.

No wonder those men wanted it and the deed to the property. Whoever they were, they were willing to take risks with both Jerry and me to get their hands on it. And they must have a pretty good idea how much there should be, but they couldn't know the majority of it had flown away back to Alaska.

Karen had to have known what the deed was and had left it behind. So, taking a short mental step, I could only assume that she might *not* have forgotten it, but had, with some rationale of her own, left it behind with purpose. Perhaps she thought they would assume she had taken it back to Alaska and had no idea that she was putting me—and Jerry—at risk. Perhaps, as usual, she really didn't care and was simply leaving problems for someone else to solve.

As I considered what I had found and could really only guess the meaning of, that glowing coal of anger grew fiercely hot again. Had the woman no consideration for the welfare of others?

Damn and blast you, Karen, I thought.

Considering how little I knew of the perpetrators, the manner of and seeming reasons for Jerry's forced disappearance, Karen owed both of us much more than a simple apology for her inconsideration and negligence.

Standing there I swore aloud that I would get it for him—one way or another.

Angrily I started to go in search of my cell phone, then reconsidered. It would be an hour later in Alaska—not that waking Karen in the middle of the night would stop me. But did I really want to confront her long distance at the moment—in the middle of the night? Yes, but were anger and suspicion by themselves sufficient reason?

You haven't got all four paws on the mouse at the moment, love, I heard my Daniel say. *It would be a good idea to cool off before you get her dander up as well. Letting off steam won't solve any part of the problem.*

I knew he was right, so I sat down and put my elbows on the table and my face in my hands as I took a deep breath. For the moment it would remain a waiting game—though I did want to know if she could tell me the identity of any or all of the three men hunting us.

Just before seven o'clock the next morning I was bonedeep weary in both mind and body and was still at the dinette table, half-asleep with my head cradled on my arms, which were folded on the tackle box, when Officers Bill and Bob Holt stopped by for the third time. They rapped on the door to be sure I was all right, asked if I had heard anything, and told me they were about to go off duty.

"We passed on all the information we collected last night," said Officer Bill, looking up to where I stood in the doorway. "There'll be an Officer Kealoha stopping by soon to take up where we're leaving off, so don't feel you've been abandoned."

"What should I do?"

"Nothing. Just stay put and wait. We think sometime soon these guys will try to contact you somehow. If they do, call 911 and ask for Kealoha. Meanwhile, we've put a BOLO out on the gray truck you described along with the information that a dark sedan was probably used to abduct Jerry Monahan."

When they had gone I wondered why I had not told them about the deed and the money I had found. Did I want it around in case I was forced to ransom Jerry with only part of the cash? That was at least a possibility. But I had to admit that having it, even though I then took the box and put it out of sight behind my suitcase, made me more than slightly nervous. But something had made me hold my tongue in terms of those two demanded items—and one other.

I had not told them about the handgun I had illegally, either. Just knowing it was there, within reach, made me feel a little stronger—at least I thought so, though I would have felt safer with my shotgun.

Going to the small bathroom, I splashed water in my face, combed my hair, and put it up into its usual twist. Then I put some coffee on to brew and some bacon in a skillet on the stove to fry before adding a couple of eggs. Hungry or not, it was time to eat something and get at least part of my energy back. God knew I might need it.

When the coffee finished brewing I poured myself a cup, put the rest into the thermos, rinsed out the pot, and put it away.

I had drunk half the cup and had just broken the eggs into the skillet to fry when a sudden pounding on the rear door startled me. Assuming it must be the officer who was taking over for the Holt twins, I went immediately, knowing I must get back to the eggs before they turned to shoe leather in the pan, and opened the door without asking who required my attention.

That could have been a grave mistake.

But what I found was Jerry, clutching the screen door handle as if it were a lifeline.

"Let me in," he gasped breathlessly, as he frantically yanked at the locked barrier. *"Quick! They'll be coming after me."*

When I unlocked it he all but fell into the room on his hands and knees and crawled forward so I could reach to close and lock both screen and door behind him.

"Jerry," I began, turning to where he sat panting on the floor at my feet, "how . . . ? What . . . ?"

"Later," he said, using the table to pull himself to a standing position. "I'll—tell you—later. Let's get away from here—before they show up."

"Where . . . ? How did you . . . ?"

"Never mind," he said, still breathing hard, ignoring the questions I was trying to ask. "Look out and see if you see any of them coming."

I didn't know if I'd recognize them if they were, but I took a look out the window in the door anyway. There was no one but a woman walking a dog along the other side of the street. I told him so.

"Get your keys," he said. "Let's try to be gone before they get here."

Knowing the overdone eggs behind him on the stove would soon begin to smoke in the pan, without wasting time on an explanation I pushed past him, turned off the gas, snatched the hot skillet off the stove and thrust it into the stainless steel sink, where it could do no harm, and poured what was left of my coffee over it. Shoving the thermos and keys at him, I grabbed my purse and a second coffee cup. We climbed out and I trotted after him around the camper to the driver's side of the truck, where he unlocked the door and we clambered in, Jerry first, so he could slide across to the passenger's side.

As I started the truck, he watched in the rearview mirror to see if anyone showed up behind us. No one did, so I pulled out of the space in which I had parked and headed down the hill to where the easiest and quickest turn was a left on Alii Drive.

At that hour of the morning traffic was, thankfully, light. A few shops had lights on inside and the hordes of tourists we had seen the day before were just beginning to show up. It took half as much time to get through downtown Kona as it had on our way in. Very soon we came to where a sign told me that turning left again would take us uphill to Highway 11.

"Should I turn here?" I asked him.

"No, don't go that way," he said, still watching behind us in the mirror. "Highway 11 is the main road in and out of Kona. You really can't leave the area without driving on it, so if they're looking for us—and they will be as soon as they see that we're gone from where you parked—they'll try both north and south on it first—probably split up to do it. Keep right, on this one for now. We can get back to that one farther along this road, if we want to."

That made sense, so I continued out of town along Alii Drive, which ran very close to the shoreline and was lined with condos and apartment buildings, one after the other, all with ocean views that must have been pretty spectacular for the residents in terms of sunsets and beach access.

"Mightn't they search this road next?" I asked Jerry after a few minutes.

"Yeah, they probably will."

"Then let's find someplace to get off the road for a while," I suggested. "This rig will be pretty easy to spot, so parking anywhere near the road won't be a good thing to do. There must be somewhere behind a building or some trees that would hide us—but close enough so we can watch to see if we're being followed and which direction they're headed if we are."

"Good idea."

I slowed slightly, looking, and we soon came to a three-story apartment building with a parking lot on the ocean side, so the building would be between Alii Drive and the truck. I pulled in, parked, and shut off the engine. In the sudden quiet, with both cab windows open, it was possible to hear the surf splashing rhythmically on the rocks of a small point at one end of the lovely crescent of white sand beach and the shrill cry of a gull that swooped above it, coasting on the breeze.

"We'll have to get out to see the road from here. Why don't I find a place to watch, either outside or in the building—while you finish making breakfast?" Jerry said, giving me a mischievous grin. "You *were* cooking bacon and eggs when I so rudely interrupted, right? Be a shame to waste 'em."

What a blessing that Jerry could, in present circumstances, maintain a sense of humor. I had to smile, but immediately turned serious again.

"I want to know what happened to you—everything about last night. Where did they take you? Are you really okay? What do they want? How did you . . . ?"

"Food things first?" His question was really a request, without the teasing. "I haven't eaten anything since dinner last night on Captain Beans' boat and I'm starving. I'll tell you all about it while we eat, okay?"

His appeal seemed entirely reasonable and I was hungry too, so I agreed to wait long enough to have answers to my questions over bacon and some new fried eggs. He went inside to see if there was a place from which to watch, but in a few minutes came back out shaking his head. He found a place outside that gave him a view of the road and there he settled behind some shrubbery.

When the food was ready I took both our plates and sat with him on the grass to eat.

"Two of those guys grabbed me the minute I left the gangway of the boat," Jerry told me after a sigh of satisfaction over the plate I had brought him full of eggs, bacon, and hash browns, and now empty. Seated on a curb at the end of the lot while he ate, he had gone on watching the road from his vantage point next to a concealing shrub full of white flowers. I had sat down next to him and listened as we both peered out around the foliage.

"They marched me to a black car, pushed me into the backseat, and got in beside me on either side. They told me that if I gave them trouble they'd go get you, too. In just a few minutes another guy came and got into the front seat, and we took off."

"A guy with dark glasses?"

"Yeah, did you see him?"

"He pushed past me and said they wanted 'the deed and the money,' before they would 'trade' you. I had no idea what he meant—then."

"But you do now?"

"I think so. I used a tire iron to break into that old tackle box of Karen's that was her late husband's, and found an appreciable amount of money and the deed to some property Karen and Lewis supposedly bought and were going to build a house on. I don't know the status of it. Those things seem to fill the bill for what the note demanded, but I suspect that Karen took a lot more money back to Homer with her."

"They didn't tell me anything about that. They just said that when you gave them what they wanted they'd let me go. Then they locked me in a closet in the apartment they took me to."

"Where was it?"

"Less than a mile up the hill, in a residential area. One of the guys with me in the backseat tied a blindfold over my eyes and I think they drove around for a bit, so I wouldn't know where I was. I didn't see any of it until I got loose and got outside. Then I could tell where I was because I could see the bay at the bottom of the street."

"How in the world did you get away?"

"There was a bag of golf clubs in that closet. When two of them went out for food and left one guy there alone, I took one of the drivers, kicked the closet door open, and hit him with it as he came to stop me—knocked him cold. Then I got out of there in a hurry and ran to where I hoped you'd stay parked, and you had. I thought they knew where you were."

I told him about contacting the police and having the Holt twins show up in answer to my call for help. "But there was nothing really that the police could do when they found out how little I actually knew about it, or who was responsible—just that you'd been abducted. They came back several times to be sure I was holding the fort successfully, with no trouble. Nice guys, but not much help."

He nodded thoughtfully.

"Could you identify those three guys for the police?" I asked him. "I might recognize the one with the note again if I saw him. He had on dark glasses that covered almost half his face. It was so odd that he was wearing them at night, but I guess that's what he meant them for—a disguise, but there was something about him . . . H-m-m."

"I could maybe pick out the voices of the two I didn't already know," Jerry said, frowning. "But the other one was that guy from the gray pickup."

"Are you sure?"

"Absolutely. I'd know him anywhere—if all I could see was his shadow. No doubt, it was him."

It was no surprise to me. It had already crossed my mind to think that Mr. Gray Truck, the *idiot,* must somehow be involved.

"What shall we do now?" I asked. "I think I should let those two Kona policemen know what's been going on—that the guys are still after us, if they are. The Holt brothers are . . ."

I stopped in midsentence as Jerry leaned forward to look more closely at a vehicle passing on the road beyond the building that sheltered the camper and us.

"There," he said. "That's it—I think. That black car that just went by."

"I saw. But it's going *toward* Kona."

"They must have been down Highway 11 already looking for us and are on their way back. It could be a good time to make a run for it in the other direction. What do you think?"

"I think we'll have to be very cautious, and that they'll check campgrounds and commercial parking lots, so we'd have to find another safe place for tonight, unless you think we should drive all the way back to Hilo. But if we did, where would we go? We can't go back to Karen's house."

Jerry considered that idea thoughtfully, then said, "That would put us out in the open on the road between here and there. Besides, you know, if the guy in the gray truck is one of them, he might think that is exactly what we would do—go back to Hilo, where he knows we started, because he followed us from there, yes? He might not know we have nowhere to go now in Hilo, but it wouldn't matter if they found us on the way."

I nodded, interested.

"So—where do you think we should go?"

"I think we should go to that refuge place you want

to see anyway. I doubt these guys would expect us to play tourist with them hunting us, would they? There's a small campground near it that I've been to on snorkeling trips—Ho'okena Beach Park. It's not widely known and is used mostly by locals."

"I have a camping permit for that one. We could stay there and with some other motor homes or campers as cover we might be able to avoid them if they came looking."

"There may not be many of those. It's usually pretty empty on weekdays and this is . . . what? Wednesday?"

I nodded.

Could it really be only Wednesday? I felt it must have been longer than that. So we still had two days until our plane left for Alaska—two days to avoid our pursuers and try to figure out what to do about the money and tackle box. I wished we had had time to contact the Holt twins before leaving Kona. I wished I knew what Karen had been thinking or doing. Remembering the phone call I had overheard on my return from that first trip to the grocery store, I now wondered if it was related and thought it probably was—somehow. *Don't call here,* she had said. *I'll call you again when it's safe—when she's . . . She's here. I'll talk to you later.*

"Well, I think Ho'okena's worth a try," Jerry was saying. "Let's go there and see how it goes. At least there we'll probably have *some* company. But if we wind up alone we can always find somewhere else to hide—off on a side road somewhere maybe."

It seemed an acceptable plan, for the moment.

TWENTY-FIVE

"JERRY!" I SAT STRAIGHT UP IN MY BED, WHERE I HAD BEEN almost asleep, and called out his name.

"What?" His response was filled with alarm as he jerked to a sitting position as well. "Did you hear something outside?"

I could just make him out in the vague light that found its way in through the window over his dinette bed.

"No—no, not that. I just thought of something that could be important—maybe. Do you remember that guy who passed us too close on the motorcycle on the way into Kona yesterday?"

Could it have been only yesterday? It seemed much longer than that to me.

"Yes, I remember. You had to brake to keep from hitting him."

"I think he was the one who talked to me on the *Tamure* last night."

"The what?"

"The boat—Captain Beans' double-hulled catamaran."

"Oh, yeah? You sure?"

"Pretty sure. It all fell together as I was drifting off to sleep. I saw him earlier in Hilo, from a spot where he could have been watching the house, and then again in the grocery store a little while later. That's why he seemed so familiar to me, but I only saw him from a distance and wasn't sure."

We had found a place to park for the night at Ho'okena Beach Park, as planned. It was a tucked-away sort of campground, two miles from Highway 11, at the end of a narrow winding road with a few bumps, and right next door to the refuge I wanted to visit at Pu'uhonua o Honaunau National Historical Park.

There we also found an unexpected and welcome surprise—the Martins. Lloyd, Shelly, and their two boys, Michael and David, who greeted us with friendly, welcoming waves when they saw us driving in.

"If you pull into that space on the other side of their larger motor home," Jerry suggested, "we'll be hidden behind it from the entrance—and anyone giving this campground a cursory look. Back in and we'll be able to look out the door at the ocean and the sunset."

Clever Jerry was right, and I did as suggested.

The Martin boys, both in swimsuits and T-shirts to protect their shoulders from the sun, came trotting to greet Jerry and he soon had one sitting on each foot, their arms wrapped around his legs at the knee, as he walked around alternately lifting them off the ground with each stride, eliciting giggles, especially from David, the younger, who finally laughed so hard he fell off.

"Hey," said Shelly, who came around as I unlocked the rear door to the camper. "This is great. Lloyd and I will have some adult company for a change."

"Maybe one adult at least," I told her with a smile

and a nod toward the current interaction between Jerry
and her boys. "Have you been here long?"

"Just last night," she told me. "But we like it so much
we've decided to give it one more. You?"

"Yes, I think so. We were in Kona last night, but this
looks like a good place for tonight and I want to see
the Refuge next door before we leave. The history of it
caught my attention years ago."

"Come and see the beach," she invited. "It's got some
history too and the remains of an old pier that used to
be part of a busy port a hundred years ago. This was a
real town with over two thousand people living here
back then."

We walked down the beach to the edge of the ocean,
where gentle waves were lapping the sand into a darker
color of gray. I leaned to pick up a dry handful and
found that it wasn't really gray, but black and white, a
combination of ground lava and crushed coral, Shelly
told me.

"On down the coast there's a beach with green sand."

"Green?"

"From olivine crystals."

"Are you a geologist?"

She laughed. "No, I just read a lot."

There were only a few people on the beach, seemingly picnickers, or mothers who, like the Martins, had
brought their children to swim and play in the sand. Off-
shore, I could see a couple of snorkelers slowly moving
along facedown in the water, sometimes going under to
swim with the fish they must be finding.

"There's a reef out there where the fish hang out.
Lloyd swam out yesterday to see. Sometimes there are
dolphins that come into the bay and swim around with
whoever's in the water."

It sounded like fun and might, I thought, tempt Jerry back into the gear he carried in his pack. If we were lucky, we wouldn't be found by our hunters and could spend a quiet, restful time, without harassment.

For me the last hours had been fraught with worry about Jerry's disappearance and it was a huge relief to have him back and to find a lovely quiet place and good people with whom to share it. But I still found myself glancing regularly toward the campground entrance and noticed that Jerry was doing the same. Once I was startled enough to swing around and stare toward the sound of tires on gravel as another car pulled into the parking area and four teenagers got out with snorkel gear.

"Is something wrong, Maxie?" Shelly asked me hesitantly.

I shook my head. "I'm just jumpy," I told her. "Didn't get enough sleep last night."

More like none, I thought, but didn't say so, seeing no reason to share concern for something that would make them uneasy and which they could do nothing about.

Sitting down on a low wall near the center of the beach, I examined the remains of a ragged rectangle of lava rock that ran from the sand out into the water—support for a pier with planks long gone that must have covered it.

"The ocean floor must fall off steeply as it goes out from the beach," I observed. "Otherwise it wouldn't be deep enough for ships to reach a pier this close to shore."

"Oh, it does. We're careful not to let the boys go swimming without life jackets and at least one of us with them. They could be in trouble fast if they slipped into the deeper water by mistake."

The next thing out of my mouth was an enormous yawn.

"Why don't you take a nap?" Shelly suggested with a smile. "I'll keep an eye on our *three* children."

Glancing down the beach I saw that Jerry was helping Michael and David build castles with wet sand that they collected in their red and blue plastic buckets and upside-downed into turrets and walls. As we watched, he showed them how to drip a mixture of sand and water from their hands to make it pile up as the water soaked away and left only a sand tower standing.

"Yes," Shelly reminded me, "Jerry should be a teacher."

I took her advice on the nap, told Jerry where I was going and why, and headed for the camper, where I was asleep in my upper bed practically before my head hit the pillow.

"Go ahead," he had told me. "I'll keep watch and let you know if any of 'them' show up."

"You must be tired too."

"A little. But I wasn't pacing the floor all night last night. That closet they put me in was too small for it, so I lay down and napped. It was dark and I hadn't anything else to do."

As I thought: irrepressible.

I woke three hours later that afternoon.

As I slept, the weather had started to change. I stepped out of the camper to see that a layer of clouds had come sweeping in from the southeast, over the long gentle slopes of Mauna Loa, to cover half the sky a stormy gray color that suggested rain was probably already falling on the Hilo side of the island. The sky was still clear to the west and the sun bright on our beach, but it would soon begin to tend toward sunset and the gray sand turn a brownish tan in its golden late afternoon glow.

The color of the water, however, reflecting the sky, had changed to a gray-blue, rather than the startlingly clear and brilliant combinations of turquoise to cobalt that I had enjoyed earlier. A light breeze was blowing and swayed the fronds of the palms that gracefully inclined their trunks toward the water. A coconut in its heavy outer husk lay rocking slightly at the edge of the water where the sea had carried it floating onto the sand.

Shelly came across to hand me a sandwich and some potato salad on a paper plate, covered by a damp paper towel to keep it fresh.

"I managed to save you at least some of the lunch," she said, laughing. "Though it was a struggle with four hungry men at the table."

"Oh, you are a darlin' girl," I told her, realizing I was hungry and breakfast long past. "Will it be enough if I promise to remember you in my will?"

"Better to remember me now," she returned. "Jerry mentioned that you have apples."

"We do indeed. Come on in and I'll pay my debt immediately. And thanks for feeding Jerry."

We climbed in and I retrieved the bag of apples from the refrigerator. She took four, one for each of them, I brought a fork for the salad, and we sat down across from each other at the table.

"Where are Jerry and the boys?" I asked, concerned that I hadn't seen my tour guide.

"I put the boys down for a nap. Jerry went out just a few minutes ago to cruise the reef," she said, gesturing toward the ocean with the apple she was holding in one hand—less a couple of bites.

Facing the door, I leaned to look out over the water. Far out in the bay I could see him, a facedown swimmer, his back just breaking the surface as he moved slowly forward, gently kicking his fins. The snorkel attached to his mask bobbed above his head as he looked down at the fish and other residents of the reef. As I watched, he made a swift kick and disappeared from view, but was back to the surface a few feet farther on in less than a minute.

"Do you snorkel?" I asked Shelly.

"Yes, we both do. Once you've had a look at the fish, coral, and, sometimes, turtles and dolphins, it's hard to resist with water so perfectly clear and warm for swimming. We take turns when we bring the boys with us, but often leave them with a sitter so we can snorkel together. When they're a little older and can swim well enough we'll teach them. Then we can all go."

"Are they anxious to learn?"

She grinned. "Michael swims like a fish, but all he currently wants is a boogie board. David? Well, he doesn't really like to get his head wet yet, but there's plenty of time to let him take it at his own pace and comfort level. We take them kayaking with us and they both like that."

I glanced out to sea again and was surprised to see Jerry swimming hard toward the beach. Then, he suddenly stopped and hung in the surf at least forty yards from the beach, treading water, looking inland. I stood up and, going to the door, opened the screen so he could see me. Immediately he waved an insistent arm, clearly pointing toward the entrance to the campground. At the same time I heard the crunch of gravel under the tires of a vehicle.

There was only one reason he would make such a gesture. One or more of our pursuers had just driven into the campground looking for us. Whirling, glad I had backed into the parking spot, I went quickly forward to peek out the small window that was placed so that one could look through into the cab of the pickup from inside the camper and, therefore, out through the windshield as well.

I expected to see the black car, but instead it was the gray pickup that rolled slowly into view, with two people inside. The nearest, the passenger, wearing his dark glasses, was the one who had given me the demand at the pier, and who I had identified as keeping a watch on Karen's house in Hilo. The other, behind the wheel, was the man who had parked that truck next to us in the Volcanoes campground. On seeing our camper parked next to the Martins' motor home, he slowed almost to a stop, then drove on out of sight, to turn around and come back, I imagined.

"Maxie, what's wrong?" Shelly, now on her feet, asked me. "There *is* something, isn't there?"

For a second or two I had no idea what to do. Pushing past her to get back to the door, I looked out to see that Jerry was once again swimming strongly toward the beach, but he had a long way to go and wasn't going to make it before they parked and came to make trouble. Thinking fast, I turned to Shelly.

"Will you trust me to tell you later and do something really important for me now?"

"Of course," she said, immediately interpreting my frown of concern. Thanks be that she was quick-witted and knew when action was required, not questions. "What do you want me to do?"

Grabbing my purse, I fished out the keys and held them out to her as I told her.

"Through no fault of ours, Jerry and I are in some serious trouble with the men in that car that just drove in. They're hunting for us. This rig is marked with Harper's

Rental logos, but it could have been rented by several others this week. Will you get out, go to the cab, unlock the driver's door, and get in—all so they can see you plainly? I want them to think this rig is your rental. Can you do that?"

In a breath, as I heard the gray truck come back and stop in front of ours, blocking it in, Shelly had the keys and was standing on the ground outside. I saw her go by the window without so much as a glance up at me to reveal that there was someone in the camper.

A door slammed in front as one or both of the men got out of the gray truck. A quick and cautious peek told me it was the man in dark glasses and that the driver had remained at the wheel, keeping the motor running. Knowing there was no time to close the curtains and that if either of them looked through a window I would be seen, I did the only thing possible: I put my trust in Shelly, and stepped into the small bathroom and closed the door to a thin crack through which I could hear what transpired through the open window over the galley sink.

I heard her unlock the cab door, felt the truck rock slightly as she climbed in, and was glad I had not put down the stabilizers for the camper.

"Hey," I heard a man's voice say, "this your rental?"

"Yes," Shelly answered calmly. "Why?"

"You with an older lady and a tall, skinny kid?"

"I'm with my husband and two small boys."

"Nobody else? You *sure*?"

"I think I would be sure of my own family. What business is it of yours anyway?" she demanded with a hint of irritation in her voice.

"Well, now . . . ," he started to answer back, but another voice interrupted—Lloyd's, which almost gave me a heart attack, since he had no way of knowing what I had asked of Shelly.

"Is there some kind of problem?" he asked.

Before the man could answer, Shelly spoke right up.

"I was just assuring this man that this is *our* rental camper and that there is *no older woman or young man* traveling with us, right?"

Good going, Shelly! Give him all the cues he needs and, if he's as smart as I think he is . . .

There was a pause that I waited through with my heart in my throat.

Then Lloyd—slower of speech than Shelly, but clearly not slow on the uptake, at least in terms of unspoken communication with his wife—agreed with her.

"Yes, it's our rental—the two of us and our two boys—and our business. Why would you want to know?"

"And you rented it from Harper's in Hilo?"

"Does it say 'Harper's' on the door in front of you?" Shelly chimed in.

"Yeah, but—"

"Look fella, you're annoying my wife, which has a way of annoying the hell out of me. Take a hike."

"Hey—sorry—no offense meant."

"Then—when you're gone—none will be taken."

Nothing else was said.

I heard footsteps in the gravel, then the door slammed shut on the gray truck and I heard it drive away, picturing Lloyd and Shelly watching closely as it did.

"What was that all about?" Lloyd asked as Shelly climbed out of the truck and they walked around to meet me at the back door of the camper, where I could see Jerry just walking out of the water onto the beach in a hurry. "Shelly, I came damn close to showing you up for a liar."

"Maxie will explain," Shelly assured him.

"Come on in," I told them both, reaching for the Jameson. "And we'll tell you all about it. You two have definitely earned at least that and a drink, along with our thanks."

Twenty-six

After Jerry and I explained the situation and all that had transpired concerning the three men we were attempting to avoid, all four of us kept a pretty close and slightly nervous watch, but none of the three men showed up again in the Ho'okena Beach Park.

Lloyd was convinced we should call the police, but what could we tell them that would be proof of anything? I did not tell them about the deed and the money I had found in the tackle box, feeling that about that, too, there were huge questions. I thought again of calling Karen, but not with others within listening range.

Jerry invited Lloyd to go back out with him to snorkel the reef, while Shelly and I watched Michael and David.

"Why don't you go too?" I suggested to Shelly. But she declined.

"Honestly, I'd rather talk to you. Tell me about your travels in your motor home. I think you're brave to take off on your own, driving all the way down that long highway from Alaska to—well, wherever you decide to go. Whatever made you think of doing that and where have you been? You must have seen some interesting places."

I told her about my adventures in Colorado and the other southwestern states of the Four Corners region and why I liked the way I traveled, with only Stretch for company. She smiled when I told her how my daughter and attorney son-in-law in Boston disapproved of my gypsy lifestyle, and my son and his lady in Seattle balanced that out with their wholehearted approval.

"Don't you ever get lonely?"

"Oh, yes, sometimes, but not for long. There are so many great people to meet in RV parks and campgrounds, and I'm a gregarious sort, so I don't hesitate to introduce myself and share experiences."

I reminisced about meeting Jessie Arnold on one trip up the Alaska Highway, and Shelly was interested in Jessie's vocation as a sled dog racer and kennel owner. "I'd love to come and see the Iditarod sometime—maybe when the boys are older."

Michael and David had gone back to building sand castles and making roads around them on which they ran small cars and trucks brought out from the motor home after their naps.

Eventually, Lloyd and Jerry came dripping out of the sea and I noticed that they stopped for a few minutes' conversation at the edge of the water and that Jerry seemed to be answering questions and doing most of the talking, while Lloyd listened intently. I couldn't help wondering what they had discussed before they came to happily share that they had swum with a sea turtle and to give us a running verbal list of the fish they had seen. Both the boys left their play and came to listen, then to coax Jerry to see the towers they had built of sand and water with roads between for their tiny cars.

When all the men and boys had washed off salt water, dried, and dressed, we pooled our edible resources for dinner together at the picnic table next to the Martin rig and watched the sun go down in a glory of colors that dyed the ocean beneath to match, with sparkles from the last rays of sunlight. As we watched the colors fade, I heard an odd clicking sound from one of the palm trees near where we sat.

"It's a barn owl," Lloyd told me. "They were brought in from the mainland to help control rodents and they hunt at night. It's probably got a nest in that palm tree."

Sure enough, in a few minutes we saw the sizable bird glide silently away over the parking area, heading inland to hunt for its dinner, its white face easy to spot even in the dusk.

By ten o'clock Jerry and I had said our good nights and were inside the camper, ready for an early bedtime—both tired after the previous twenty-four hours of stress and activity on top of little sleep the night before. I had filled Jerry in on what had happened earlier with the men in the gray pickup.

"Nice people, the Martins," Jerry commented. "It was good luck that they were there to say what they did to those guys."

"They're fine people," I agreed. "You have a real fan club in Michael and David."

"I always wished I'd had a younger brother or sister," he said thoughtfully. "It's fun to play with kids that age."

"Shelly thinks you'd be a great teacher."

"She does?"

"Yes, and it wouldn't be a bad idea. You're very good with them."

He smiled, but said nothing, though I could tell he was pleased at the compliment.

Though we both tried to read, we could neither one keep our eyes open, soon slept, and were awake early the next morning.

By eight o'clock the Martins were packed up and ready to leave for their home in Waimea, north of Kona.

We traded addresses and phone numbers, and I invited them to visit me in Alaska anytime I wasn't on the road somewhere—and even then, if wherever I was suited them.

"Where are you going next winter?" Shelly asked.

"Virginia maybe. I have some genealogical research I'd like to do there. But then, I've always wanted to see dinosaur country in Alberta, so—we'll see. I've the rest of the summer to make up my mind. Let's keep in touch anyway."

"Oh, yes," Shelly agreed.

Lloyd nodded as he shook hands with Jerry. "That was good snorkeling yesterday. And I'll remember that thing you taught me," he said. "You're very good at it."

"Thanks," said Jerry with a grin. "I knew you'd pick that trick up in a hurry."

We watched them all out of sight, both small boys once again waving energetically through the dinette window, where they were seat-belted in safely for the trip, one on each side of the table, with coloring books and Lego blocks to keep them occupied.

"It's Thursday," Jerry said as we climbed back into the camper and settled at the table with the last of the morning coffee. "Tomorrow we need to be back in Hilo. Let's pack up and go to that refuge you want to see."

Drinking the last swallow from his cup, he took the keys and started out to retrieve his fanny pack from the storage compartment on the outside of the camper, but stopped at the door and turned back to me with a serious expression.

"If you'll give me that tackle box, I'll put it back where you had it stored. If they didn't find it when they searched here once, it's probably the safest place for it, especially since we'll be away from the camper. Don't you think so?"

I did. Retrieving it from the closet where I had hidden it, I gave it to him and turned to put away the last of the breakfast dishes, which I had already washed and dried.

He came back shortly wearing his fanny pack and handed me the keys with his usual smile. "Mission accomplished. Let's go."

It was a bright sunny morning, with no hint of the storm clouds that had darkened the sky the evening before. As we drove the short distance to Pu'uhonua o Honaunau, the Place of Refuge, though we looked carefully, we saw no sign of those we wished to avoid.

The Refuge is a National Historic Park, so I once again showed my Golden Age Passport and we drove to the parking lot, which, at that early-morning hour just after opening, had only a few cars and a single tourist bus. The driver was sitting on a low wall outside his bus with a cup of coffee in his hand, watching people come and go as he waited for his passengers to return.

"If we park next to it," Jerry suggested, "there'll be someone to see if anyone tries to break in again."

The driver gave us a smile and a nod as we walked past him.

"Will you be here long?" I asked.

"Probably at least an hour or so," he told me. "It's a big place and the seniors in this group like to take their time. I'll keep an eye on your camper."

We thanked him and went off to the nearby visitor center, where I picked up several brochures on the Refuge, and some pages of information on plants, birds, and the instructions to a game similar to checkers that was played by the ancient Hawaiians.

Opening the brochure on Pu'uhonau o Honaunau, I found a drawing of the Refuge and saw immediately why it took time for visitors, senior or not, to see the place, for it was much larger than I had imagined, and spread out along the edge of the ocean. Over half of it was based on the flat of an old lava flow and was enclosed on the landward sides by huge walls built of the same dark lava stone. The rest was on white sand in groves of palm trees, which could not grow on the lava. A small sheltered cove and two ponds lay between the two areas.

"A lot of people must have lived here," I said to the woman who had given me the brochure.

"Actually, not many," she told me. "The area inside the wall was a very sacred place and outside them was a royal residence, but few people actually lived here unless they came for refuge during a war." She showed me a description on the back of the brochure so I could read it as Jerry and I walked slowly down a gentle slope to the white sand area.

Honaunau Bay, with its sheltered canoe landing and availability of drinking water, was a natural place for the ali'i—royal chiefs—to establish one of their most important residences. Separated from the royal grounds by a massive wall was the

*pu'uhonua, a place of refuge for defeated warriors,
noncombatants in time of war, and those who vio-
lated the kapu, the sacred laws.*

There had been no palace, like the one I had seen
in Kona. Instead, the royal residence had consisted of a
number of thatched buildings in the coconut palm grove
of the white sand area, where the *ali'i* lived with atten-
dants and servants to care for him and his family. The
canoe landing in the cove was for royal use only.

We wandered about in the grove, where there was
one model house to show how they had been made—
lashed together with coconut fiber and thatched with *ti*
leaves. It was cool and pleasant under the palms and,
with no wind, the shadows of their fronds made lovely
wheel patterns on the sand beneath them.

Under one such tree we came upon a couple sitting
on opposite sides of a flat stone with rows of regularly
spaced shallow holes for the light and dark pebbles with
which to play konane, the ancient game for which I had
the instructions.

"That looks like checkers," Jerry commented, watching the woman jump a dark pebble over a light one of
her opponent. She looked at least part Asian and was
dark-haired and very pretty.

"It's similar," she told him, looking up with a smile.
"But there are more pieces and it's the person who
makes the last possible move who wins, which at the moment seems to be me."

"Well," her companion responded with a grin and
a glance up at Jerry, "it's early yet. We'll stay till I can,
maybe, at least break even, but Lu is very good at this."

We watched for a minute or two, then went on to walk
around the small cove toward the area inside the huge

stone wall—the *pu'uhonua,* sanctuary, made sacred by
the bones of the chiefs, who possessed spiritual power.

Halfway around the cove, Jerry suddenly stopped me
and pointed out into the water at the edge of the surf.
"Look," he said. "There's a sea turtle."

"Where?"

"Right there—under the water next to that big rock."

I could see the shape of it, half-swimming as it pushed
its way toward the shore over some submerged stones.
As the clear green waves rose and fell its curved shell
was momentarily exposed.

"It'll crawl out and bask in the sun to warm up," Jerry
said. "I wish you could see them in the open ocean.
They're incredible distance swimmers."

The bus driver had been right. There was a number
of what my Daniel always called "the oldies" wandering around in groups of two or three, following the self-
guided tour described in their brochures.

We passed several people headed back toward the
parking lot, one a younger man who greeted us with a nod
and a "Good morning."

On the southern side of the cove we came to a thatched
reproduction of the Hale o Keawe, a very sacred temple
that had once housed the bones of twenty-three *ali'i*—
royal chiefs. Surrounding it were several hand-carved
wooden figures that the brochure called *ki'i,* but that I
had always known as tiki. Two or three were life-sized,
and there was something threatening and more than a
little fierce about their posture and expressions—fierce
and beautiful—that reminded me somehow of the fero-
cious quality of the red-hot lava pouring from the volcano. There, at the edge of the Place of Refuge, it was
as if they were not only guardians of the sanctity of the
chiefs' bones and power, but the sanctuary beyond them,

the refuge itself, so no one would dare pursue farther those seeking safety and forgiveness for their transgressions, whatever they had been.

The whole idea of refuge appealed to me. There are of course different kinds of refuge and meanings for it to different peoples. To this people it had been the opportunity for a second chance at life itself, since the punishment for breaking any *kapu*—and there were many—was always death. To reach this refuge the person in trouble would have had to outrun his pursuers or swim across the bay—probably hounded by men in canoes—and come to land within the confines of those huge stone walls. There it was decreed that blood should never be spilled and the person who dared break that *kapu* would himself be killed.

Before Columbus ever thought of sailing west, Honaunau was already hallowed ground. Not until 1829 were the bones of the great line of deified chiefs removed from that temple. They were gods, and they held the ultimate power of life and death—and forgiveness—over their people.

To me, refuge had always meant sanctuary, of course. But more than that—safe haven, shelter from whatever storms might come in life. A good marriage is a refuge for both partners, and I was lucky enough to have found refuge in both Joe and Daniel and, I believe, to give the same comforting security to them and to my children. Not everyone is so fortunate.

The house in which I live is another kind of refuge, the sort that makes you feel you can be totally yourself within its walls and share that sense of shelter and warmth with friends and family. When things aren't going well, it is shelter and comfort to be in your own space, with your own familiar things and people around you.

Intending to follow Jerry around to the side of the Hale o Keawe temple, I had just reached the corner when he reached to grab my arm and pull me into its shadow.

"They're here," he said in a low voice. "And I think they saw you."

I didn't need to ask who he meant by "they," nor did I doubt his word enough to stick my neck out to take my own look around the corner of that thatched wall of the temple. We fled away from it together into the vast sanctuary of Honaunau.

Refuge it had been and—I could only hope—refuge it would be for us.

TWENTY-SEVEN

JERRY RAN AHEAD, AND WHEN I STUMBLED OVER A HALF-buried lava stone in the white sand trail, he slowed enough to reach back and grab my hand. Women in their sixties do not run as fleetingly as such long-legged young men, so the assistance was welcome, though a time or two he came close to yanking me off my feet.

We came to a place where the trail dropped a foot or two and, though we were crossing lava flats where no palms grew, here and there were a few low shrubs in the cracks and crannies of the stone. Jerry slowed, glanced quickly back in the direction we had come, then pushed me behind a fairly thick one that grew waist high in a wide fissure in the rock, let go of my hand, and turned to go on.

"Stay here and keep your head down," he told me.

"But ..."

Without a word more he was gone in long strides, jumping over stones and cutting corners on the wind-ing track. I saw him hesitate, then leap off it to vanish around the corner of a huge platformlike structure built of lava stones.

A few seconds later I heard the pounding feet of someone else coming in my direction on the trail and huddled down behind my bit of sheltering shrub, making myself as small and still as possible. I had been carrying my purse and now, as I clutched it tightly, arms wrapped around it, something poked me sharply in the ribs. Afraid to move, I endured, wondering distractedly what I had inside that was hard enough to cause hurt.

Through the leaves of the bush I could see just enough of the person who ran by to see it was the man from the gray truck. Heart in my throat, I watched him speed along the path, following Jerry, who had obviously decoyed him away from me.

Then, as I crouched there, not far behind him another man came jogging past—the driver of the bus we had seen in the parking lot—*with a gun in his hand*!

Until then I had, as commanded, stayed hidden behind the bush. But with two people chasing him, one with a deadly weapon, I was not about to let him double the odds against Jerry.

His handgun reminded me that I had one as well and it was undoubtedly what was poking me in the ribs. I took it out, dropped my purse, and stood up from behind my bit of shelter.

"Hey, you," I yelled at him, aiming my gun in his direction with both hands. "You stop—right there."

Something in my voice must have told him I was serious, because he stopped.

"Now, turn around—slowly."

He did and his eyes widened to see I was armed. "What the hell?"

"Drop the gun. Then you're going to walk this direction, past me, to go and find the police."

He did not drop his gun, though he did not raise and

aim it at me. Instead, he glared at me in aggravation. "Lady," he said, scowling in frustration, "I *am* the police. Give me that thing."

"Prove it," I demanded, keeping the gun barrel as steadily pointed at him as possible, still afraid he might raise it and be able to shoot faster than I would. He was also just far enough away that I wasn't sure I could hit him if I had to shoot.

"I'm going to show you my ID," he said. "It's in my pocket and I'm going to reach for it now."

He carefully took a wallet with identification and a badge out of a shirt pocket, flashed it at me, and started to step forward.

"Don't," I warned him, not moving the handgun an inch from where I had it aimed. I had seen as many cop shows on television as anyone else and thought I knew what to do next. "Anyone can have a fake badge. Toss it over here."

It flew through the air to land close to my feet. Cautiously, without taking my attention from him, I took one hand from the gun, leaned to retrieve it, and could tell at a glance that this officer's name was Walt Cornish and the badge was real!

I lowered the gun and stared at him. "What . . . ?"

"Give me that," he snapped, stepping quickly to snatch the badge out of my hand, replace it in his pocket, then take my handgun away from me.

There was a sudden cry and the sounds of a struggle from the direction of that huge lava platform and we both turned to see that Jerry and the gray-truck man were grappling with each other on top of it—the much heavier man evidently trying to shove Jerry over the edge to fall to the hard lava flat below, a drop of at least eight feet.

Without a word, Officer Cornish, a gun in each hand, was off and running toward the platform, ignoring the trail to go in great bounds across the rough stone that was really anything but flat. He reached the platform, but there was no way to go up along that sixty-foot-long end. He could either search for an access somewhere out of sight along another side, then try to climb the hand- and footholds between the naturally shaped stones that had been carefully laid together without mortar, or do what he did—stay below, ready to break Jerry's fall should his adversary succeed in pushing him over the side. From where he stood he could see only part of the fight, but could at least hear what was going on over his head.

I could see, and watched in alarm as the pair above him wrestled back and forth, near the edge of the platform. Jerry, young and fit, was mostly holding his own, but his opponent had greater weight and, clearly, fighting experience and was using both. He threw a heavy punch at Jerry, who jerked his head back to avoid it, and the blow landed on his shoulder instead. As he stumbled slightly, off balance, the other man moved in swiftly to wrap his arms around Jerry's torso and one arm, and dragged him, struggling, toward the stone brink. With his free fist, Jerry was battering the side of the man's head, to little effect.

Just as I was certain that either Jerry or both of them would go over the edge, in a quick move, Jerry managed to hook a leg behind the other man's knee, causing him to lose stability and stagger back, relaxing his grasp in the process. Unable to regain his balance, he sat down hard.

Cornish had moved back just far enough from the wall to be able to see that Jerry was standing alone and shouted something from below. When Jerry looked down, the officer tossed one of the guns he was still holding up to him. It sailed through the air in an arc and was easily caught, held, and immediately aimed at the man with whom he had been struggling.

The fight was over. I sat down on a large lava stone at the side of the trail, took a deep breath of relief, and began to feel my adrenaline rush fade along with the fear I had felt for my young tour guide. Officer Cornish had disappeared around the side of the platform to find a way up while Jerry kept guard on the other man. He evidently found one, for in a few minutes I saw them together, then all three men disappeared and I supposed they would be down soon.

Behind me I heard someone else coming along the trail and turned, hoping it would not be another of the three who had been chasing us. It was, instead, the couple who had been playing konane. They stopped beside me.

"Are you okay?" the woman asked with concern, laying a hand on my shoulder.

When I said I was, she smiled and surprised me by pulling another of those police wallets out of the pocket of her jeans to show me. "I'm Kaimalu," she told me. "But everyone but my mother calls me Lu."

"That's Hawaiian," I said, thoughts still coming slowly.

"Yes, it means peaceful sea."

There was a chuckle from her opponent at the konane board.

"Sometimes she actually deserves the name," he said, holding out a large hand to shake mine in introduction. "I'm Dale not-so-peaceful Miyashiro, also an officer."

"How did you two happen to be here—and Officer Cornish? I assume it wasn't just chance."

"No. We knew you were coming and have been here

since before the park opened this morning," Lu told me and sat down next to me on the stone.

"How could you know?"

"A Lloyd Martin called last night on a cell phone and relayed a message from Officer Monahan," said Officer Miyashiro.

That Lloyd Martin had called was a surprise until I remembered his conversation with Jerry as they came in from snorkeling the reef the evening before. But—*Officer Monahan*! I was so astounded I could scarcely ask, "You mean Jerry is . . ."

"A policeman? Yes. He works undercover in narcotics, so we'd like you to keep that bit of information to yourself. But he'll tell you all about it."

"How can he be old enough?" I asked.

She smiled. "He's older than he looks. That's part of what makes him so effective. But don't say anything to give him away to this guy they have in custody, okay?"

"There were two others," I said quickly before the three reached us.

"One of those escaped in the car they drove here. We have one of them and the third—the one Cornish has now—ran after you two when we accosted them near the visitor center." She indicated the man in handcuffs as he came up to us in the custody of Officer Cornish. Jerry, walking last, reached to help me up off my stone seat, as the other three officers took their prisoner away.

I never did learn his name, nor did I care.

By midafternoon I was driving the truck camper back over the road we had traveled to reach Kona, this time headed for Hilo, with Jerry, as usual, beside me. I was glad to have his company and to learn exactly what had transpired without my knowledge and why.

"It's a long story," Jerry had said earlier in the Refuge, reaching to help me up off my stone seat. "I'll tell you everything on the way to Hilo."

"You're going back with me?"

"You bet. I'm going to make sure that you get on that plane for Alaska tomorrow with no further trouble."

I was glad he felt that way.

"So you had Lloyd call the police last night and tell them that we were going to the Refuge this morning?"

"I had to confide my police identity to him," Jerry said. "Sometimes you have to trust someone, and he was the sort I knew could keep it to himself."

"But how did you know they would come after us there?"

"Well, I really didn't for sure, but it seemed likely they might be having second thoughts about the ownership of this camper, having seen it in the campground yesterday, and make another attempt at us. It was worth a shot at catching them—something we've been trying to do for some time now."

"Why? What is this all about?"

The story he related to me was convoluted and frightening, and explained some things about Karen and her nervous attitude, but not why she had left the tackle box with its valuable contents.

The man in the gray truck, the one in the dark glasses, and another, the last of the three who had kidnapped Jerry and threatened me, were involved in land grab schemes, mainly on the Big Island of Hawaii. The value of real estate in the Hilo area, for instance, had been rising fast, with properties selling for as much as triple or quadruple their price of five to ten years earlier.

"They've kept it very simple," Jerry told me. "With a mortgage company as a front, they falsify paperwork and deeds. The would-be owner believes—and his or her paper-work says—that the payments and interest will remain the same. What is kept in the company records is markedly different and shows that when the value of the property under consideration rises, the amount of the payments goes up and the rate of interest will go up accordingly, to three or four times what it was. When that happens, it makes it impossible for most to meet even the interest payment and, therefore, they lose the property by default.

"At that point all these guys need to do is get their hands on the buyer's deed, alter it to match what is on record at the company, and forge the signatures. If for some reason they are unable to obtain the original deed, they blackmail the victim one way or another for the amount of money they would make if they had obtained and revised it—sometimes, as in Karen's case, for both cash and deed. This was why they were trying to make Karen—or you, after she was gone—turn over the deed *and* the money. They usually prey on widows, low-income would-be homeowners, and those on limited budgets—especially those who have little knowledge of things financial. Karen certainly filled that bill for them and was too embarrassed to confide in you, though she was smart enough to retain her copy of the original deed. So they tried breaking in to find it.

"But you were asking another question. Not only did you have no idea that any of this was happening, you would have figured out that something was wrong with the original deal in a heartbeat."

"So it all boils down to money. But how did they know we had the tackle box?"

"I don't know. If Karen was trying to keep it away from them it would have made more sense for her to have taken it home with her, wouldn't it?"

I agreed and thought that she and I would most certainly have a conversation when I got back to Homer.

Jerry was quiet for a minute or two, thinking.

"I'd sure like to know the identity of the one who got away," he said finally. "He never even spoke in more than a whisper when they snatched me from the dock in Kona; he drove the car, wearing gloves and a hat with a brim that hid his face, and I was blindfolded most of the way. He never came into that apartment where they kept me in the closet. So I never got a look. Now it's for sure that they'll find the car abandoned and he'll be in the wind with no way to trace him."

As we passed the turnoff to the Hawaii Volcanoes National Park and continued on down the road, I had some other more personal questions for Jerry.

"So, how old are you really?"

He grinned.

"I'm twenty-five, if you have to know and won't tell anybody. Looking younger is helpful in my job—actually helped me get it. But it can't last much longer—the eighteen-year-old part, I mean, not the police part."

"Are you really from Fairbanks?"

"Yes. I was born and lived there until ten years ago."

"And your stepfather doesn't mistreat you."

"There isn't a stepfather. My parents died in a car crash when I was fifteen. My uncle brought me here to live with him and my aunt. He's a policeman, so it was natural that I would want to be one too."

I smiled as I thought back to the day I met him with Adam the plumber. "You were keeping track of Karen, weren't you? Not really a plumber's helper at all."

"Right."

"And when I met you in the botanical garden?"

"Followed you there on purpose and had to work like

the devil telling lies to gain your sympathy and get you
to decide that you should hire me to help pack."

He leaned back in the passenger seat, laced his fingers together behind his head, and grinned appealingly.

"So now," he said, "once again: Home, James, and
don't spare the horses."

I parked the rig in the driveway of his uncle's house that
night and Officer Jerry Monahan saw me off at the airport the next day, after I returned the truck camper to
Harper's.

"We'll take care of the gun and the items in the tackle
box with your friend Karen," he assured me, and I didn't
debate his use of the term *friend*.

"Would you like to venture a guess as to the identity
of the third man chasing us?" he asked.

"I've more than a guess, I think. After reviewing all
that happened, who would know more about Karen and
her business—and that she was a recent and vulnerable
widow—than the landlord, Raymond Taylor?"

"You're right. Clever lady. That's why he kept both
of us from seeing his face in Kona. If you ever want an
undercover job, let me know."

"If you ever come back to Alaska, you must come
and visit me," I invited him.

"One of these days I'll show up on your doorstep in
Homer, I promise."

I had an idea that he probably would, and it pleased
me.

Twenty-eight

I HAD ARRIVED LATE FRIDAY NIGHT, HAVING NAPPED MY way across the Pacific from Hawaii, waking just before the wheels of the plane hit the tarmac of the Anchorage airport. Spending what was left of the night in a nearby hotel, as planned, I had been ready to reclaim my car and head for home when Alex showed up with Jessie to meet me that Saturday morning for the drive down the Kenai Peninsula. Before we left he had assured us he was taking some vacation days and would arrive to join us on Wednesday afternoon. "I have a friend with a boat who's volunteered to take me out halibut fishing Thursday or Friday. So prepare yourselves for a fish feast on Saturday."

"That's optimistic," Jessie had teased him.

"Not from what he says. Supposedly they're reeling in some good ones this year."

He had waved us off, and Jessie had made the drive to Homer a pleasant and seemingly shorter one as we caught up on everything that had been going on in our lives since last we had an extended time to spend together. Tank, upon seeing me, had looked around for Stretch, but finding his buddy not in evidence, had willingly occupied the backseat and either watched the landscape we passed, or curled up comfortably and snoozed.

It had been good to pull into my own driveway that afternoon. Very shortly after that I stood, once again, on the deck of my Homer refuge, looking south over the afternoon sparkles of Kachemak Bay and, though my garden had not gone completely wild in the time I had been gone, feeling remiss over the work I enjoyed and had abandoned half a month earlier. I had no intention of talking to Karen about what had transpired after she left Hilo. Jerry had said that the police would contact her and set things straight.

Stretch and Tank, reunited and shedding all concern for the dignity to which they both aspired, were playing keep-away in the yard with a couple of sticks, while Jessie Arnold cut some tiger lilies and delphinium from a bed near the house to grace my dining table.

"These are lovely, Maxie," she said, coming back up the stairs toward me with her hands full of gold and blue.

"Lot of weeds in that bed," I observed, half-distracted by my own assorted thoughts. "I should have been here to pull them."

Somehow this homecoming was less reassuring than I had anticipated and had felt on arriving at the end of my trip up the Alaska Highway. It was not disappointing exactly, but as if there were something incomplete about it—something that remained to be settled, or done, though I couldn't think what it could be. The most satisfying of homes for me it was and would remain, but this time it was not as complete a safe harbor as usual, or the refuge of an entirely peaceful mind—fears forgotten, cares cast aside, and the welcome company of a friend.

Jessie came across to where I stood and laid a hand on my shoulder.

"Are you okay?" she asked. "You look sad."

I turned to her with a smile. "Just thoughtful. I'm fine, but something keeps hovering in the back of my mind that I've forgotten and can't get hold of. It'll come to me if I leave it alone. Let's go in and I'll get some dinner started."

We had no more than crossed into the kitchen, and Jessie had asked for a vase in which to arrange the flowers, when the sound of tires on the gravel of my drive caught my attention. Stepping to the window, I saw a car I didn't recognize pull to a stop behind my own. The driver's door opened and I nearly dropped the vase I had been filling with water for the lilies when I recognized the man who climbed out.

"Joe!"

Leaving the vase on the counter, I hurried to throw open the door and saw not only my son, but also his lady, Sharon, coming up the walk, both with wide smiles.

It always startles me how much he has grown to look like his father: tall, long-legged, eyes as blue as the waters of the bay, with a similar sparkle.

"Hey, Mom," he said, and swept me into his usual bear hug.

"Wherever did you come from with no warning at all?" I asked, leaning back to look up at him, knowing he was aware that he needed no advance invitation, ever. "Why didn't you call me?"

"We tried," he said, turning me loose so I could hug

and greet Sharon as well. "But the answering machine was all we got, so we came anyway—once almost a month ago. This is our second trip up this summer. Hope you don't mind that we stayed in the house a couple of nights last time. We tried to leave it as we found it."

"Of course I don't mind. That's why you know where to find the key I hide outside. It's your home too, Joe. You know that."

Something tickled my memory as I embraced Sharon, but in my pleasure in seeing the two of them, I let it pass.

"You'll find the kitchen floor extra clean," Sharon said, as we went inside. "On that first trip I dropped your dishwashing soap and the bottle cracked and spilled, so a cleanup job was necessary—not that the floor wasn't clean already, of course," she rushed on to assure me. "I replaced the soap."

So that was where the odd brand had come from—one mystery solved.

"This is my friend Jessie Arnold," I told them, as she came smiling to meet them. "Jessie, this is my son, Joe, and his good lady, Sharon."

"The *Iditarod* musher Jessie Arnold?" Sharon asked.

"Yes, I've been known to run a dog team or two."

"I remember. You came up the highway when you and Mom got tangled with that runaway boy, didn't you?" This from Joe.

We agreed that she had.

Hearing new voices inside the house, Stretch, ever curious and confident of receiving his own recognition, came trotting in the door from the deck and went straight to Joe for appreciation and got it, Tank following closely behind him.

"Is that one yours?" Sharon asked Jessie.

"My lead dog, Tank."

The two women followed the dogs out onto the deck, where Stretch brought one of the sticks with the obvious expectation that one of them would throw it for him to retrieve. Tank, recovering more of his dignity, sat down at Jessie's feet.

The two women were a pleasant contrast, with Jessie's honey-hued curls and Sharon's dark locks.

Joe and I smiled, sharing that thought.

"Both peaches," he commented.

"What brought you here almost a month ago—and now, of course?" I questioned, as I took out the Jameson and also the gin for Sharon, who I knew preferred it, with tonic.

"Both times I've been working with your crime lab on a complicated case that started in Seattle and ended in Anchorage," Joe told me. "Sharon decided to come along, so we came a couple of days early that first time and drove down—just slipped in and out when you weren't here."

"I'm sorry we missed each other, but you're back now and so am I."

"So, how was Hawaii?"

"Interesting," I told him. Then, shaking my head, "Not without its moments, but—well—Paradise and Hades mixed. I met some great people—and some not great at all. I'll tell you about it later. Let's just enjoy the evening for now, okay?"

We each took a couple of glasses and joined the pair on the deck, now sitting in two of my green chairs.

As I reached over her shoulder to hand Sharon her drink, I caught again the scent that I had half-noticed on greeting her. Recognition dawned this time and I had to laugh as the solution to the scent mystery was revealed.

She glanced up with an unspoken question in her slightly puzzled expression.

"You left traces on that first trip that confused me and made my caretaker afraid that someone was staying here uninvited," I told her.

"I did?"

"You've changed the scent you're wearing, haven't you?"

"Yes. Joe gave me this one for Christmas. Do you like it?"

"I do, and noticed it just once, a bit of a hint on the air when I arrived from the highway trip. It must have drifted out from somewhere."

I turned to Joe, who had inherited my love of reading.

"And you," I said, "were reading *The Heaven Tree* while you were here."

He gave me a surprised grin and nodded. "Are you psychic? How the heck could you know that?"

"You put it back on the shelf in a different place."

Jessie shook her head at me. "Is there any mystery you can't solve, Maxie?" she asked with humor.

I had started a disclaimer, when a knock at the door turned me in that direction. Opening it, I found a local florist's deliveryman on the step, with a large, carefully wrapped arrangement in his hands. "For you, Mrs. McNabb," he said and handed it over.

"Thank you, Darrel," I told him—the son of a family I have known for years. Homer is a small town where everyone knows everyone else and the post office is a center of our social life—so much that we keep refusing to have our mail delivered so we can see each other there regularly.

"What's that?" Joe asked, coming into the kitchen,

where I had placed the arrangement on the counter and was in the process of unwrapping it.

"I don't know."

"Have you got a secret admirer?" he teased.

The wrapping fell away, as Jessie and Sharon both joined us to watch the unveiling. What appeared were orchids—many orchids, large and small, in glowing white and magenta, several of the Chinese variety tucked in with the rest, clearly sent all the way from Hawaii, the colors blurring due to the tears in my eyes.

And without help from the accompanying card, I knew who had sent them, but opened it anyway, and read:

> *With many thanks and much affection*
> *from your plumber in training,*
> *undercover tour guide,*
> *and good friend—J.M.*

Did I happen to mention that I like the boy?

ALEX AND JESSIE PULLED INTO THE LONG DRIVE, TANK once again riding shotgun by the window.

Fastening the dog's collar to the tether attached to his box, Jessie followed Alex up the steps and into the house.

"Want a cup of tea?" he asked, hanging both their coats by the door and joining Jessie in removing the rubber boots they had worn.

"Sounds good. Maybe a couple of those Double Stuf Oreos to go with it," she suggested, crossing sock-footed to the stove, where she added a log to the fire, then stood rubbing her hands together in the welcome heat. "It's stopped raining and the temperature's dropped a bit. I may be able to run the guys with the four-wheeler tomorrow, if it isn't too muddy."

"As long as you don't run late. I forgot to tell you that we're invited to dinner with Cass and Linda tomorrow night," Alex called from the kitchen, where he had put two mugs of water with tea bags into the microwave.

"We are?"

"You bet. Have you forgotten what tomorrow is—or are you trying to ignore it this year?"

She frowned for a second or two, then realized. "Oh! It's my *birthday*!"

"Right!"

"I had totally spaced on it. Where did October go?"

Coming back with both mugs in one hand, package of cookies in the other, he gave a mug to Jessie and they settled, one at either end of the sofa, which was purposely large enough so there was room for each to stretch out their legs—Oreos within reach of both.

"October," Alex answered, "probably went as usual, but you've been pretty focused on getting back out with the dogs, after a long, frustrating delay."

"Well, I *was*—until this rain made an appearance. Sure hope it's about over. We're all tired of being either cooped up or soaking wet."

"How's old Pete doing, by the way?" he asked with a frown of concern.

Pete, one of the oldest dogs in Jessie's yard, was a favorite, though he was no longer allowed in the teams of a dozen or more at a time that she trained for racing. He went at the front of a sled, when there was snow; otherwise he pulled one of the two four-wheelers she owned. He had sprained a foreleg badly about the same time Jessie had torn a tendon in her knee in a fall down the side of a mountain a year earlier. They had healed together through the winter, but she knew Pete would never be strong enough again to help pull any of her sleds over the hundreds of miles necessary for training and distance racing.

"The leg's okay," she said slowly, a sad and concerned expression on her face. "But the vet says he's got heart and breathing problems that are only going to get worse. He's such a sweet old guy that I'd really miss having him around, but I may have to have him put down before spring. Can't have him struggling just to get by. That's not fair, however much I hate it."

"Would it help to bring him inside to sleep?"

Jessie shook her head sadly. "He'd just want to go back out with the rest. I've been bringing him in with Tank during the day—especially with this rain—and I moved Jeep and put Pete in the box next to Tank. They're good buds. It'll be okay, if I watch him close. But every time I take a team out for a training run, it's all I can do to leave him behind, looking longingly after us with those sad eyes. He doesn't understand at all—just wants to be back where he thinks he belongs."

Alex was not surprised to see tears in Jessie's eyes, knowing that she loved all her sled dogs, but that Pete was special, for he had been with her as long as any in her kennel and had sired many good pups, some of which were now racing in what Pete felt was his place. Strong, even-tempered, and ready to do whatever was required of him, he was not at all happy to be left behind. Besides running many shorter races, he had been a member of the teams that made the long, thousand-mile runs in the longest and most famous races of all, the Iditarod and the Yukon Quest, more than once in the former.

"I'll help keep an eye on him," Alex said, setting his half-empty mug on the floor beside the sofa and swinging his legs to stand up. "Hey! You want your present now?"

"But tomorrow's the day."

"That's okay. I think you should have it now. Besides, maybe you'll want to use it—have it—maybe even wear it—tomorrow," he called back, taking long strides to the bedroom. Jessie heard a drawer open and shut; then he came back with a kid's grin that was so infectious it made her smile, too, as she wiped her eyes. Stopping beside her, Alex handed her a box that was about a foot square, clumsily wrapped in bright yellow paper, with an excess of Scotch tape, and festooned with multicolored curly ribbons. "There ya go! Open it up, almost-a-birthday girl!"

Jessie examined the decorative object in her lap for a long minute as Alex sat down again on the opposite end of the sofa, swung his stocking feet up, retrieved his tea, and sat waiting, eyes dancing in anticipation.

"Wrap this yourself, did you?" she asked.

"What could possibly have given you *that* impression?"

"Well—it's—ah—very artistic in design," she teased.

"Maybe I should advertise—make more and autograph them? Or—on second thought—maybe not. Just bear in mind that I considered the funny papers first, so this is first class."

Under the paper was a box with a lid, which Jessie removed to find . . . another box with another lid. Three boxes later, each smaller than the last, the tears had vanished and she was giggling as she took the lid off what turned out to be the last—a black velvet–covered jewelry box. Inside was something she immediately expected and found.

"Oh, Alex! They're beautiful! You replaced the diamond earring I lost on Niqa Island. But—wait a minute—these two look different than those. Did you get *new* ones? You didn't need to do that."

"Well—yes, Jess. As it turns out, I did. What I learned in the attempt was that you can't just pick up a diamond post to match one you already have. They're matched in pairs for size and quality and color and—who knows what else. It was easier to trade in the one you didn't lose and get a matched pair than it would have been to try to find another, or have one made. These are almost exactly the same, but slightly larger and set a little differently—with screw-on backings, so you won't lose one this time. I hope you don't mind that I raided your jewelry box for the old one."

"Mind? Alex, I love them!" Jessie said, getting up to give him a huge hug and a kiss. "Thank you, dear man. And you're right, I'll definitely wear them tomorrow night to dinner. Linda will be green."

With a swallow that emptied his tea mug, still holding Jessie, Alex stood up and set her on her feet

"I'm for bed. It's been a long, damp day, with an earthquake thrown in, so I'm ready to hit the hay." He gave her a sideways leer and twirled one end of his handlebar moustache suggestively. "I recommend that you come, too, and thank me properly."

Later, in the dark bedroom at the top of the stairs, Jessie lay with her head on his shoulder, his arm holding her close.

"You know," he said drowsily, "my mother has a poem she always said at bedtime on birthdays when I was a kid."

"What?" she whispered in his ear, knowing his penchant for poetry and quotations.

" 'When your birthday is over, and you've wound up the clock, and put out the cat, and fastened the lock, may you say with a smile that's contented and glad, "This has been the best birthday that ever I had." ' "

Jessie giggled.

"In my case, I think it should probably be changed to

put out the dog! But, since this isn't really my birthday, will you promise to say it again tomorrow night?"

"Sure thing."

Half an hour later both were slumbering soundly, lulled by the repetitious rhythm of rain on the roof overhead and drizzling from it to the ground below.

Familiar with living next to over forty dogs, neither heard the long howl of one that, disturbed from sleep by something moving in the nearby trees, had ventured into the downpour outside its box in the row farthest from the house and nearest the woods that lay to the west. As that wail slowly faded, another dog answered from the far corner of the lot with a similar cry that rose and fell into a series of yips and yowls.

There was a distant sound of movement in the trees as something crashed hurriedly downhill through the brush. The noise terminated upon reaching Knik Road and was heard no more.

Both dogs shook themselves free of much of the rainwater that had dampened their coats, and disappeared once again into the shelter of their respective boxes.